THE
HUNGRY
EDGE

T0078295

THE HUNGRY EDGE

ASHOAK UPADHYAY

PARTRIDGE

A Penguin Company

Copyright © 2013 by Ashoak Upadhyay.

ISBN: Hardcover   978-1-4828-1208-4
             Softcover   978-1-4828-1209-1
             Ebook   978-1-4828-1207-7

This is a work of fiction. All of the characters, names, incidents, organizations, and dialogue in this novel are either the products of the author's imagination or are used fictitiously.

All rights reserved. No part of this book may be used or reproduced by any means, graphic, electronic, or mechanical, including photocopying, recording, taping or by any information storage retrieval system without the written permission of the publisher except in the case of brief quotations embodied in critical articles and reviews.

Because of the dynamic nature of the Internet, any web addresses or links contained in this book may have changed since publication and may no longer be valid. The views expressed in this work are solely those of the author and do not necessarily reflect the views of the publisher, and the publisher hereby disclaims any responsibility for them.

Author photo by Paul Noronha

To order additional copies of this book, contact
Partridge India
000 800 10062 62
www.partridgepublishing.com/india
orders.india@partridgepublishing.com

O! Who can hold a fire in his hand
By thinking on the frosty Caucasus?
Or cloy the hungry edge of appetite
By bare imagination of a feast?
                              —William Shakespeare.
                              Richard II Act 1 Sc. 3

We reside only in memories
Stone yields to the breeze of time.
                              —Girijaa Upadhyay "Sepia"

One hot and humid afternoon a young man walked into The Wayside Inn and without knowing it into a relationship with three men that was to change their lives in ways none could have imagined. The restaurant was packed with earnest looking executives from the cluster of foreign banks in the vicinity frowning into their beers, an occasional poet or two no one recognized, women shoppers with outsized sunshades perched on their nurtured hairdos, and college students from across the car park with cell phones and darting eyes.

The young man hesitated at the entrance squinting into the cool dark hall, a frown creasing his face until he caught the eye of a woman staring at him, whisking her eyes away after their glances locked for a second. He stood rooted to the spot as a door opened to a terrifying thought that she had returned from some dark void. Her eyes! The same dark brown, the whites contrasting with the black eyeliner that accentuated their size, giving her a look of open wonder and he knew his imagination was playing with him, that it was not her but a mother of three noisy children making a mess of their food and having a good time doing it.

The clatter of forks and spoons, the tinkle of laughter and the occasional belch, the steamy mix of fried chicken and onions, and stale beer, brought back other painful memories and he shut his eyes, aware that waiters rushing to and fro with food trays were eyeing him curiously. He opened them reluctantly then noticed someone at a bay window table at the far end beckoning. Three men, two of them absorbed in their food, heads bowed as if in homage to some divine power, with a corpulent middle-aged man, smiling at him over their heads. He made his way to the table. The fourth chair seemed almost destined for him, he would later think. Mistaking his preoccupied air for irritation, the fat man, napkin tucked into his shirt, left hand holding a fork pierced into his steak and onions said, 'You needn't glare at us like that; there is a chair at our table if you want the view so badly.' The newcomer's features relaxed—he smiled and joined the group.

He ordered sausages and a platter of sautéed vegetables. He had a lean face, a prominently hooked nose off-centre, thin lips pulled down at the corners, dark blank eyes with a slight squint in one of them, and a wide forehead ending in thick black-brown hair specked with grey parted in the middle. Each part of his face seemed at odds with every other, but the result was quite striking; some would even describe it as a handsome face with a saturnine set to it. Occasionally the others would steal a glance at him, wondering why his right eye twitched, noticing the indifference with which he ate or the way he hunched his shoulders or, more curiously, the tremor of his left hand as he raised a forkful of sausage to his barely open mouth. No one spoke and the young man was thankful for the lack of curiosity.

'Would you care for some tea?'

He looked up from his empty plate at the fat man with his back to the window, his huge head silhouetted against the bright afternoon light, his several chins quivering as he spoke, small black-browed eyes deeply buried in their sockets, pink labia-like lips. The voice was measured and slightly sibilant and reassuring. He peered over the bald dome fringed with dyed jet-black hair out to the open parking lot and beyond, the Art Gallery. He heard the scrape of chairs and scamper of feet, and she came into view in the parking lot. She threw a final glance back at the window table with a wistful and puzzled smile, her bangled hand on the door of her Ford Escort, her shades still perched on her forehead, and then stepped in, her sari riding up a plump leg.

'Yes, yes of course.'

'We have seen you before . . . you came last Saturday too, did you not? But it was full and you left.' The elderly white-haired man spoke softly.

'I tell you! That dead poet took the seat, and chewed our ears off. Did you give him the loan for his new flat at Dombivli? My God! Dombivli! That's like living in a manhole!' The young man, the third diner, spoke with mock exasperation.

'You youngsters! All south Mumbai-born, father's money, false attitudes! What do you mean *Dombivli*? It's a perfectly respectable suburb. A lot of south Indians, trade union leaders, journalists, live there—self-made citizens.' The old man sniffed.

Mr Editor, don't get so worked up. It's just that I would rather take all the shit from my brothers and live where I do than in Dombivli. You want to reduce the population? Hunh? Pile every pregnant woman into a rickshaw and . . .'

'That's foul, Arvind, perfectly despicable!' the defender of Dombivli exclaimed.

'Exactly! The fellow who makes the rickshaws should be arrested for poisoning the air. I believe Dombivli is worse than three Bangkoks.'

The corpulent diner seemed to awake from a dream. '"The Banker", that is what they call me, also known in less august circles as Ranjan Kapoor.'

The young smiled shyly at Mahesh. 'Arvind Purohit, Bookseller. I own the shop down this street, two buildings away; Konarak Books.'

He turned to nod at the young man with the scars of old pimples on both cheeks. Arvind was balding at a rapid rate despite help from hair oils and the graphologists he regularly consulted. He wore horn-rimmed glasses and his eyes drooped at the corners giving him an air of perpetual sadness. But he was actually very happy to be here among these men eating his omelette and toast, slurping his cream of tomato soup.

The fourth man at the table munched his food carefully. He was a sparse eater his plate had a single fried egg, boiled carrots and unbuttered whole wheat bread. He lifted the last of the bread to his mouth chewed slowly, sipped some water wiped his mouth with a paper napkin a small burp escaping his lips. His face was wrinkled with deep crevices running from the corners of his eyes to his jaw, on the way puckering up his mouth as if he had swallowed something very sour or lost his dentures. A thick crop of white hair, neatly combed and parted on the left gave him an oddly school-boyish look till you saw his small intense eyes behind thick black-framed glasses that made him look like an-out-of-work college professor.

'Dev Reddy, Editor. Glad to meet you.'

The others waited expectantly. He was their guest, so to speak; he wasn't up to it. Perhaps he was apprehensive about unforeseen journeys. Reddy frowned into his tea, Arvind looked up at the ceiling humming an aimless tune, then at the early beer drinkers at the next table. They could hear the plaintive litany of the crippled beggar and his family near the car park.

'I-er-Mahesh Vatsayana, work for a Consumer goods firm . . . marketing . . .'

They nodded and waited. He sipped his tea without another word.

Ranjan broke the silence.

'I know this sounds silly, but do you expect to come here next Saturday?'

The Banker smiled hastily, a weak smile as he raised a fat hand to stop Mahesh, who had looked up.

'I ask because we are . . . "The Group of Three" . . . meet every Saturday for lunch and some aimless talk about whatever strikes us and holds our attention—something that has escaped our notice in the papers, or hasn't been reported. Of course there is some banter as you would have noticed, but it's really quite an interesting way of passing lazy Saturday afternoons. We always wanted to be a "Gang of Four".'

Reddy chuckled.

'That just goes yakkity yak over lunch—as if that ever changed the world.' He sat back grinning.

'Stop dreaming, Mr Editor! Bill Gates has already changed the world without shooting anyone.' Arvind the bookseller laughed and leant forward.

'Look at our lives . . . even the Chinese never had it so good. You think Mao Dse Dong . . . ?'

Reddy pursed his lips, they almost disappeared into his mouth and Mahesh saw a very old man shake his head.

'Capitalism! *Tchah!*'

'Well, yes, yes, it's a pretty good idea—the group of three, I've never been part of . . . you know. Yes . . . yes . . . money is all there is to . . . life, love . . . Look, can you excuse me. I have a headache. Waiter, bill please.'

They watched him leave, an unhurried stride but with his shoulders hunched forward as if he were walking into a strong wind.

'He's carrying a load.' The Banker had shut his eyes.

"Oh, is it so? Why not, it's Saturday night and he has to find a girl, he's probably not married, too quiet for any woman, I think, but young, like me, so all power to him, I'd say.' Arvind nodded sagely. He was impatient to leave.

The Banker did not respond. He saw Mahesh cross the parking lot and walk past Lund & Blockley Opticians and Elphinstone College and soon he was gone from sight.

'That man, he has a story in his heart.'

He planned to turn right and cut by the old Watson Hotel with its warren of offices—a shabby remnant of what was, nearly a hundred years ago, one of the grandest hotels. But he had time on his hands, the light had still not faded and he did not think they would be out this early. So he walked into the Gallery of Modern Art and idled past a retrospective of a long-forgotten painter, not really seeing anything, his mind cloaked in a fog. He wished he had stayed back till The Wayside shut at seven, when it would have been dark enough for him to find what he was looking for. He walked out into a muggy early dusk, the sky, a dirty blue-black, a starless canopy over the mindless rush of cars and buses trailing plumes of sulphurous smoke. The muggy heat wore him down; he felt he was wading through thick mud. A little out of breath he made his way past the Institute of Science, shoulders hunched, a thin trickle of sweat running down his lean face. He passed the Old Secretariat, the old campus of the university with its clock tower, a smaller Big Ben, till he saw them—a small army of whores and transvestites pacing the length of the broad sidewalk—their ramp—solitary silhouettes against the illuminated stone facade of the brooding High Court, its arched blind-eye windows like empty sockets, the palm trees slicing up the street lights into shadows.

He smiled to himself.

He walked past the faceless figures at the darkened railings, tantalising almost intangible forms. Nerves tingling, heart pounding, he scanned a pair of legs disappearing into miniskirt, a cleavage revealed as a sari slips off a shoulder, young boys in shorts with painted lips. The fog in his head cleared. Then he spotted her, face hidden in the shadows of a palm tree. It was the way she held herself, hands by her sides, like a statue or a parade-ground soldier, staring out towards the Oval, her bare short-skirted legs ending strangely in a pair of Reeboks.

The sheets had been washed and ironed but he could trace the stains of past encounters in the oddest of places. A strong smell of insecticide hung in the air. In a corner he saw one of its victims, a full-grown roach belly-up in the last throes of asphyxiation. He swallowed the rising bile and watched her strip to her black, faded panties and white bra stained under the arms. Her face had the immobility of death, her lips full blown and blood-red a fresh wound on her bleached, puffy face. But she smiled shyly as she slid off her panties, shrugged off her bra and climbed into bed. He stepped out of his pants and hung them on the stringy coat hanger next to last year's calendar. She turned on her side away from him, foetus-like, and he lay next to her letting his stiff cock rub gently against her buttocks. She quickly turned and he climbed on her and she opened her mouth in feigned ecstasy and he turned away shut his eyes and pictured a cliff edge where a woman, her face hidden by a *duppatta* blowing in the wind was calling out to him and in one juddering moment of helpless release he cried out, 'No-o-o-o-o' and it was over. He rolled off her, gasping, his eyes still shut and tried to remember the name of some god, but all he could whisper was 'O God, O God'.

Arvind Purohit, hurried to lock up The Konarak bookshop. After seeing off the last salesman he went to the cubbyhole at the rear of the shop that served as his private office, opened a drawer of his walnut-wood desk and leafed through his brown paper-covered collection of pornographic downloads. Every time he flipped the sheets of coloured printouts he had spent hours scanning on his computer, he felt a shiver of excitement and loathing. And like many a young man in this city raised in a joint Hindu family, married at twenty-five to a fresh faced bride out of the small towns across the country, he fantasized about the terrifying possibilities that these hairless pudenda and pendulous breasts, offered. Today is Saturday night he thought to himself. Can I get Raju and Ashok to spend an evening at the Golden Gateway? There is one waitress that he had imagined would be willing . . . If only his pals had been with him!

Ranjan Kapoor boarded the 10.31 local for Bandra and the two-bedroom flat he shared with his daughter and wife, feeling pretty content with himself. He had dropped Dev Reddy to Churchgate station from The Wayside Inn, the old man reluctant to leave but Ranjan had insisted; the inquiring eyes behind the thick glasses that glinted in the bright lights of the Asiatic department store had registered churlish disappointment. But he had climbed out of the taxi.

As the head of credit-recovery operations in a small cooperative bank that had branches in select commercial areas, especially near the stock market, servicing depositors, petty traders and small businessmen, Ranjan Kapoor took the view that everyone in this city had a dark secret. This view had not come to him from any deep introspection on the follies of the human race, much less of that section of it living in this huge 'garbage heap'. It came from a simple conclusion that if he had one or two stories, so would others. He carried his own secrets with a dreadful unease that gave him sleepless nights and blood pressure so high that his doctor marvelled he had not yet suffered its worst consequences. He could put a stop to the little but highly lucrative racket that he ran, all by himself, in the department. But the urge to satiate his fantasies drove him inexorably into a furtive existence that he tried to reconcile with the public image of him as a family man.

Ranjan Kapoor, The Banker was considered an honourable man because he looked and felt like one; portly and courteous, his temperament calibrated to the occasion. He dished out his observations on this world and the hereafter with an urbanity and gravitas that impressed and, comforted the listener. Not many would remember what he had said but they would carry away an impression of having been in the company of a dependable man.

Ranjan walked down the dark passage towards his apartment, rang the bell after fumbling with the latchkey, heard the shuffling footsteps of his wife, gave a sigh and stared into the face of a woman who had shared his bed for thirty years, of which the last fifteen had been spent both sleeping with their backs to one another.

'How was your day? It's pretty late.'

'Where is Deepika?' He asked idly.

'Still partying I suppose . . . does she ever tell me> So, how was your day?'

He undressed in the bathroom, staring at his blue-grey jowls hanging like half-filled water balloons. His breath felt garlicky, his tongue thickly coated. He used the tongue cleaner, brushed his teeth, rummaged in his trouser pocket, memorized an address scribbled in Hindi and tore the yellow slip of crumpled paper into small neat pieces, flushing them down the toilet. He walked back to the large outsized bed, to his side of it, and lay down.

'I survived.'

Dev Reddy's pique gnawed at him all through the journey home to Virar, northernmost suburb of Mumbai. He knew he was too old to figure in Ranjan's nocturnal plans that he was certain did not include a seminar on waste management. This was the fourth Saturday in a row that he had abandoned him; normally they travelled together on the 6.45 fast, with Ranjan getting off at Bandra. They would continue where they left off at The Wayside. He wanted, no, *needed* his company for as long as it was possible. In Ranjan he found a bridge to life, as he had not lived it, a dangerous balancing act that excited his frayed imagination. Take for example, Ranjan's view that 'nations do not live by principles, but for opportunities.' Or his conviction that mankind cared less for truths or falsehoods than for the persuasive statement. For Reddy, reared on a diet of Marxist history, the idea that, by implication, even revolution was nothing more than a game of dice, or a 'window of opportunity' to use the currently fashionable terminology, was nothing short of heresy; yet was it not a more appropriate description of the drama of revolution than 'historical inevitability'? And that dark skinned young man with those blank eyes, what did Ranjan mean, 'he has a story in his heart'?

In the frenetic swirl of people buses and auto-rickshaws he hunted for the three-wheeler monstrosity that Arvind had derided. He could not have agreed with the young man more. Every ride home in the noisy vehicle, driven by manic drivers, their eyes everywhere but on the crater-pocked road filled him with dread. The narrow streets were also lined with buses, cars, handcarts, trucks and almost every mode of transport mankind had invented. As the smoke-belching rickshaw careened wildly, Reddy felt his dentures shake and his heart rattle. What did he have to look forward to at home? He had told Ranjan a lot about the emptiness in his life, but for all the silent sympathy, he knew he alone had to cope with his failure to have seized the chances that came his way or to have looked for them when they did not. An angry bitterness burst through his churlishness as he thought of his one-bedroom flat, his diabetic wife, Rajani, once a comrade-in-arms, and his younger son Sripad. He supposed there would be no dinner; they would have eaten the remains of the afternoon's meal. He stopped the rickshaw at a south Indian eatery, a block away from home and ordered Curd Rice to quench the fire in his belly. His doctor, an old comrade-friend had told him he had hyperacidity aggravated with '*Hurry, worry and curry.*' Must be the curry he thought. He fancied himself free of the worries and the hurry that beset virtually everyone in the city, and his friend The Banker, because as he reminded himself he was a revolutionary; well, if not that, at least a radical editor; all too often these past few years he thought himself just an old man with fading memories and painful regrets.

Working out of a small office in the textile mill area, Lalbaugh, in central Mumbai, Dev Reddy, had spent the best part of his youth and formidable writing skills penning graphic descriptions of rural poverty and peasant uprisings in eastern and southern India, especially Andhra Pradesh. He had left his village in the Telengana districts of that state, the centre of a brief peasant uprising as a young college graduate eager to escape the drudgery of small towns and smaller villages, imbued with an unformed ambition to make it in Mumbai in the heady days after independence when the city had jobs going a-begging, what with the English packing their bags. He could have walked into any of the old colonial offices in Ballard Estate, many now owned by oil merchants from the inner city and asked for the designation of his choice, so short were young, English-speaking Indians. He almost did. Then an old communist from his village, asked him to edit a new journal 'dedicated to the spirit of the Telengana uprising.' Reddy yielded; he could not resist the lure of fame and immortality the old veteran of countless polemical battles and seductions threw his way.

His fire and brimstone rhetoric, the declamatory style, peppered with lurid images of rural poverty brought him instant popularity and sealed his fate; over time his acquaintance with leading bureaucrats and academicians who wanted to write for the new radical journal and the unctuous respect they paid him for that favour blinded him to his existence on the edge of poverty.

Not a single worker let alone a peasant read the English-language journal. The textile workers were least interested in the deprivation of the Indian peasant having fled that poverty in their own time. And, as city workers, they had their own nightmares to cope with, what with many textile mills on the verge of closure because of failing markets and the misappropriation of funds by owners.

When the globalization fever hit Indian shores the purveyors of public opinion, enamoured by the flow of wealth and glamour into the cities, quickly forgot the peasant. The owners and financiers of the Fourth Estate were loath to spend column inches on anything more than the urgent demands for more freedom to spend and an incessant cataloguing of the ways to do so.

The journal's circulation plummeted; funds began drying up. Reddy had to flow with the sentiment for urban news stories or drown. He was ready to swim with the current after a brief struggle with his ideological beliefs. His elder son Hemendra, was about to graduate, unfortunately with an indifferent academic record and would need funding for further studies; the younger fellow Sripad, was still in high school. But how was he to feed the appetites of the new generation readers? Desperate, Reddy offered his writing skills to the textile workers' unions next door. He had to learn about the workingmen's lives from scratch after spending two decades living virtually next door to them. He could barely feed his family.

Then he met Ranjan Kapoor, through a common friend in the union of a factory that was about to close down, the owners having squeezed it dry. Their arrangement was sealed over tea at an Irani restaurant at Byculla close to the branch of the bank that Ranjan had joined at the time as Head, Research. Their relationship appeared like divine intervention to Reddy because he was being offered enough funds, 'courtesy sympathetic friends in the banking community, you know' to continue writing his radical editorials in support of peasant uplift if he would agree to do background research on companies as and when asked. 'Get to the bottom of things Reddy; let's expose the corruption in capitalism. Traders, all of them, all they want is to break the laws and siphon off our money. I mean the bank's money.'

Reddy's dying embers of radical politics were rekindled. Blinded by his good luck and the Samaritan's kindly appearance (yes, The Banker was portly and suave even then) and ungifted with an inquiring disposition into human motives, Reddy's journey into another fantasy began then. How was he to know that it would start unravelling that afternoon at The Wayside Inn after Mahesh Vatsayana joined them for lunch?

Mahesh hurried home in a foul temper. The girl had wanted money for a taxi to her tenement in the Mazgaon dock area. He volunteered to drop her but she was evasive. Contrite at his abruptness, he offered to buy her a takeaway dinner, a pizza; she refused. All she wanted was this last contact, the money to take her home. Under the pallid light she looked haggard, the eyes dark empty sockets. She stepped away perhaps aware of its treacherous quality; she wanted to leave him with a better impression. In a softer tone she again asked him for a hundred rupees. Silently he handed it over turned on his heels towards a waiting cab. At home he showered, threw himself on the bed face down, arms akimbo but sleep would not come, his body coiled tight, his head in a vice-like grip.

The Rajabai Tower clock chimed: four a.m. He walked unsteadily to the open window looked up at the starless sky dark and faintly ominous, the metronomic tick of his bedside clock adding to his unease. To his left beyond the halogen lights of the Marine Drive the Arabian Sea appeared like a dark and deep void. He dressed and head bowed, shoulders hunched, headed towards the promenade. A lone cab parked at the curb groaned to life as he stepped onto the parapet wall, the old Fiat rumbled some distance ahead of him and stopped. He hastened toward it, perhaps he could chat up that cab driver, share a cigarette swap stories. But the taxi moved again. He stopped, stepped off the parapet, and made his way home to wide-eyed solitude.

Ranjan woke late that Sunday morning, alone in bed, his head weighing a ton and sandpaper on his tongue. He wondered when Deepika, his daughter of twenty-one, had returned from her party. He heard Madhavi, his wife with multiple sorrows, out in the kitchen and hoped she had not yet made his morning tea. He loved it richly brewed and milky and she insisted on serving him tepid dishwater with Equal.

She had already made the tea. He sipped it distastefully.

'When did she get home'?

'Hanh! Better you ask in what condition.'

No! No! He screamed to himself. *Not again!!!*

'Didn't you hear her stumbling against her door like an elephant on high heels?'

He sat on the toilet seat head in hands, his bowels frozen.

Just twenty-one! A drunk already? How am I going to get her married? No wonder her mother hates me, that old hag.

With a self-assurance that had blinded him to the consequences of his 'rationalism' he had let her drop out of college after just one year so that she could 'discover' her 'true calling'. Three years later, Deepika was no more than a personal assistant to a prominent socialite who somehow never remembered her promise to introduce the young college drop-out to the world of design.

Ranjan Kapoor had promised his wife he would talk sense into her because she constantly reminded him, not without some malice, that their daughter's wasting ways were the result of his solemn blessing of three years ago: 'You are now a citizen of the Indian Republic with voting rights, so go forth . . .'

But he did love his daughter with an aching devotion, so he pulled himself together and knocked on her bedroom door. Getting no answer he gently pushed it open and almost fainted as the stench crashed into his face.

Vomit.

Pools of dry vomit caking the floor.

Deepika was snoring through parted lips.

He held a towel to his mouth, picked up a halter-top from the windowsill and stared at his lovely daughter, frail and beautiful in her pink flowered nightgown that had ridden up her thighs, tears rolling down his stubbly cheeks.

No one dreams in this city; everyone fantasizes. On Sundays some semblance of humanity returns to the besieged inhabitant. The fantasy machine winds down and the grim recognition of a frenetic yet empty existence in the slums, poky flats, ugly high rises cheek by jowl with pavement dwellings creates its own claustrophobia. The precious few beaches on the western side of the island and the promenade on Marine Drive are choked with hapless inhabitants of tenements or *chawls* from central Mumbai desperate for a whiff of sea breeze and the illusion of open space.

Dev Reddy had no need for the fleeting freedom of the Marine Drive promenade or the city's narrow beaches. He never stirred from his small apartment in a sprawling complex of five-storied buildings named Paradise Residency at the edge of a foul-smelling swamp, the remnant of the old mangroves steadily chopped away by the city's builders. The five hundred square feet flat consisted of a tiny bedroom, a larger living room at one end of which was a narrow strip of a balcony just half the width of the room and in which Sripad, his younger son sought refuge from his father's disaffections in the tattered copies of Shakespeare and American poetry. Against the opposite wall of the living room next to the black and white television set that Sripad was now trying to switch on was Reddy's 'study', a square wooden table that doubled up as dining table on weekdays for his wife and son. On Sundays it was his vehicle for voyages into the dark souls of businessmen that owed Ranjan's bank. Above were two plywood slabs nailed to the wall on which rested the collected works of Lenin and Stalin and above them, a framed reprint of Marx staring down balefully at the dispirited lives in this cramped quarter. Next to the synodal decrees, lay Rajani his wife's cookery books; on weekdays Sripad's film criticism and Great Literature paperbacks from lending libraries rested grandly on all. Saturday night, he morosely moved them into the balcony.

Here in Paradise Residency, while the editor was labouring over "contingent liabilities", Rajani was busy in her own refuge from a disenchanted existence—cooking. She too had had hopes but they faded faster than her husband's once the sons came along. She had been part of a group of feminists at Mumbai University in the late sixties, a doctoral candidate in Sociology whose passionate embrace of Vladimir Ilyich Lenin's view of change had scared off her free thinking thesis supervisor fresh from Bryn Mawr. While other women from her group drifted with effortless ease into feminist studies znd crabby academic faculties, Rajani had to make some hard choices: street-fighting activism or motherhood? She chose the latter with the same zeal she had embraced feminism and revived her skills in south Indian cuisine. Her sons were growing fast, their appetites were voracious and their demands on her time incessant. She washed their clothes, ironed their school uniforms, supervised their studies and cooked for them. She did not complain because she loved them enough to forgive them their uncaring boisterousness. But she did mind that Dev never helped. Then Hemu Reddy the eldest went off to Presidency

College in Calcutta, the hotbed of leftist politics of every hue from pink to purple, made inflammatory speeches and sometimes spent weekends in filthy jails. She wept silently for years after he joined the Communist Party (Marxist), even though he hacked his way through the dense thicket of party bureaucracy towards politburo membership. She wept not for Hemu as tragic replay of the father but for his yet-to-be-found wife as inheritor of her burdens.

She sat in her spotlessly clean kitchen, a small woman with salt-and-pepper hair tied in a knot at the back, her stern face softening as she looked around the neatly stacked steel boxes containing the ingredients of her fine art, fresh flowers at the feet of a silver-plated statue of Lord Ganesha. She felt a momentary peace in her heart.

'Sripad, tell your father lunch is ready.'

Sripad was watching the HBO channel on silent mode. He hated Sundays, alternated between boredom and exhaustion and did not reply. Hunched over a file marked 'Confidential' Ranjan had given him the previous night, Reddy did not hear his wife either, only the echoes of Ranjan's words.

'Okay, Reddy get to work on this gentleman. The bank has a heavy exposure on the company and we want the money back.'

Arvind Purohit, the young owner of the Konarak bookstore near The Wayside Inn, hated Sundays because he had to spend them in the sprawling flat in central Mumbai with a family far too big for his comfort; two elder brothers and their wives, not to mention runny-nosed nephews and nieces and the old patriarch, eighty-five with a far-from-senile brain. His eldest brother, Devendra, a silent and taciturn man who walked slowly, as if treading on eggshells, and spoke even slower, as if measuring the rates of return on his words, had dark hooded eyes on either side of a beaked nose that he kept pinching when angry. He ran the family stock-broking business. He considered his youngest brother's love for books about an India he was convinced never existed, a mark of ill-formed character. Arvind wasn't sure how much he loved Devendra but he knew he feared him; especially when he would think aloud . . .

'Maybe we should rent the store out. What do you say, *Bapu*? I know some foreign banks would give their right arm for that location, ha! Ha!'

The old man would bestow upon his youngest son an affectionate smile, his rheumy eyes lighting up with an ancient compassion. Then with a brutality that rocked the brothers back against their chairs, the old man would reply, every Sunday:

'We don't need to. Arvind loves his work, which is more than I can say for you, Dev. The only difference is that you don't know what else to do. And that goes for Amol as well. Where is he by the way?'

Obese at thirty-two, Amol, the middle brother suffered the benevolent and sometimes malicious despotism of his father and brother with cheerful fatalism. Too lazy to work his way into the old patriarch's confidence through hard work, he aligned himself with his elder brother's views on life, commerce and disdain for Arvind's "arty farty" proclivities.

After exchanges like this, Arvind felt warm affection for the old man he had never been close to. The youngest of the three brothers and four sisters, Arvind had far too many surrogate parents to feel the absence of his father or his mother who had died six weeks after his birth, exhausted by child-bearing and diabetes. He carried all the burdens of the youngest sibling on his frail and sloping shoulders. In adolescence and later, he bore the constant bullying of his brothers with indifference because by then he was being tormented by his urges; playing Peeping Tom on his doting sisters in various stages of undress. As a married man he did not feel the shame anymore when he fantasized about Sheetal, his elder sister-in-law, Amol's wife, a cheery, open-faced spirit with wide hips and quivering bosoms that silenced the most animated conversation and brought Arvind close to hysteria every Sunday at mealtimes when the sisters-in-law served the Purohit men. He had developed his voyeurism in tremendously risky conditions so it had the quality of a precious gift that he savoured in brief spells. There was always the danger that his eldest sister-in-law, Parvati, a thin and austere woman, or Poornima his wife, a shy girl-woman with bright and curious eyes would catch his own feverish orbs casting about in hot pursuit. But he could not help himself; Sheetal leavened an otherwise tortuous day at home with its ponderous hierarchy, the aimless cheer of maids, retainers and his overbearing brothers.

At 10.45 on Monday morning, commuters desperate to get off the densely packed compartments before the train moved on, rudely pushed a young man onto the Grant Road Station platform. Sripad Reddy felt his damp and crumpled cotton shirt and cursed himself for not having taken the earlier train from Virar. The 9.42 seemed to bring the entire working population of that northernmost suburb and stations en route to Churchgate. But he wouldn't be late for his 11 o' clock appointment and he was happy for that.

He walked past overflowing garbage dumps, pavement dwellers cursing, shitting and cooking or just getting stoned, mounds of shit, dried rivulets of piss, banks of cars and scooters baking in the hot sun and a stretch of scooped-out road, the stench of trapped sewer water mixing with other odours.

Fifty years ago Sleater Road had been lined with gulmohar trees and stone townhouses. All that remained were some of the trees dying of asphyxiation; one townhouse that had been turned into boarding rooms and 'social' clubs that were really gambling dens. The rest of the mansions with their courtyards had been razed to make way for high rises with tiny balconies.

An idle curiosity had brought Sripad to this crumbling street redolent of a gentile past. He was on his way to an interview for a job as the estate manager of a new residential colony. Not that he wanted it. For four years after his Master of Arts in English Literature, he had got away without one and at twenty-six he took pride in that fact. He made some money writing film reviews for an English daily newspaper; his name was familiar to those few readers of the small film review section that appeared on page three, twice a week. He spent long hours at the British Council and The American Centre libraries, reading up review magazines, film scripts and poetry for a new angle, a weighty quote. The price he had to pay for this happy indulgence was getting a bit too high these days; his mother wanted him to rise early and exercise, his father wanted him to help with *The Last Frontier*.

He resisted; in his father he saw the corrosive effects of a consuming obsession, the banality of reality and its irredeemable horrors. As he confided to Vispy Irani, his only friend, owner of Connaught Café near Princess Street:

'Vispy, my father cannot understand why I don't read Nehru's *Discovery of India*. Why the fucks should I? I learn more about India from *Discovery Channel* than he has learnt after writing about the Indian peasant forever.' Sripad wrinkled his forehead.

'You told him that?' Vispy's eyebrows had climbed into his hairline. Sripad just stared at his old friend.

As he waited at the wrought-iron gates for the security guard to finish shouting his name into the intercom to someone who shouted back even louder, he thought of his father's gaunt and lined face after he had told him that Shakespeare had more to teach the striking workers than

Karl Marx; like an open window through which he saw a vast empty landscape stretching to the horizon, a parched earth where the wind had stopped howling and the cloudless sky was stripped of all mystery. He saw his father, perplexed and angry shake his head in disbelief, 'You are mad!'

He walked up a slight slope between two five-storey buildings, towards the tallest in the complex, twenty-five floors high. The wind through the corridor rocked him back a little. He thought of the black monolith in Kubrick's *2001: Space Odyssey*. He climbed a short flight of shallow steps, stepped into a cool black marble-walled foyer at the end of which stood a bank of elevators. To its left was a plain glass enclosed "Office" Behind a wooden desk piled with papers sat a man with a handle bar moustache, ramrod stiff, leafing through a small sheaf of papers in front of him. He beckoned with his index finger, gestured for him to sit and continued reading.

His father did not speak to Sripad for a week. Usually, most verbal communication was one sided, Sripad doing all the listening; so silences were welcome. But after this incident the son felt a pain, a grievance transmitted through blenches, flinching of expression, a tension waiting to explode at the mention of Ezra Pound or Bob Dylan.

He was intuitive enough to sense in his father a loss, like the face of a cliff slipped into the sea and he felt a remorse that surprised him. It was at this point in his relationship with his father that Vispy gave him the idea.

'Look you have to get out of their hair, show them you are more than just a smart-assed guy. So here it is. How about a job that doesn't tax your meagre intellect, requires little physical activity apart from admiring some scenery and that gets you a decent check every month end for doing all this or even less?'

'Balls! Vispy, there is no such job unless you are want me to marry one of your rich aunts!'

'You'd be no good for them Sripad! They want men with hairy forearms not eunuchs like you. No, listen, there is this swanky apartment complex on Sleater Road, you know Grant Road Station West . . . ?'

Curiosity, just curiosity and a need to make Vispy feel nice, had brought him to this office. He, a film critic now an *estate manager*?

'So-o-o . . . Sripad Reddy, *hmm.*'

Colonel Biswas, secretary of the Pyramid Heights Cooperative Housing Society, retired Infantry officer, twice decorated in long forgotten wars, harrumphed

'Son, are you sure you want this job? Master's in Literature, film critic on weekends, you say? Well? We certainly would like someone like you, the last bloke we had . . .' The old man sniffed, shook his head. 'Drank on the job . . . could have had him shot at dawn. *Ha . . . Ha* . . . Just joking. The army, you know. It never leaves you.'

Sripad nodded. A sudden tranquillity fell over him, like fresh morning dew. He could hear children out in the landscaped garden, crows cawing maniacally and pigeons cooing like demented lovers out in the open parking lot to the right of where they sat. Off in the distance the clackety-clack of the suburban train rose and fell. He liked the twinkle in Colonel Biswas' eyes even though the old man spoke as if he had a potato in his mouth. What the hell, he thought, why not step onto the straight and narrow; he could always hop back on the wayward highway whenever he wished.

'I'll take it.'

Arvind jerked awake, swung his legs onto the floor and stared at the stain on his pyjamas, his inner thighs sticky and wet. He turned furtively, unsure if his wife was asleep; she faced the other way a slim inert arm over the curve of her hips. He heard his sisters-in-law in the kitchen. Somewhere a flush was worked. On the TV Sudhansu Maharaj droned about inner peace to an entranced patriarch. A wistful sadness crept over him; all he could remember was Sheetal in a tub of . . . buttermilk was it? On a dimly lit stage and he running toward her but never getting close enough. What was that between her legs, a lotus? And when did this explosion . . . ?

'Warappen? Arvin?'

'Nothing. Nothing, go back to sleep.'

She stretched, yawned hugely and held him in her gaze, clear as a summer sky.

'Arvind . . . did you scream or what, hunh?'

He hurried to the bathroom His irritation mounted, he felt trapped as he dabbed at the stains.

'What happened? Why is your pyjama wet?'

'Tchah! Nothing. Just careless, washing. Get me my trousers will you? I'm having a bath.'

Poornima stared at him open-mouthed. 'Without tea *first?*'

At two o clock that afternoon, after her elder sisters-in-law retired for their afternoon nap, Poornima sat on her bed to write a long letter.

'*Dear Mama,*

It has been so long since I heard from you Mama and I still feel miserable in this house. I know I have been married almost two years and I can hear you muttering how that is enough time for any bahu, even the youngest, to settle in. But Mama, I can't! This house has a million people, really! You can't walk an inch without someone bumping into you or tripping over one of the brats. My eldest brother-in-law Devendra bhaisahab gives me the shivers Mama, with his snaky eyes and smirky lips. And the city, mama! All that noise and crowd! Why do the men always walk into you? Yes, I have said this a hundred times and yes, you have asked me to adjust, how do the other women in the city manage to keep from colliding into strangers, but Mama I miss you and Dilipbhaiya's pranks and my St John's College friends, I hate this city. And that brings me to the reason for this long letter. Arvind . . . ! Mind you . . . I am not complaining. I know you told me marriage is hard work and that husbands don't please easily. As far as I am concerned, husbands are boors. Mama, I mean it! He never touches me, never makes me feel like a woman!! Arvind doesn't even look at me! And mama, listen carefully, I am not making this up, I have seen his eyes glued to Sheetal's backside! He sits at lunch with his mouth open like that dog we had? I can almost hear him panting'.

So tell me, is this Romance? Of course you'll say, look beta, 'It's marriage!' And I say, I serve them all at the Sunday lunch don't I? And yes I lie dutifully on my back and my husband pants and grunts above me in the dark, once a week, yes? But let me tell you Mama, he is not there! Physically yes, but he is far away and you know what, Mama dear? This morning, he thought I was fast asleep, but I know his pyjama was wet BEFORE he went to the bathroom. What do you think? Have I married a baby wetting his bed? I don't know, Mama, what should I think? Please write soon. I'll stop here. I know I have already taxed your brain. Okay, so I won't tell you anymore, okay? Give Papa my humble greetings, and tell that brother of mine to visit me. I miss him so much!' ps. I have to run down to the post office before the brats return from school,.

Your loving and confused daughter Poornima.'

But she did not post it. She stared at the words for clues to a hidden self. Opening her heart with such candour, Poornima wondered if she had confessed too much, even to someone who was close to her, like sisters, people used to say of daughter and mother. Should she write to her best friend Gyan, with whom she had shared all the secrets of yearning and romance in far off places, away from the rough and tumble alleyways of Agra with its restless youth full of wasting energy instead? The letter seemed to codify in cold print the confusions tormenting her young heart but she was frightened at the finality of its indictment.

She sought refuge in self-pity, despairing of her loneliness in this crowded house and the city with its teeming bodies and hot hands. She ran to the mirror and stared at an oval face, a wide mouth with full lips, small pointed nose with diamond stud and wide-set eyes. She ran a finger over her lips, cupped her flushed face, eyes glistening with tears . . . "Little Big Eyes", that is what her schoolteacher, an Anglo Indian had called her. She wiped them, kneaded her temples gently and asked herself: So this is it: a life of benign neglect, the inadvertent touch and indifferent affection?

No! She cried to herself. She was beautiful and intelligent. First class MA in Sociology from St John's

College Agra with a collection of Dhaka cotton saris the envy of the neighbourhood! She did not need Madhubala or Nargis, celluloid goddesses of rapturous seduction to guide her!! She would seduce Arvind! She would teach him . . . things. She would improvise on the job.

It was getting close to five and she could hear the kids clamouring for pizza and cheese toast. She would not post the letter, she decided. She did not tear it either. She shoved it into a drawer in her dressing table and scurried out.

Mahesh Vatsayana walked into his office in the Ballard Estate area overlooking the harbour greeted his secretary, Mrs. Bisell, an old Anglo Indian Bible-reading widow, who whispered:

'Mahesh, that new manager-recruit's waiting for you. You know, the one you wanted to meet before he left for Lucknow? Yogesh Sinha?'

He looked at her blankly; his hand on the brass knob and then remembered. He nodded walked in and around to his swivel chair. The young man rose to his feet.

No!

'Mr Vatsayana? Pleased to meet you, Sir, Sinha, Yogesh Sinha.'

It cannot be!

'Mr Vatsayana? Are you okay?'

Except for the voice it was he, come back from whatever unquiet world his soul roamed in. Mahesh shut his eyes tight, took a deep breath and shook the offered hand now limp with uncertainty.

'Sit down.'

He stared at the fresh and eager face, the same thick black hair, the back of which was done in a cross hatch after the current fashion; he had noticed that. Slightly long sideburns and a well-trimmed moustache above full lips.

Oh God, *Hey Ram!*

He sat back and raised his eyes to the fan whirring languorously, like some dark bird of prey.

'Yogesh, you married?'

'Yes Sir! I've . . . just this last summer. A management graduate like me Sir. In Lucknow; she will be a housewife. See, Sir, we . . . ahh . . . plan to have a family and, maybe after a couple of years she can start working.' The young man looked up at the saturnine face unctuously.

'Perhaps you Sir, I mean this company could, I mean would, have use of her talents?'

'Do you love her?'

"Of course! I . . ."

'Enough to kill somebody, anybody perhaps even her or yourself to preserve that love?'

'Mr Vatsayana! I do not know what you mean! I came here to seek your blessing for this new assignment.'

'I know and you shall have it. After all you are going to report to me and you are the best candidate for the job.'

'Thank you, Sir.'

'So . . . Do you?'

'Whar, what Sir?'

'Have a safe journey and all the very best, Mr Sinha.'

With a spring in his step Yogesh made for the door, sweat trickling down his flushed cheeks. He paused, turned to stare at the fan above Mahesh's head, mesmerised by its lazy movement. An involuntary shiver ran through his plump body then he smiled at Mahesh standing against the open window, staring at him. His voice was hoarse and seemed to come from far away.

'Thank, thank you Sir! If you should come by Lucknow . . .' Then he was gone.

Mahesh slumped against his swivel chair utterly drained. He did not know what had come over him except that he wanted to feel young once again, perhaps to believe that this was not a spirit or some other restless ephemeral being but he himself. That by some tripping of fate lines he had come in like form to tell him that all was well. But he was denied that respite, it was a Monday afternoon and he was fantasizing.

The buzzer on his phone trilled and he was reminded of another appointment. He asked Mrs Bisell to reschedule it and pulled out a faded sepia photograph of his parents. A grim looking man dressed in a double breasted wide-lapelled jacket with a bow tie askew squinted back at him: a pair of spectacles dangled carelessly from his right hand. His mother, in a brocaded sari, head covered, modest, subordinate, her face already haggard, no make up not even Afghan Snow, so popular those days with Indian middle class men and women desperate to lighten their skin, starkly exposed, brutally frank in her portrayal of service to this short-sighted man. There was no date; a wedding photograph? What were those hills in the background?

He was their only child but he could not recall the intimacy of a mother's caress, the warmth of a father's companionship. Mahesh's father lived in his own world before his retirement from the Central Defence Accounts branch office of the Ministry of Defence. He rarely came home before son and mother had eaten their dinner, in silence. After his career was over, he spent his days shuffling around in carpet slippers, an old vest and faded, striped pyjamas, face drained of cheer. Night after night, Mahesh heard them in their bedroom, he raging with suppressed anger, she trying to calm him.

They lived for and off each other. So infrequent were his interactions with his father through childhood that he could count the number of times he had helped him with homework. Old Vatsayana had a head for figures, Mahesh did not and he tried to get his son through complex equations and Pythagoras' Theorem. But their moments were always marked by urgency on his part to get it over with. Then he died leaving his son with the mystery of torments and his widow, with her anguish.

One day as Mahesh returned from school, his mother pulled him to her room and told him a story. She told him of a man who had come to Bombay from the north, a runaway, seeking fame as a scriptwriter in the city's film studios in the years following Independence and the communal riots that rend an ancient land painfully adjusting to its new destinies.

With Imtiaz Shaikh, a poet and friend from Agra, that city with its Taj Mahal and its cantonment, the symbols of two imperial powers and two kinds of poetry really, Alok Vatsayana had knocked on the doors of producers, budding and famous actors, and directors looking for a good story. He had a few, Imtiaz, a couple of poems. They knocked in vain. Money was running out, but food was cheap and they shared a dormitory in a lodge near Victoria Terminus, the railway station run by a man from their town, a kindly soul. But creeping poverty was taking its toll; the stories became less hopeful.

Then one day, armed with a reference from an exasperated producer eager to get rid of them, they knocked on the doors of a literary salon of sorts run by a rich lawyer. There, a famous scriptwriter whose name his mother never disclosed, asked them for their offering and Alok Vats, ("the shortened surname he wrote by had a nice creative ring to it" she said with a wistful smile), handed over a tattered handwritten manuscript.

It was a tale of a young man's odyssey to the big wicked city, a rags-to-riches saga of love and rejection and a disillusioned return to the village.

All this was told to him in a low voice, urgent, slightly breathless. Perhaps for the last time, Mahesh felt his mother's breath on his face, her eyes mirroring her disappointments, urging her son to believe and perhaps forgive them their self-absorption and he, the son, sensing adventure as the story unfolded, trying to sketch a portrait of his father as a young writer in those tumultuous times . . .

They were asked to come back the next day. A maid handed them an envelope and shut the door in their face. The famous scriptwriter was to the point; he offered to buy the story and Imtiaz' lyrics with full copyright, for Rs 3000, at the time, a princely sum. If the terms were agreeable they were to ring the bell again and the maid would hand them the cheque. If not, she would return their manuscripts.

Alok Vats, did not want to accept, because he felt short-changed; Imtiaz, the poet was willing. He wanted the money to move across to the new state of Pakistan. He confessed to a rage at the riots ravaging the city even after Partition. He told his shocked collaborator that he could no longer write about love and hope, that the words he wanted to pen were full of revenge and he did not want to write that way, at least not in this land he had been born and raised in and loved and now hated . . .

Mahesh's father found this a betrayal but kept silent. What could he say to alter this man's mind, their destiny? This was his reward then, abandonment in every sense of the word. He dared not consider a life of storytelling without his lyricist, his muse, poet-in-arms hustling for fame and God knows what else. They took the money, both angry and bewildered. Imtiaz Shaikh left for Pakistan, Alok Vats, watched his dreams vanish around the nearest bend. She had been on that platform too, a young pampered girl who wanted to spend the rest of her life with this tearful man, erasing all memory of betrayals.

For the first, and the last time, Mahesh learnt of his mother's love, a compassion really so overlain with, perhaps mistaken for, acceptance of every turn in his declining self-esteem that she could not push him to write anymore. He did make a few half-hearted attempts but the phenomenal success of a film sealed his fate. It is a film that has made box office history with its songs and story line. It made the protagonists millionaire-stars overnight; the famous scriptwriter, who had paid two starving and confused writers, became more famous. But Alok Vats was crushed; the story was his, though the famous man had changed the bleak ending. He ranted for days, felt cheated by fate, all the more so because the poet's songs had been faithfully rendered. They were to reverberate down the decades in restaurants, marriage halls and taxis.

He needed Mahesh's mother more than ever before but her father would only approve if he took a regular job. That was the final blow. Alok Vats sat for a competitive examination. Aloknath Vatsayana was selected for the Central Defence Accounts as a junior officer. The urge to write was smothered though it was to rekindle briefly and irresolutely. .

'We will always be what others make of us.'

To Mahesh, then a boy of sixteen, her account had a flavour of the epic. For his father he felt a profound gratitude and in himself the faint stirrings of ambition but by the time his mother got to the end of the story he was devastated; her words a harsh sentence on human endeavour. And he carried that legacy of fatalism into mature age. Till, at the age of thirty-one, he met Abhijeet and Meenakshi.

Dev Reddy clambered onto the already full 9.15 fast, seconds before it pulled away from Virar on its one hour and a half run to Churchgate. He managed a seat on the edge of the hard, wooden bench, looked around nervously at the dense crowds simmering with jagged restlessness. There was a time when he could take the suffocating heat, sweating bodies, the aimless affability and pointless rage of commuters condemned to their temporary incarceration in his stride. What had leavened the ordeal was the conviction that the "peasant revolution" would liberate him and his fellow passengers from the urban nightmare of which commuting was the most horrific part. The dream faded, age was now leading to infirmity, and every day he felt panic rising in his chest as he ran over the permutations of his death in this mobile prison.

'Move over, uncle, share the seat!'

As the train rushed into Lower Parel he peered through the grilled window at the crowds whizzing past and for a moment he had the feeling that they were gathered in such numbers to welcome the chronicler of their ordeals and failed struggles. Then the tidal flood pushed him back and he tried to fight back, to get off that damned train, this living hell, before it moved on again. He despaired of the train's irrevocable certainty, its mindless devotion to punctuality, why couldn't it wait just a few seconds longer, why the hurry, we are all going to die but I don't want to fall in the gap, and he pushed with all his might at shoulders and arms and then, miraculously, a hand propelled him forward he could not keep step but he was off the train, shaken but in one piece, his glasses askew. He ran a hand feverishly over the smooth leather of his beloved shoulder bag. There was a slash, his wallet was missing, office files and lunch box untouched. He sat on a bench, his mouth open, staring at nothing.

At eleven thirty on Tuesday morning, Ranjan Kapoor greeted Balchandra Gandhi with a courtesy he reserved for his chairman, whom he met sometimes, or the Prime Minister of the Indian republic who he had never met and did not think he ever would. Accompanying Gandhi was Nasreen Treasurywala, the managing director of the company he owned, a buxom, pasty-faced lady with heavily mascaraed eyes behind smoky glasses, thick greying hair tied in a severe knot. She was dressed in a midnight blue chiffon sari with a matching, low cut blouse. The gathered top end of her sari would often, during the course of the meeting, fall off a plump shoulder. The man in front of him, with a trim white beard flecked with grey, the upper lip overshadowed by a thin patrician nose, would frequently stare down its length, head canting to the right in abrupt movements, suggesting long hours before the mirror perfecting attitude and posture. Gandhi was now very angry for having been kept waiting over an hour.

'Tea, Mr Gandhi and, er, Ms. Treasurywala? Or maybe some fresh fruit juice? The canteen . . .'

'No, thanks, Ranjan.' He looked down his nose a bleak smile playing around thin lips though his eyes did twinkle.

Nasreen laughed, a hoarse, rasping bark that ended in a simper.

'And let's get down to first names, Ranjan. This is the first time we are meeting. I knew the guy who was handling my portfolio, Ranga, quite well. I never seemed to have met you, er, in which department?'

'The privilege is entirely mine, Mr Gandhi.'

'Bal . . . '. The beard quivered as the head canted.

'Gandhi . . .'

'Bala . . .'

'And call me Nasreen'. Ranjan nodded a bit impatiently.

'Yes, yes, no problem there. Anyway, I can assure you that we shall get along quite well, I can see that. Yes, I was earlier in Chemicals and Insurance. It's only last month that I was sent your files.'

'Moving up the ladder, heh? Stick by me and you'll grow . . . That's what I say to all the creditors who come knocking . . . I mean . . .'

'Yes, that's what I wanted to know, er, Bal, you see, the bank's exposure is, let's see, Rs 75 crore, all told with penal interest for non-payment etc. etc'

'Is it that much, Nasreen, US$ 15 million . . . ? *Har, har,*.Ranjan, I prefer to talk dollars you know, part of the global network. Ahh, Nasreen, what do you say? I thought it was only 6 million.' He struck the pose at Nasreen.

'No-o-o-o-13 more likely.' She nodded vigorously, her spectacles slipped down her nose. Bal stared at her for a second, then turned to Ranjan.

'Anyway, Ranjan, that's neither here nor there, actually we're waiting for our financial director, you know him, Ravi Sarathy, he should have been here an hour ago. I don't know. His cell phone's switched off. Maybe he's gone to meet *mama*, This is ridiculous!'

'I beg your pardon?'

Nasreen broke in.

'He means his mother. She wanted Rs 5000 for the temple and Ravi has taken it to her. Don't you remember, Bala, you told him to take her the money *before* coming here. He has the files.' She barked once more.

Ranjan clicked his tongue.

'Anyway, we have the records and they are right here not in some temple. So, tell me Bala, how do you plan to return our money? As you know, the Reserve Bank of India is pretty shirty these days about bad loans, sticky portfolios and we are particularly worried about clients that—'

'Oh, we are turning the corner, believe me.' Bala sounded peeved.

'—do not respond to several reminders from our loan recovery officers.' Ranjan let his bleak eyes rest on the haughty nose.

'Nasreen, are you aware of this? Why wasn't I told?'

'At least a thousand times we talked and you asked me to get Ravi to prepare a draft reply. God! Don't you remember . . . anything?'

She shook her head once more and rolled her eyes up at the ceiling.

'Nasreen! This is ridiculous! I told you to take care of this matter.' He stopped, his eyebrows furrowed in thought.

'Ahh!! Now I remember. Ranjan, I've been busy with our annual function, you know, Best Hunk of the Year Award, and believe you me it's no easy task. Then the party, selecting the sponsors; BodyArt has to get the right ones to protect its image of a clean and ethical outfit. Can't have condom manufacturers, tobacco peddlers.'

'Though if they are generous enough . . .' Nasreen chipped in with a snigger.

'Anyway we have the right sponsors now. Hope you and Mrs Kapoor can make it; October 3rd you know, at the Ritz.' Nasreen leaned forward and her sari slipped off her shoulder.

'Yes, Ranjan, we wanted to have it on October 2nd, that was the only day the Rooftop banquet hall came cheap at The Oberoi, but then we were told it was a dry day—no liquor on Gandhi's birth anniversary . . . for God's sake! *What the fuck!* I mean, where's the fun in a party with all those rippling muscles and no blue label, only Fanta? I mean, for God's sake! And you know—just joking, God, *I'm so tired*!'

Ranjan stared so hard she flinched, turned away; two pauses later she pulled her sari back into place.

'So tell me Bala, what's happening? Apart from the party of course . . . the bank would like to know.'

Gandhi pulled a small chit of paper from his trouser pocket and shuffled forward on his chair. With supreme confidence he reached out for a pencil from a holder between them and scribbled furiously, tongue curling around the edge of his lips.

'Okay, Ranjan, and this is between you and me . . . till we're up and running, if you know what I mean . . .'

The Banker pinned them down. Where had the money gone? Where were the assets to show for the loans raised? They sputtered, dissembled, uttered clichés Ranjan was sure had been picked up at cocktail parties. 'We hit the deck running.' 'Stuck to our knitting.' Or, one that mystified him, 'Got our knickers in a twist.'

Gandhi was flustered. Ranjan's question was not part of the script. Most bank managers he had faced in the last few months were happy just to meet this courteous man, full of risqué jokes, a faint British accent with Nasreen in tow. Most bank officials were only too glad to echo the banalities to their superiors; 'Mr Gandhi is committed to turning his company around, our money is safe, rescheduling would help.'

Ranjan's avuncular smiles suggested warm empathy at the hardships they were enduring. But he was smiling because they had confirmed his suspicions of greed and generous swipes for personal profit, extravagant spending, slack schedules and cost overruns, emptying coffers replenished with fresh loans. Crony capitalism. As he saw them off at the door to his small office, he knew that he would be meeting them again . . . after that report from his old friend Reddy.

The Ladies compartment of the 8.43 Andheri fast that night wasn't crowded and Deepika hesitated before entering; there is safety in numbers especially in the Ladies and even more so at night. She quickly clambered on as the low growl of the train started and sat at the window looking out at the lights on Marine Drive. She was tired and depressed. Aditya, that inebriated lout who had made her an offer of a "lifetime career" as he called it, had spoilt a perfect sunset evening by the United Services Club promenade. But she admitted the fault was hers. Ever since she had left college midway through the first year she had drifted with an odd mix of decisive inaction, or as was the case now, with futile activity. She felt her grasp on the opportunities she thought existed to be so tenuous as to almost frighten her into a state of paralyzing despair. She did not like the idea that Aditya had suggested. *'Hospitality' indeed!* She did not think she wanted to smile at fat greasy Japanese or Americans, not as a floor manager at The Taj Mahal hotel even if the 'art' of hospitality was taught her free. She thought she should ask her father to pull some strings and get her back to college. That boring world of studies and examinations was so much more reassuring than this hospitality thing. *Catering?* She had wanted to be a fashion designer! And what Shernaz B had done was to send that boring drunk Aditya. She felt cheated. She envied her father his Saturday sessions at the Wayside Inn. Suddenly she wanted him close by her, his huge hand stroking her hair, his voice so comforting.

The Wayside Inn was packed with the usual mix of students from Elphinstone College, poets huddled in a corner smoking their cheroots and drooling into their beer, housewives bored to death from shopping at the newly opened Westside department store. At one table, four middle aged ladies, exhausted from their campaigns around Ladies Innerwear, Cutlery and Household Linen, waited for their steaks and chicken in wine sauce and assorted pastries, with varying degrees of tetchiness.

At the table by the window, Ranjan, Reddy and Arvind were eating with an air of studied detachment. Occasionally one of them glanced towards the door, out the bay window. They were waiting.

'Hello. We were waiting.'

'Thank you . . .' He looked around for the waiter distractedly.

'What a week! One blast after another . . . Bombs at the Taj, where were you? Then the arrest of the police commissioner, rapes, so many single women in this city! God I can't believe this!' Arvind smacked his forehead.

'What, Arvind, what is it you can't believe . . . That police commissioners cannot be tempted? Rapes . . . ? Daily fare. Forget them.' Ranjan looked upset.

'It's so demeaning, all the same.' Reddy ran his fingers through his thick white hair.

'Makes you lose faith in everything, democracy, justice . . . I remember Marx saying, "The educator must be educated.'

'Mr. Reddy, we are talking of flesh and blood.' Arvind leaned forward for emphasis.

'So you think it's all fine for the chief guardian of the law to shield criminals?' The Editor was addressing the Banker. Ranjan smiled pityingly.

'My dear Reddy, why blame a cop who has another six months before his pension spins him into grubby anonymity?'

'That's true boss, this fake stamp racket . . . the guy running it has the blessings of the former chief minister . . . and the current deputy chief minister is—'

'Yes Arvind; in hospital with chest pains. So you see Reddy there is some reckoning in this world.' Ranjan attacked his steak vigorously.

'Tchah! This is cynicism of the worse kind! Arvind and you reduce democracy to a circus!'

'But, Reddy, in this country it is one! You think your man on the street, or the poor peasant in your village in Andhra, votes with his head? You think parties contest issues . . . in English . . . ?' Ranjan stared at him in stagy amazement. .

'No. Of course they do! In the regional tones, lack of drinking water, electricity, sanitation, people dying like flies, multinationals. Come on you, we, know the issues, Ranjan, unlike our young downtown Mumbai friend here, with his head in ancient India.'

'Mr. Editor, Sir, who cares for the WHO, multinationals? The voter in the village wants to know if the candidate belongs to his community or caste. Democracy means community, which is the joint family. I should know, even if I am a townie. Add them up and you get India!'

'Frankly Arvind I think you are cross eyed and so are we.'

Reddy looked for help.

'Mahesh?'

Ranjan broke in impatiently.

'Look, Reddy, of course you are right about the basic problems in the villages. But that is exactly my point! Wretched and yet they vote! Why? They love it! All that ceremony! It's a festive day at someone else's expense. We can only guess at who they think's picking up the tab, interpret the gestures. Religion? Community or caste? Who knows? Who can tell?'

Mahesh let the waiter shove the fried eggs with a side order of sliced raw tomatoes before him. He ripped some bread, dipped it into the yolk, swirled it round, the yellow ooze spilling onto the plate. He brought the bread to his mouth and followed it up with a tomato sliver. He kept silent.

'But we need to know, to separate statecraft and religion!' Reddy broke the pause.

'That's all fine in London and Paris. Here religion and community have tied people for thousands of years, and torn them apart ever so often. Separation! T*sk .tsk,* an empty word here.'

Arvind was nodding excitedly.

'Boss, that's correct, some of the stuff I have; there are books you know that talk of ancient Indian societies getting it all mixed up nicely. Politics, religion, sex. a revolving door.'

Reddy's puckered mouth was twitching agitatedly.

'Ranjan! That's anarchy! We need codified laws that bind people, to . . . to an idea of what is right and wrong . . . Why . . . *you!* You of all people—should know that!'

'And what if you don't have it, or can't decide which is which?'

He muttered these words, his voice soft and immeasurably sad.

The Banker looked at the dark inscrutable face, an eye twitching. He heard Reddy's impatience.

'Yes, yes! Morality . . . A poor man steals to feed his starving children. Theft is understandable after all we are more enlightened than in Dickens' time. But the due process of law—'

'And what if your morality also fails you?' The voice remained soft but probing.

'Hunh? I don't know. I think that is ridiculous! Even tribals, I remember, in Dahanu, just outside the city barely 150 miles away, they have a code of honour, yes a code, not written, but one to live by. You sound like a nihilist.'

'Editor Sir, I for one do not know what you mean but I think there's a good yarn looming on the horizon.' Arvind smiled at Mahesh and turned to the silent corpulent Ranjan. 'What do you say, Mr. Banker, interested?' Ranjan did not reply. Unfazed, Arvind turned to Mahesh.

'Okay, Mahesh so tell us . . . Spin us a good yarn. All this sermonising after a Saturday lunch is depressing.'

Suddenly Mahesh felt embarrassed. He was unused to so much attention. But a new stirring in his blood propelled him.

'I don't know if you've ever read this story about Radha, a girl of sixteen in a remote village in Orissa that was eaten by a python?'

They stared blankly.

'One afternoon Radha's younger sister came home in tears and told the parents that she had come upon Radha sitting under a tree when this "*ajgar*", crept up behind her, opened its jaw wide, and in one swift motion had gulped her down and then vanished into a pit in the thicket. Repeatedly questioned by unbelieving parents, the young seven year old, tearfully stuck to her story that Radha had been "swallowed" by a huge snake. There was some suspension of belief here, because villagers knew or thought they knew that pythons don't ordinarily eat their fare this way, in one long and quick swallow. But by nightfall and the next day when Radha hadn't returned the parents called a meeting of the village council, the panchayat and a team of angry young men marched off to look for a bloated python.'

Ranjan seemed to be dozing, Arvind's jaw had dropped but Reddy was impatient and kept turning around to look at the other customers. He also signalled the waiter for some more tea.

'They found her slippers and shawl at the foot of the tree.'

'Oh God!' Arvind exclaimed in disbelief

'Oh, for Heaven's sake! What is this!' Reddy burst out.

'They followed a dirt track into the thick jungle . . . and in a pit they found a python but it wasn't the one they were looking for. This one was rather lean and showed no signs of having devoured a five foot three young human being. But their fury was so primal that they killed it nevertheless.'

'Isn't this story . . . what does it have to do with law, justice; Ranjan?" asked an exasperated Reddy.

'Quiet, Dev. Drink your tea and think Mao's thoughts.'

'Who's the author . . . ?' Arvind had pulled out a small spiral pad.

'Hunh? Alok Vats.' It just slipped out.

'Vats? Never heard of him.' Arvind set aside his pad. Ranjan opened his eyes turned to Mahesh.

'So . . . what happened?'

'They called in the police who called in the forest department and the environmentalists who promptly began to disagree amongst themselves as to the plausibility of the young sister's story. But the parents were broken with grief their belief in the unity between man and nature had been torn apart so abruptly.'

'But had it?'

Mahesh looked startled. Ranjan's eyes were almost shut and he barely heard the whisper.

'The story spread like wildfire . . . the python became the most evil manifestation of the dark spirits that tribals had feared and placated for centuries. Word spread that the culprit if you will, was a huge python with a belly like a cow's, sighted a year ago in the neighborhood. Memory and myth served up an awful potent of sudden and violent death.'

'You know I don't think I like this story too much . . . it has too much mumbo jumbo.' Arvind wondered how to respond without sounding disrespectful.

'Sir, please!. But this story is great. Alok Vats? What else has he written? Can I order some stock?'

'A week later the parents were visited by a peasant from a neighboring village; he had a tale to tell. He had been walking along the riverbank a few days ago. On the far side he saw a young couple bathing. They were . . . frolicking in the shallow water . . . the sounds of their laughter carried on a faint breeze across the placid river. He mentioned this incident, uncommon as it was in these times when truckers from the highway nearby posed such a threat to young women and even men, bathing in their scanty clothes at this lonely stretch, to his village elders. They had sent him here.'

'Oh, *ho ho*! Wow, so that was it!' Arvind looked around at the others, nodding all the while.

'Yes, she had faked her death in connivance with her young sister. The young couple were traced the boy was beaten within an inch of his life. Radha had eloped with her lover because she did not wish to get married to the man of her parents' choice. Of course, she pleaded and begged, telling her parents to kill both of them if they would not sanctify their relationship, now a week old. The parents did discuss that possibility with the village elders because it was a matter of honor. The panchayat understood that death was an honorable and noble exit for Radha and her lover. But it had a different agenda. The village council wanted to reinforce a code of conduct based on a collective morality by example. So they banished the boy from the village the girl was to spend the rest of her life serving her parents. The boy migrated to this city where he now lives and works on a construction site.'

'God, to forsake your parents, your identity, your life . . . for love?'

'Yes, Mr Reddy, for love. They did not run away, to a city, to another district or town; they created a mythology of love in harmony with their own concept of love conceived in 'death' and rebirth. Was it suicide? Murder? And what about her accomplice, the young sister, acquiescing in her sister's fiction of a grotesque death, perhaps seeing this as dress rehearsal for her own reinventions, just seven years, mind you. And what about her lover, a young man willing to shoulder the awesome responsibility of creating and sustaining a new life for them both, for all time till death or new fictions tore them apart?'

'Don't forget the python!'

Arvind hurried back to his shop, reluctant to leave but Ranjan edged him away. Reddy, silent and a bit morose, lost in thought, stood listlessly at the curb along with Mahesh and Ranjan. No one made a move to hail a cab; each stood there at the edge of the pavement, staring across at the Art Gallery. The streetlights came to life, casting a pale sheen over them. Ranjan turned to Reddy and whispered . . .

'Reddy you better get a move on. I have to meet someone, for a drink or two. So don't wait for me, okay?'

Reddy did not stir. His mind was racing once again; why was Ranjan fobbing him off? What was he up to, and this time with that crazy fellow Mahesh? He didn't like this at all.

'I was hoping we could, you know, talk about that Gandhi case.'

'We'll talk it over Monday afternoon okay, old friend? I am a bit tired and I do have to meet this gentleman in a short while. Here's a taxi. Okay, off you go. And give my regards to Rajani.'

They watched the taillights disappear as the taxi rounded the plaza and vanished in a trail of blue exhaust towards Churchgate station. Mahesh wanted to leave but he also felt an inexplicable desire to linger with this overweight man. Then Ranjan spoke.

'I was wondering if you'd care to join me for a drink? Not too far from here; they serve some good chicken *tikkas.*'

Mahesh looked around at him, a sudden agitation evident in his voice.

'I, hunh, I don't drink, I mean I used to when, no I haven't touched a drop in years. What is it you want of me?'

'Nothing. You don't have to—have a coffee or something . . . I just found your story interesting . . . and, I want to talk with you, you know, without the others. I don't think they would understand. So what do you say? Just an hour or so?'

Suddenly Ranjan wasn't sure. What was he going to say to this dark inscrutable young man with his sudden bursts of anger, his silences? But the story had troubled him. God! The waywardness of youth! As the taxi drove up Shahid Bhagat Singh road towards The Drumbeat Bar Ranjan suddenly turned to Mahesh.

'Listen . . . that story. It wasn't real was it? I mean, I understand it was written by some fellow Vats, never heard of him myself, but it wasn't true was it? I mean, there is no tale written like that is there? You invented it on the spur of the moment didn't you?'

'Alok Vats, was my father. He searched for the truth in stories.'

'But were they true? Can one imagine any human being and that too a young girl, erasing her life by a fiction for such a frivolous thing? To frolic naked in a river, unaware of the havoc created around her? Was she mad?'

Mahesh smiled as they alighted and Ranjan paid off the taxi.

'Perhaps. But she followed her heart. I should say . . . the writer looked into her heart and found it a festival of colour.' Ranjan stared at the smile that creased that young old face with its hidden sorrows and suddenly wanted to get away. At the door to the Drumbeat, the fat concierge with his peak cap with gold braids and dark trousers below a huge belly had a smile on, hand on the door. Ranjan looked at his watch.

'Er, Mahesh . . . see . . . hunh, I'd like to get home. Not feeling too well. We must have that drink someday'

He wasn't used to walking in crowded streets; his wheezing increased as his short legs pulled him through the flood of evening commuters, pavement vendors hawking everything from garments to watches. Ranjan hadn't felt this confused in a long time. He could not have said why he had walked away from that young man he wanted to share a drink with, perhaps tell him a bit about Deepika. But he also wanted to get away to a world he understood and felt in control of. Heart? He knew about the head and the need for men like him to satiate the urgings of the devil below his waist. He felt in need of someone young, with no heart but a soft body that he could feast upon with his eyes and hands. He pulled out his mobile and called a number.

'Hello, yes, I was given this number by a friend and I was wondering if there were any roses . . . What? Yes, yes, okay . . . At the Yacht Club, near The Gateway, in half an hour I'll look out for a white Maruti 800 last digits 981. Okay. goodbye,'

Ranjan was driven into a high rise in the Cuffe Parade and escorted to the thirteenth floor. At the end of the passage, Albert, his contact man, rang the bell whose soft chimes had barely sounded before another swarthy man in white shirt and trousers, opened the door and bowed to Ranjan. He was led into a large living room, made to sit on a plush sofa into which he sank with a grunt. A small coffee table by his side held a jug of cold water and glasses. His mouth was dry and his heart was pumping faster than usual. Just then a stately-looking woman in her forties, decked in a black sari and gold bangles walked out of an adjoining room with a large smile on her powdered face.

She had small eyes that liked what they saw for her smile got broader.

'So glad you came . . . *arrey* Thomas, get *sahab* a drink or something . . . ? No? Alright, Sir, now how can we help you?'

'I beg your pardon?'

'You like boy or girl friend? Housewife; fortyish? Oh, but how silly, let me introduce you to them. You can choose. Come with me.'

She walked him down a small corridor, her hand in his, small and nervous like a quivering sparrow in a giant paw he thought, past framed reprints of garish mountain streams and oceans with small ships bobbing on them, into a neat room with a large double bed. The air-conditioning had been turned on so the room was cool. He smelt room freshener. The sky-blue curtains were drawn, the lighting was soft and off to one side was a shelf, half way to the ceiling, filled with paperbacks. He was still in a daze, and felt an irresistible urge to sleep. He felt dizzy on his feet so he sat at the foot of the bed and watched the girl traipse into the small bathroom, throwing him a shy smile. as she shut the door. He felt a deep shame and a yearning that frightened him. Why did that image of the tribal couple frolicking on the riverbank haunt him so much? He was panting and he could feel his cock beginning to harden. This girl was older than Deepika; that had been his first thought when he chose her over a pleasant looking plump housewife who fingered her *mangalsutra* at her neck nervously. No names had been mentioned and the lady had explained that there was to be 'no penetration'. He had felt embarrassed at this crudeness but oddly also re-assured.

She emerged from the bathroom in a nightgown with floral prints that made her look very prim. Her small feet peering beneath the trailing edge of the dress lent her a vulnerability that he found endearing and, exciting. She had slanted eyes, a flattish nose and a faint black down on her upper lip. But her smile was bewitching and she had a very measured voice, as if she had learnt English at some correspondence school. She sat next to him and stroked his face and he smelt mint on her breath. As she put her hand between his shirt buttons and felt his ponderous belly and his soft chest he cried out in delight, and turned to her and kissed her on her full swollen lips, and as she closed her eyes and shoved her tongue into his mouth he cupped her small breasts, free under the nightgown and as if on cue she reached for his trouser zip and he imagined himself as that slender, naked tribal boy embracing his ebony-skinned girl, her bouncing breasts and coffee-dark nipples flattening against his own lean hairless chest. Ranjan rose to his feet with a grunt, the better to pull his trousers down. She backed off and looked the other way as he muttered the name of Alok Vats under his breath, like an invocation. With his trousers and drawers gathered at his ankles, he looked up from his massive and taut cock and caught a momentary fear in her eyes and the spell was broken and he saw her for what she was, a young college kid playing grown up games for the money. He stared at her, imprisoned in his trousers and Jockey shorts, his swelling refusing to die on him and sadness overwhelmed him, a wave of melancholy for the whole world and for his daughter and most of all for himself and the enormity of his desires that taunted this frail girl in the floral nightgown. But she had regained her composure and sat on the edge of the bed, facing him. Gamely she reached for his throbbing tumescence, her other hand round his ample waist, stroking his flabby buttocks. He groaned and called out for mercy and before he knew it, he felt her warm, wet mouth slide over his straining penis and his heart would have burst through his chest had he not by some mysterious act of will, pulled free of her and stumbled into the bathroom, reaching the sink just as the world exploded. He stood there forever it seemed, staring down at the water washing away his ecstatic frenzy, the draining water sounding like a waterfall that he would have liked to sit under for all time with all memory erased. Then he looked up and saw in the mirror a haggard face with its dewlap folds. Then as in soft focus she came into view, hand on doorjamb, her face mirroring confusion and compassion and he was ashamed of his corpulence but most of all by his naked passions. But she kept looking into his eyes and held his gaze in the mirror as the sobs died and then she smiled and held him from behind and pulled him out into the room and made him lie down and slid her nightgown off and hugged him close and stroked his hair. He whimpered in pain or desire he wasn't sure but he knew this fantasy was over and paid for. He felt a desperate need to run from this place and almost called his daughter on the mobile after he had dressed. She did not leave the room with him but lay in bed, her legs wide apart an open invitation but he felt a self-disgust that startled and perhaps frightened her. He shut the door before she could stop him. .As he rode the elevator this time without any escort, his mobile rang

'Ranjan, where have you been your mobile is not working or what? I have been trying you for years! Where is Deepika? Do you know what time it is? She hasn't come home and neither did she call. Go look for her! What kind of father are you, *hunh*?'

Arvind's head spun as he hurried back to the bookshop. God! What a story that was, that Mahesh, *really*! Alok Vats? Never heard of him but boy! What a couple; were they stupid or what? You want to elope you have to run as far as legs and wheels can carry you. Can't play that trick and live next door! Frolicking in the river, naked! Hey Ram! You can do this only in *Lady Chatterley's Lover*. He locked up reached for his mobile and set about organizing the evening. Being an efficient sort of fellow, he also called home, asked for his sister-in-law Sheetal and told her he would be late. He knew she had an incurious mind, usually giggled into the phone whenever he called. She appeared so self-contained.

The din was unbearable. Nursing his third lime and soda, Arvind fought creeping nausea; for a panic-stricken moment he thought he was going blind. A thick pall pf cigarette smoke hung over the cavernous, dimly lit hall on the mezzanine of the Golden Gateway. At the far end, four girls in short blouses and below-the-navel skirts gyrated clumsily to remixes of film songs. Strobe lights splashed garish colors across their bodies creating the illusion of disembodied body parts keeping time to the metronomic beat. Arvind's friends were boisterous with lewd whistles and catcalls. But for him the enchantment lay in the waitress with the braided ponytail. Reed-thin, she moved awkwardly on high heels, her sari, a dark blue rustling behind and around him as she waited on them. She had gifted him a ruby-red smile as she placed his fizzy glass before him, he was certain. He sought meaning in the way she set out the quarter plates, stretching out to the other end of the table over his shoulder, rather than walking around to it. He wanted to snake his hand up her legs; he thought of ravishing her behind the Gents revolving door, her sari hitched up to her waist, a face-to-face, on-the-feet fuck but he found the furtive contact of her warm thighs when she stood up close behind him, arms across a serving tray, an auspicious start.

Suddenly, his bladder swelled; reluctantly he rose and she stepped back as he made his way to the toilet down a small passage across from the kitchen. Through its swinging half-doors, he glimpsed rows of pots and pans stirred by sweaty cooks in dirty singlets and shorts, and his stomach churned faster as he pushed open the heavy closet door of the narrow toilet with its urine-splashed, damp cigarette ends-strewn floor. When he returned, his lady-love-in-blue had moved to another table, now standing behind a visibly drunk man with a puffy face and raspy voice conversing in a guttural Marathi with his cronies who all seemed to be in a similar state of inebriation. Then he saw the man across her beckon. Squinting in the dim lights he thought he saw him slip her something.

Outraged, Arvind bit into the Chicken kebab; this gorilla had tried to buy her! He was oblivious to the girls on the dance floor, now peeling off to the encouragement of hundred-rupee notes hurled at them. His friends too were flinging balled-up notes; *one-rupee notes for sure, the stingy bastards!* Had he liked this sort of thing he thought bitterly, he would have walked up to one of the dancers, held her hand and pressed a thousand rupees into her palm, kissed her passionately and told her to get herself a haircut and a new sari.

Carried away by his sense of nobility, he felt he must rescue that frail waitress from those louts and, for certain, multiple gang rape. He stared at her but she had eyes only for the drunks she was serving and his chivalry contorted into a fury at this betrayal. The manic strobe lights distorted body shapes and the music sounded like dogs barking at someone throwing up. He peered into this miasmic hell and thought he saw her vanishing into the kitchen. Blindly, he lurched through delirious men on their feet waving their incomes away, and stood a little way off from the kitchen doors banging open on creaking hinges, his heart pounding. The roar rose to a crescendo as one of the dancers pulled at the drawstrings of her diaphanous skirt and held the two ends between her teeth in a kaleidoscope of flashing colors. He turned back just as she walked out with a tray full of drinks and he took a step forward; she was startled then she smiled, stopped in her tracks and waited to pass, head tilted thin eyebrows raised inquiringly. He opened his mouth to make his profound observations on life and love. Just then his mobile rang.

Hey Ram! I forgot to switch it off!

Panic paralysed him; the waitress with a shake of her head, squeezed past him, tray held high. Frantically, he reached into his pocket, squinted at the display and almost fainted. *Poornima!*

He ran towards the entrance waving the trilling mobile in the direction of his friends, took the landing two steps at a time onto the street.

'Hu, hullo?'

'Arvind! Is that you Arvind? Where you are? I can't hear, are you in the vegetable market or what?'

'No, no, I, I am . . . at the station, yes, Grant Road Station seeing off a friend.'

'Grant Road station? Why Grant Road? Churchgate station would have been better for you, isn't it?. *Tcha*! Arvind, come home, no one here except Old Broomstick, I mean Paravthiji and she is looking at me quite funny. Sheetal and Amol have gone to Renu Kaki's house to coo over the new baby and I am feeling scared alone here. Will you come home? And soon?'

'Oh for heaven's sake calm down, why don't you both watch TV? She is just an old lonely woman. What was that you called her?'

'What was that? I called her what? I don't know . . . Parvatiji that is what we call her, right? What? What did you hear?'

'Never mind. Coming in about an hour, okay?'

'What? Round midnight? And what do I do till then? Catch flies? Old—I mean Parvatiji is pacing up and down the corridor and I think I hear the car so Sheetal and Amol are back. Only my husband is at Grant Road Station seeing somebody . . .'

'What do you mean *seeing* somebody? I told you, listen with your ears wide open—I am seeing someone off, okay? At the station, in fact I hear the train coming. Bye now, I'll see you soon.'

Arvind ran up the stairs; dancers had left the floor, and his friends were quarreling over the bill. He looked around for the waitress in blue, shading his eyes against the harsh glare of tube lights. He looked in vain and he was sure she had gone off with those goons. The waiters were sullen and the one that took their bill gnashed his teeth when he noticed the tip.

Arvind felt immeasurably cheated by life; all lost because he had not switched off his mobile.

Reddy woke with a foul temper. His sleep had been fitful, disturbed by Mahesh's story and images from a foggy past. He remembered the night before; his headache began then. Rajani usually greeted him with a stoic silence that discomfited him for just that moment. This time she managed a weak smile and he stiffened.

'You are not going to believe this but Sripad has found himself a job. Estate manager.'

He looked at her blankly, his thoughts still on Ranjan and Mahesh.

'What's that? Sripad has a job? But, how is that possible?'

'What do you mean? Some people take their responsibilities a little more seriously, you know.'

'Estate manager? What on earth is that? He is managing private property? *My-y-y son?* Whose property?'

'Sometimes, Dev, I wonder if you know which planet you live on? He has promised me half his pay. That should settle the mounting society dues and maybe, who knows, maybe we could have a holiday? I've always wanted to get away from this swamp—even for a few days!'

Her sob went unheeded. Reddy still couldn't believe his ears. *Estate manager?* His son is mad! If he is not reciting some gibberish about foul promontories he is *protecting property?!*

He sat at the dining table and held his throbbing head. He pulled the BodyArt papers open and, unmindful of Sripad snoring on the carpet behind him plunged into the murky world of corporate finance. His restless night lent his work a fierce clarity of purpose. He rose, an hour later to reward himself to some strong coffee, heard Rajani stirring in the small bedroom and hurried back to his worktable. As his weak eyes scrolled down the company's balance sheets the old editor heard his heart singing in joyous wonder. In these papers he was discovering more than evidence of flagrant misappropriation; he believed BodyArt was reconfirming a faith, edging him back from the brink of apostasy; for that, he felt strangely grateful to the very person he was stalking.

Behind him, his son was waking up with noisy yawns, small farts and grunts. Reddy's smile vanished; he stopped scribbling, pencil held over the percentages and flow diagrams, and waited for the sky to fall.

'Morning, *Babu*, you heard from *Amma?* I got a job as foreman—.'

'Hunh? I thought you were some kind of property—.'

'Just kidding. You know that song about a guy getting a job as foreman and the working class can kiss my—.'

'Foreman? What on earth are you talking about? Can't you see I'm busy? Roll up your bedding and try not to sing in the bathroom, okay?'

'Come on, *Babu* this is Sunday, let's all take in a film, some rubbish thing, popcorn, ice-cream, what do you say?'

Reddy turned in his chair. He saw a fresh face, clear eyes, tousled hair, hands busy scratching beneath the T-shirt. For a moment he softened at this picture of innocence, and he wondered when and where his own innocence had gone. And, much against his will and to his horror, his mind spun back to Mahesh and the story by—what was his name? Alok Vats—what kind of name was that? He watched his son stride past him, a tribal clinging to a waif with flowers in her hair. He looked up at the ceiling, BodyArt scurrying away from his mind as it flooded with memories of apocalyptic times and a moonlit river and a silhouetted breast, of other missed opportunities for fleeting but hot love He heard Sripad singing in the bath.

> "*Can't you see I love you-u-u-u,*
> "*Please don't break my heart in two-o-o-*
> "*O Sole mio . . .*"

Reddy put down the pencil and began to cry.

Alone at the curb after Ranjan had abruptly changed his mind about the drink invitation and walked away, Mahesh felt relieved. He had a painful remembrance of evenings spent in places like The Drumbeat. Every whiff of stale tobacco smoke and whisky that wafted out as the door was swung open, every single glimpse of a brightly-lit interior, and the sound of tinkling laughter abruptly cut off as the concierge shut the door, made him think of Abhijeet alternating between euphoric joy and sudden despair, both abrupt but intense. He hailed a taxi standing nearby. He paid no attention to the driver's incessant chatter about police corruption. Like an air bubble, a conversation with his mother, days before she died, broke through his recollection of the evening. In the midst of her sever osteo-arthritic pain that confined her to bed, she had told him about a suitcase that contained his father's "writing material".

'That suitcase is yours. But open it only after I am gone. Promise me that.'

He had. A month after her death he rented the house to an old couple friend of his parents who were happy to let him lock the master bedroom. He had fled to Dadar. The suitcase had remained in his parents' room ever since.

At ten o'clock that Sunday morning he was on his way to his childhood home for that suitcase, a voyage of discovery that would force him to confront his past.

It was an old tin suitcase, battered in parts but the lock held surprisingly well. The keys had been tied to the handle of the box. He carried it back to Churchgate with nervous excitement. A musty mothball smell rose as the lid creaked open. Notebooks, of the school-exercise type, bound with a thick rubber band, a case full of unsharpened pencils, a box of fountain pens some of the tips rusted. An old scarf, a crumpled hat and two pairs of spectacles in their cases, an old copy of Wren and Martin's English grammar covered in flaky brown paper. There was a photo album with the picture of a dazzlingly beautiful Madhubala on the cover. He flipped the pages, thick soot-colored leaves with dog-eared pictures; the glue had given way in many places. Some of the smaller photographs slipped from the album. He put them back and laid the heavy album aside. He opened one of the notebooks. The first page had this inscription.

"Memories of a fragmented life."

Then on the next page:

'My father wanted me to study Mathematics at St John's College, Agra like him but my heart was not in it. I wanted to read Literature, and when I told him of my desire he looked at me in a strange sort of way, and shook his head. But the first "native" professor of Mathematics at the local college at the young age of twenty-four, the first Indian in town to own a bicycle did not protest. And so I entered the portals of that imposing building, glad that I would be able to spend all my time reading the great Masters, Dickens, Austen, Conrad, George Eliot, Tagore, blissfully ignorant of what I would do with all that knowledge"

Mahesh stopped. Literature? Dickens? Books? Maths professor? When were they all erased from his childhood? It was like reading a stranger's diary. Then he reaches the part about the poet and a tangled destiny.

"*. . . There was only boy in my class, a pimply-faced, gangly student who interested me enough to want to get to know. Needless to say, I left the initiative to him. One day in the library, engrossed in Conrad's "Outcast of the Islands", the dense language making me almost dizzy, I heard a thin reedy voice whisper behind me.*

'An outcast, reading about an outcast?'

'I turned. Imtiaz Shaikh had a wide grin that showed dirty teeth but his eyes danced. I did not know what he meant but I was intrigued. We became friends, attracted to each other by a common dislike of the restless activity that marked college life."

Son of a carpenter? Mahesh read on with racing excitement.

'Imtiaz wanted to be a poet; his interest in Literature had lead him into what he described as "massive confrontations" with his father who felt cheated by a son frittering away an opportunity to get on in life, an opportunity funded by a local trader of wines, an English widower named Swindon his father worked for and who had taken a liking for the precocious boy . . .'

'. . . Two years later we had graduated, he with Honours, and I with difficulty. He had still not shown me a single poem or story. But his fervor was undiminished. We met in the cafeteria for what turned out to be a decisive moment in our lives.

'So what are you going to do? The war is over, the Allies have won, and the British have lost the Jewel in their crown. Soon India will be free. What a time to graduate! All of us at the crossroads. So what do you do, my friend?'

'I had no idea. Imtiaz gave me one.'

'Bombay! This part of the country has nothing to offer. We'll get into films. You write the story I'll do the lyrics. Why have we done Literature? Films are our destiny!' Alok Vats. 20 July 1946. Bombay

Mahesh shut the notebook. Were these fragments part of the story the famous scriptwriter bought off them? The epic that was, in fact, the undoing of their collaboration and friendship? Had his mother got the narrative right? Or was she improvising?

He rummaged in the suitcase, pulled out a tattered map of Bombay torn out of the Census report of 1931, an empty packet of Red and White cigarettes, its lettering faded. He leafed through bills and receipts, and one caught his attention; a hotel bill for Rs 110. On top of the fragile pink paper, in Gothic letters all upper case was inscribed, "Brighton Guest House, Ballard Estate, Bombay" and was made out to one Sidney Brown. Who on earth was that; another character for a story never written? A possible patron?

He picked up the album and found a photograph of three young men standing outside the arched gateway to an old stone building. Above the entrance were inscribed the words, "Brighton Guest House." The picture was grainy and the harsh sunlight flattened facial details but he recognized his father standing next to a fair-skinned man in a hat pulled cockily to one side. A cigarette dangled from the corners of his thin mouth, giving him a raffish air. Sidney Brown? On the other side stood a tall dark figure, lantern-jawed sporting a clipped moustache that gave him a slightly military air. But he had wavy hair and a smile that almost creased his face in half. His father, Alok Vats, wore no hat, but an oversized shirt and trousers. Even then he had a guarded expression; his head tilted slightly, his eyes on the camera as if readying for a sudden assault. He put it back into the album. From a thick brown envelope newspaper clippings dating from 1947 through the nineteen fifties, mostly from the old *Bombay Chronicle* and *The Times of India,* the newsprint almost yellow, brittle scattered onto the floor. Only two other notebooks had been scribbled in; he opened the one packed with hurried scrawls racing across the single-lined pages in a frenzy, words tripping one over the other, often obliterated with furious scratches, margins trampled upon by the invading army of words and more words. He turned to the last page.

Aloknanda Vatsayana. 1952. Bombay.

He turned to the last written page in the third exercise book: *1954.* Twenty pages were left blank. The rest, five notebooks were as good as new though the outer edges of the leaves had discolored. Was this the last of his writing? A reluctant testament to his son or pieces of narrative discarded and forgotten? Had his mother set them aside, in that old tin suitcase that she insisted he open only after her death? *1954.* Mahesh would have been four years old when his father penned those last words. Had an intimation of a drought made him stop after that frenetic scrawling? A foreboding that his last battle for immortality had been irrevocably lost?

Mahesh sat back, the silence in the room broken by the ticking of the wall clock, 2.30 pm. He felt a peculiar sensation, as if he were trekking up some mountain slope. With quivering hands he turned back to the first page of the second notebook. The writing was almost indecipherable. Entire sentences had been deleted; paragraphs angrily crossed out. There were dangling sentences sometimes no sentence breaks, swirls of blue-black ink on a once-white page

'why do I feel deserted? Imtiaz, words . . . Waste? Dead as a doormat. Be nice to everyone and watch yourself die. She

loves me, yes, like death . . . Sold for a song, my jewel, my blood—'

'Why did the bastard change it? There is life in renunciation! Was money to blame? I almost loved him . . . ? Can I make something of this cruel ordinariness?'

'Set it in CDA? Why has Imtiaz not written to me? I must try. Get down to the blank paper with pen. That young lady? .No, no. Let us see—' April 1950

'The bus is late, a rare event. This is the starting point for its northward journey to Worli depot. There she is, getting off at Churchgate station, two stops before mine. .for a local to some suburban office? (Check. But how?).She has worn a starched cotton sari, full sleeve dark green blouse and she keeps glancing my way. Two years at the same bus stop most mornings. I know she lives in the new apartment blocks further south. Sometimes I have glimpsed her riding past me in a blue Landmaster a puffy faced man in a shark-skin, cotton (?) at the wheel. Husband? Brother? (I hope so!) Then the bus rolls up. She is the first one in and I follow her, the soapy smell of her shampooed hair trailing behind her. Afghan Snow, lots of it. On a sudden impulse I sit next to her even though there is a window seat ahead. She turns to me and quickly looks away as the bus starts.*

'As it swerves right, I feel soft flesh against mine. My heart thumps wildly as the pressure increases ever so slightly even though the bus is sedately steady. I grip the bar of the seat in front, knuckles white against the dull steel, shut my eyes tight, wishing this moment to last forever, to end this second. I feel exposed, like some animal that has emerged from a long hibernation into the sunlight. I picture that thigh under the sari and petticoat, a rounded, not bony knee. She has always intimidated me with her self-confidence and her aggressiveness today confuses me because I cannot see her face. She is peering out of the window at the scenes below, the trams passing by in stately procession from the Prince of Wales Museum on to*

Hornby Vellard road and Victoria Terminus. I cannot move, I must shift my weight towards the aisle, perhaps flee to the lower deck, at any moment she will turn and her blood-red mouth will form a scream. I can smell her sweat beneath the perfume—' February 1952.

Mahesh set the notebook aside, his head reeling. He couldn't believe his mother hadn't read this and not felt devastated. If she had that would explain why she kept it hidden from him in her lifetime. But she did want her son to judge his father well; the notebooks would restore his worth. Mahesh felt grateful for that gesture, but also cheated by her silence. He would have been able to put a face to her sorrows; confronting moral ambiguities far earlier would have made him less vulnerable.

He held the notebooks as if weighing the pain they must have caused, this legacy of smothered lust and incomplete expiation. He flipped the pages and the image of his tormented parents vanished beyond the penumbra of clouded memory. He could view the fragments as autobiography or fiction; it didn't matter because they came from some inner needs and impulses that he was familiar with. The writer had had no means of coping with his demons other than the written word.

"We are always what others make of us" his mother's fading voice echoed. He had been angered by this indictment even as he took it to heart. He had got it all wrong. No, it was his mother's apology for her own silences. Aloknanda Vatsayana had ploughed his field, and had crept into his corner to die a lonely death leaving behind these word-portraits, incomplete sketches of longing and its pain, of the flesh and its torments.

It was almost dawn. Soon Monday would be upon him. He had a busy day at the office but he would call his secretary and ask her to reschedule his appointments for the following day. He wanted nothing more than to read those fragments again and again, and sleep.

Ever since his relationship with Madhavi soured because of differences over Deepika's future three years ago, Ranjan had been glad to leave as early as possible for the office, his shelter from domestic storms. Today, he was glad to be getting away from his daughter.

His moods alternated between regret and guilt over that girl's invitation the night before. So he only half-listened to his daughter plaintively wrestle with her indecisions, her desires and ambitions.

For Deepika his presence was enough, so their conversation wandered aimlessly like a drunk on a deserted beach. Had he been less obsessed with his voracious appetites, Ranjan would have seen the dangerous crossroad Deepika stood at. His counsel was not forthcoming even the next morning when she asked him, for the last time, if she should resume college.

'Deepika, you are an adult. Think clearly, is all I ask and let Mama know, okay, darling? Don't be late for dinner. And let me know if you want that call centre job.'

Disappointed, confused, Deepika, saw her father off at the door and wished she could curl up in bed, pull the sheet over her head and block out the world. Her mother emerged from the bathroom saw her slouched at the kitchen table.

'What! Now you want I should brush your teeth? Rise and shine, darling! Go on! And what have Papa and daughter decided, hmm?'

'Leave me alone, mama I'm not feeling well, okay?'

'Listen to me, my dear. Listen to me, please? Go back to college. Don't get taken in by this fashion nonsense. Its just a ruse to ensnare pretty and empty-headed girls like you. And then—'

'Mama, you don't know anything, so don't talk, please!'

'Listen I know what I read and hear. Acid attacks on girls by spurned boyfriends! I tell you, men in this city are demented. They are beasts! Read the paper. Scarred for life! And this is not a stray incident. You need to be with youngsters in college. Get a sense of purpose. What is this fashion designing? Animals! No upbringing—'

It was as if her mother had let in the light so that she saw the road sharp and clear. Late morning she called Aditya. He was ecstatic.

'Hey, baby, that's cool, man! You took years! Hope you haven't aged, *hah!* just joking, darling. Okay, so meet me at three . . . Pyramid Heights, Sleater Road . . .'

That afternoon, Deepika accompanied a swaggering Aditya into a black marbled foyer past a glass-fronted room marked "Office" toward a bank of elevators. A young man rose from behind a wooden desk and strode towards them inquiringly.

'Yeah man, Col Biswas' wife is expecting us, okay?' Aditya spat out at him.

Deepika saw a pale face, hair combed back off a wide forehead, rimless glasses accentuating inquisitive yet soft eyes. He opened his mouth to say something, then just nodded and headed back to his desk. He kept staring at her till the lift doors closed on her.

'Who is that chap, Aditya?'

'Could have gotten nosy. I'll kick his arse when we get down, don't worry Babes.'

'Never, *never,* call me that Aditya, okay, Babes . . . never again. And you haven't answered my question.'

'Oh sorry, Deepu, that's the new office manager, Sripad something. Mrs Biswas says okay guy, a bit stuck up in the sky but the colonel likes him.'

Two hours later Deepika was heading home in a state of great excitement. Unmindful of the pushing and shoving in the packed Ladies Only, she was savouring the complex sensations a voyage into a strange world creates in the very young, made comfortable by the assurance of 'expert supervision'. Beneath Mrs. Biswas' guiding lights who knew what uncharted lands she might not discover? It had not taken that old guardian of lost souls very long to clear Deepika's cluttered head of all the confusions and indecisiveness about life's myriad options for self-advancement.

'Self-discovery has a fool for a teacher, darling. For instance, some kids think they have the talent for sculpture or poetry but they're good at mending things, like computer chaps or politicians, you know? The street singer thinks of himself another Mukesh. Others like you my dear, are borne to beauty that can die without grace . . . grace needs that rare gift of making people feel, well, wanted, important . . . only then beauty blooms.'

Deepika said nothing as "Gauri Aunty" stroked her arm.

'Deepika, we can help. But take your time. If you want get back to college go ahead; if you want to know what you don't know what you can be, we can help make you know what you don't know. No degree-*shegree* here. Just soaking in a fine and lost art of, let us say, freewheeling counselling. We make you global citizens.' She smiled bleakly and held Deepika's hand.

One foot in, she had a few questions.

'Okay, hunh, what, what do I pay, I mean the fees and all that, and—?'

Mrs Biswas snorted.

'*Arre betey*, forget the fees, we'll see about that later. My husband and I don't need the money, my dear. Fees? *Tchah*!'

For the first time in his life, Sripad fell in love, comprehensively. That is the expression he used over and over again to measure his feelings for the girl with that "stud bull". He hated that fellow . . . comprehensively. Aditya made him feel amiss in those qualities he assumed women looked for in men, muscles, piercing stares and a purposeful stride that gave the world warning of a presence. But why had she stared back at him?

"Vispy, Vispy! What can I say!' Sripad exclaimed to Vispy Irani, over a beer in Connaught Café.

'She has this quality, you know, an epiphany, Ingrid Bergman in *Casablanca*, the face of love, a rhapsody shot in soft focus. I wanted to sweep her away, no, no, .the fucking moron with her would have smashed me to bits.'

'*Gilchodiya*! Fucker! What has happened to you? One look and that is it?'

'No, no! Vispy my boy, I tell you I have never felt so, so bold! I wanted to hold her back, see? 'Come with me', I wanted to tell her. You know that Bob Dylan line, *"And this is not your fate . . ."*

'*Tchah*! What an arsehole! Its Thomas not Bob and I don't recall that line. Sripad! Stick to your film heroines, my boy. *'Lovers and madmen have such seething brains/such shaping fantasies, that apprehend/More than cool reason ever comprehends.*' I bet you don't know where that came from Mr Shakespearewala? Hunh? *Twelfth Night*, The Clown.'

'Okay, shaddup. Listen. Seriously, there is something wrong in the state of Denmark, my friend. That Biswas couple; I don't give a shit, but when this girl walked into my life, man, I want to investigate, you know?'.

'So what are you going to do, Inspector Close-up? Barely a month into your first fucking job and you making an ass of yourself?'

'Okay, Vispy, don't get your eyebrows into a twist. Look at them! No, I have to think this through. I've been noticing a lot of kids walking into the foyer asking for the Biswas residence. Sometimes that stud bull leads them by the nose, you know. An hour or so later they are traipsing past me again, some smiling, others as grumpy as your grandmother. Next this . . . this living poem. So what is going on, I ask myself.'

Poonima woke late on Monday. Arvind wasn't by her side. Her first thought was he'd left early for the shop; but it was eleven o'clock. His pyjamas lay in a heap next to her. She held them up, scrutinised the front and back, nodded and threw them into the wicker basket for the maid to wash. She dressed quickly, one hurried look at the unlined face broken only by a sparkling smile and scurried into the kitchen where her sisters-in-law were finishing their mid-morning tea. Sheepishly she poured herself some.

'Having late nights, are we?' Parvati spoke to no one in particular. Sheetal giggled softly, rolled her eyes and slurped her milk from a tall steel tumbler, nodded furtively at her elder-sister-in-law and hurried out.

'He's off to earn his daily bread, or should we say spend the family's, heh!' Poornima couldn't understand Parvati's anger. She rinsed her cup and hurried to her room.

She looked everywhere for the un-posted letter; between her clothes, under the mattress. Perhaps she had posted it? No matter. She sat on the bed, propping herself against three pillows and began in her neat scrawl.

"*Dear mama,*

> *I don't know if you got my last letter. Ignore it if you have because today I am on top of the world. Last night I had a wonderful dream and I felt so happy on waking . . .'*

She looked up with a start. Parvati stood in front of her, eyebrows arching steadily, a hand on her hips, head tilted. How had she not heard her enter the room?

'So, one more letter to mama is it?'

She walked up briskly and before Poornima could help it snatched the letter from her paralysed hands.

'So-o-o-o. Hmmm? In quite a spirit are we? First blame your husband, then dream of . . . whom? And all this to your mother?'

The room spun before her, terror squeezed her heart and she thought she would faint as Parvati stalked the room, opening a drawer here, peering into the open cupboard there.

'You should have posted that letter, my little sparrow. This house is like a public park, secrets have to be kept, you know, secret; especially from husbands. Of course Arvind doesn't know. I am not so insensitive.' She paused.

'Shift! My back hurts all the time. *Aah!* That's better! Let's talk . . . like you and your friend Gayatri would have.' She laid a hand on Poornima's knee; the leg jerked, the hand stayed there.

'We women have to stick by each other. We understand why, I mean, I know what you feel, the anger, the disappointment; you are young, a girl with fire in her . . . her loins—'

Poornima whimpered; her brains had melted. She blinked rapidly, gulped the nausea rising in her throat. Parvati ran a thin dry hand over her forearm. Poornima shivered involuntarily but could not move her arm away.

'Yes, fire in the blood and tight silky skin. What else can a man ask for? You are unhappy because he doesn't bother? But my dear, which of these brothers cares for his spouse? My husband . . . he . . ."

Parvati was kneading Poornima's fingers.

'We haven't had, we haven't slept together in years. Look at me, my rosebud!'

She held Poornima by the chin and pulled her close, her withered face, sharp creases from pinched nostrils bracketing the bitter mouth inches from the terrified letter-writer. Parvati's breath smelt of cloves, her voice had sunk to a hoarse whisper.

'I was not always like this. But you know, your husband does not stroke you and the flower withers. Wells run dry I have also searched, my dear . . . for the attention, the affection of my man, then strangers, not that there were many in my life, just uncles, old relatives, friends of this large business family who paw you at weddings. Years ago . . . a year after our first one was born, at a wedding, this . . . this colleague of our dear father-in-law, he, he found me in the bathroom as I had just finished and, the door hadn't been locked, perhaps in my haste to empty my bladder. He walked in and before I could pull my sari down, he had . . . but you know what? His eyes had a pleading look as his hot and clammy hand groped. Ridiculous you'll say, and you are right; but for those few seconds time had frozen. I never forgot though I forgave him his audacity—'

Poornima was certain she was in a nightmare. This couldn't be happening to her! She tried to move away to the far side of the bed. Parvati's hand held her in a claw-like grip.

'Don't dismiss me like that . . . you *bitch!* I could have had them if I wanted to! But I was faithful, even after all those hot groping, oh, you should see them now; barely able to walk, drooling into their food but now they chase Sheetal. Oh! Yes! I know! Your husband . . . But don't take it amiss. *Ghar ki murgi dal barabar*: the grass is greener in the other garden. And it all works out . . . it is in the family, right? Within the walls of this . . . this madhouse— So who is he . . . ?'

Poornima strove to calm her thrumming nerves, ride this out in silence, she told herself. She wished she were dead.

'Get up!' Her voice sounded like a whip crack.

Poornima had turned to stone. Parvati stood before her, her eyes gleaming with a strange light.

'Get up my full moon! That's good. Feel . . . Go on, put your hand on my—, here rub them. *Ah-h-h-!* Yours are so soft and firm, but then you have yet to become a mother! For you, my rose petal, middle age and sagging balloons, old age and dried prunes are still far away. *Hey Parmatma!* We women need each other! After all the dirty hands on your buttocks, your private parts, when brothers have traded their lust for another's wife, we will turn to each other for the intimacy we crave . . . without the cruelty, the alcoholic breaths and frantic thrusts and the indifference later and . . . and . . . *Oh-h-h . . . Poornima*!!'

The young woman broke loose from the sudden embrace and ran out and into the common bathroom down the corridor. Luckily it was empty. She bolted the door, collapsed against it, sobbed, then ran to the sink and threw up in racking coughs. She let the water run long after she had emptied her stomach. The mirror reflected a puffy face, reddened eyes brimming with tears, but most of all Poornima saw fear. She buttoned her blouse, sat on the commode and tried to think calmly. But those dry hands, the claw-like grip, and the hoarse urgency, without pause, kept terrorising her.

She did not know how long she sat there. No one knocked. It seemed as if the world had forgotten her and she was glad. She looked round. The only window was small with slatted glass panes. The door stayed bolted. Of all the places in this house of prying eyes and hands, this small guest washroom, a public place virtually, was the most secure. And it was this thought that lifted her paralysing fear.

She washed her tear-stained face, brushed her hair with a broken comb lying under the sink and gingerly opened the door. The house was eerily quiet. Her room was empty. The unfinished letter lay on the bed. She tore it and flushed the pieces, watching them swirl and vanish. She rubbed some moisturising lotion onto her face, applied a light lip gloss, some eyeliner. Then she changed into a fresh *kurta* and *salwaar* and pulled out the cell phone her husband had given her.

'Arvind? Hi, what you doing? What? Why am I calling? Nothing, I just miss you, that's all. You left while I was sleeping and I—What? No . . . no, nothing, wrong. Actually Arvind, hunh, can we meet today? You know, some place other than home? Can I come to the shop, right away? No? What? No, nothing's wrong. Really Arvind! Can't we talk? I mean, meet? Just us? Married people do that all the time, don't they? No, no, not tomorrow, not Sunday. No! *Nothing doing!* It has to be tonight! This evening, okay? Right! So what about? Say I meet you at Churchgate station, next to the bookstall— What? How do I know? Come on Arvind! Okay, another place? Fine . . . Eros theatre then. No! Don't ask Amol*ji* to drive me there. I'll take a bus, yes *Papa!* I'll be careful, bye. And Arvind . . . I love you.'

At six fifteen that evening Mrs. Ahuja, hurrying to Churchgate Station like other commuters glanced at the slim lady at the corner of the entrance to the Eros theatre without much thought. Only when she had crossed the road, did she turn to gape at the red chiffon sari, sea-green blouse, hair blowing in the late evening breeze and an oval face that she thought glamorous till she recognised it.

As she told Parvati that night, after her husband had fallen asleep in a drunken stupor.

'I just gaped and gaped, Paru, I didn't recognise her! What clothes, what style! Did you people know she dressed like that? No? Why? I mean, I don't know. No, nobody was with her, but listen! Paru, she was expecting someone! That I can tell for sure; she kept looking this way then that way. Where is her husband?'

Parvati switched off the cordless phone with a smile that did not reach her eyes. She sat in the kitchen, sipping her tea. The ticking of the clock on the wall sounded loud in the quiet of the night. She was the last to lock up. She usually sat here all by herself, after all the chores were done and everyone had retired to their rooms. It was her refuge for reflection and planning. She rinsed the cup and put it away on the rack, switched off the light and tiptoed down the quiet corridor to her sleeping husband, still smiling.

Earlier that evening while Arvind and Poornima met for the first of their intensely private meetings in public places, Ranjan Kapoor was sipping his third Scotch in the exclusive Belvedere club in The Oberoi Towers, a guest of his bank's most colourful and, wealthy defaulter, Bal Gandhi.

'How's the drink Ranjan? Care for some *aloo tikkas*? Nasreen, correct me if I am wrong but haven't we made the arrangements for Ranjan's first instalment? No? But Raghu was to sign the cheques and keep them ready. You must remember? One for First Capital, the other for Ranjan's bank?'

'God! I am so tired, Rajeev, this man! He drives me crazy! Where is the money, Baloo? You want me to get your accountant to sign cheques that bounce?'

'*Tsk!* . . . What about the money that came from the latest franchisee for BodyArt equipment? The one in Port Blair?'

'God! This man, Ranjit, I tell you! Why am I doing this? I don't need the job! My whole life has been mortgaged to BodyArt . . . and what have I got? He's always been this way, Rohan . . . no money where his mouth is.'

Her sari slipped from her shoulder. Her skin appeared blotchier than the last time they met but Ranjan could feel a stirring. He shifted uncomfortably in his chair, smiled weakly at Nasreen who kept staring at him, open-mouthed. She unclasped her thick hair, shook it loose, knotted it again, clasp between teeth as yellow as old piano keys and as even. She sighed, bit her lower lip and kept her eyes on Ranjan daintily sipping his whisky. Gandhi was working himself into anger, head tilting one way then another, as if searching for the right pose, thumb and index finger twisting the tip of his freshly trimmed beard. Anger, Ranjan thought, becomes that aristocratic face.

'This is ridiculous, Nasreen! Let's not discuss dirty linen in front of our friend. And his name is Ranjan. Memorise it. You want another Coke or Pepsi? Your hot flushes are in full bloom I notice, Nasreen.'

Ranjan sensed that they had been on edge even though Gandhi strove to maintain his calm. Nasreen had tipped over the cliff pulling her boss. It was time to haul them up, restore their nerves.

'Bala, you, ahh, are also from Pakistan? From Karachi I presume?"

Gandhi had a petulant curl to his thin lips now that he had struck the attitude he desired. He rolled his eyes, took a deep breath and nodded.

'Yes, Karachi; my father really. He owned the biggest grocery shop downtown. I was born there but I don't recollect anything. You . . . ?'

'Lahore . . .'

The mood had mellowed. The club was filling up. Bala turned and waved at a group at the next table.

'Dilip! *How . . . are you?* And the golf? Haven't broken your skull yet, I see, hmmm, pity; *har, har, har, har!* That's Dilip with his colleagues from Chase, .friends from Cambridge. Nasreen? Do we owe them?'

'Shut up Baloo, I have a headache.' Nasreen held her temples. The liquor was creeping into Ranjan's brain.

'Bal . . .'

He had his smile in place; it was time. He took a small sip, sat back and half-shut his eyes, his face a picture of earnest concern.

"Bala and Nasreen, it's like this. I am under pressure from my managing director. He wants to book defaulters. Yes, Mr Gandhi, he has a few months left and he wants a posting in Washington, DC, in the International Monetary Fund. Can you believe that? This is strictly off the record and it is actually Mr Scotch talking, of course, *heh, heh . . .'* Ranjan smirked and shook his head as if marvelling at the whiskey's powers.

The two were silent. Bala had renewed his search for an appropriate pose, his head moving like a puppet's;

Nasreen's, sari was completely off her shoulders now. Ranjan noticed a button in her blouse had snapped; the white of the bra showed. .

'Yes, that's the long and short of it. My managing director—listen carefully, *wants . . . a prosecution*—'

Nasreen let out a sigh. Bala picked his nose, his beady eyes examining the results intently before wiping his fingers on a napkin he tossed over his shoulder. Then he perked up.

'He goes . . . when, Ranjan?'

'Like I said, two maybe three months, at the most, six . . .'

'So-o-o—I see. Fact is Ranjan, I'll take a little more than that to raise the funds. You see those guys sitting there? The frog-eyed chap? Well, this is between you and me—and Nasreen of course, t*hey are going .to fund me!* *T*he paperwork's done! It's just a matter of time. *We are turning the corner, Ranjan*!' He fell back as if exhausted by the sheer force of his conviction.

Then he shot upright, struck by a thought.

Ranjan, we'll make it worth your while. You are a well wisher. And well wishers—? We treat them well. You know?' Bal was nodding to himself, eyes half-shut; they shone with an invitation to better times.

'So what are you saying? Should I have another? I think I will.'

Bal smiled expansively. He threw his arms wide, as if readying to hug someone

'Of course you'll figure out a way to get us the time we need. We do want to pay don't we Nasreen? No, let me finish. Our job is to help you think how you can help us get the time we need to help your bank clean up its portfolios. So, take a break, let your hair down! Family jaunt in Europe. No? Okay we'll work something out. Just get us . . . time, is all—I say, Ranjan, are you alright?'

'Yes, yes, just dozed off. Thish, ahh, Leapfrog, whatever it is. Good malt, lights a fire, I mean—'

'That's it, Uncle!! *Hunh! Hunh!* Now you're rocking!' Nasreen was shaking her head to music only she could hear. Bal stared at her blankly.

Dev Reddy's world collapsed on Monday ten minutes after he entered the office of *The Last Frontier* in a tenement block in the working class district of Lalbaug. Till then he had been on song. He braved the ride from Virar with a spring in his step because his digging into BodyArt files had hit a lode. Gandhi hadn't used bank funds for any of the promised ventures. Now he had to discover where the money had gone.

'Good morning, Sanjay. What are you scribbling so furiously; a manifesto for the young and dispossessed . . . ? Hah!'

Startled, his editorial assistant turned and blushed. He hadn't heard Reddy come in.

'Nothing, *Sir*, just drafting—'

Reddy settled at his computer in the far corner. In the tiny pantry Ram Lakhan, the tea boy, wasn't in. The office had a musty smell, an overhang of stale tea and cigarette smoke. Reddy often wondered who smoked in here. He was too preoccupied to find out.

'Sir, a courier came a few minutes back. He would not give me the packet. He will return in fifteen minutes, he said, Pushpa called in sick and will not come today and tomorrow and day after, Comrade.' Sanjay concluded morosely

Reddy nodded absent-mindedly. Just then the doorbell rang.

Reddy would recall these moments for months later; his mild perplexity at Pushpa's absence and Sanjay's forced courtesy, the silence in the pantry, his upbeat mood. He signed for the packet, wondered at its weighty size. He read the contents slowly, at first uncomprehendingly, then with dismay and finally with disbelief. He collapsed into his chair, his knees buckling. He read again the two-page letter from the solicitors.

He had been evicted. *The Last Frontier* had two months to vacate the premises. *Vacate?* He read it again. The solicitors represented the new owners of the tenement block. He had known that the mill owners deep in debt were negotiating with city builders hungry for land in this central part of the city, the old textile district. He had refused to acknowledge the inevitable; now it had hit between the eyes.

Sanjay asked what the matter was. In that young face with its wispy Che Guevara beard, he saw a false sympathy that told him how far behind the times he was. Sanjay had known; the staff had known that is why Ram Lakhan and Pushpa had stayed away. They were jumping ship, he thought bitterly.

'What we will do now Comrade *saar?* We need a lawyer to fight?'

Reddy shook his head. He felt the end upon him. He shook his head once again at his fate that had pushed him ruthlessly to the margins of relevance. This was the final blow, to be denied a sanctuary.

The phone rang.

'Ranjan, my friend! It's all over, Ranjan. I've been evicted. *The Last Frontier* is no more.'

'We expected that Reddy. How much time do you have? That's enough; we'll figure something out. Have you got anything for me?'

As usual The Wayside Inn was full. At their table by the bay window, Arvind was gleefully describing his prank on the 'Dead Poets' to an inattentive Reddy.

'Ah! Here comes Mahesh!' the listener interjected.

Arvind leaned over.

'So, how was the week, Mahesh? Read any more Alok Vats? Boy, the things people in love will do, really! My wife for instance . . .'

They looked up from the menu.

'No, no nothing, just you know, it's nothing, forget about it. So what should we order . . .' He looked distinctly disturbed.

The waiter walked away with the soup orders. At the poets' table the conversation got loud.

'Kafka suffers from translation. Just like *Mahabharata*. At least I can read Kalidasa's *Meghdoot* in the original. But what to do with German?' Wilfred the chief 'dead poet' set his mug down carefully and wiped his upper lip.

'Ah, you old goat, you have no problem with your poems translated into Portuguese, do you? Who reads you in Lisbon?'

They felt his presence before they saw him. Ranjan sat without any greeting, his florid face glistening with sweat.

'Well, well, I see the Gang is a hungry lot these days! Sorry I'm late. Good old Advani my boss needs a dramatic ending to an indifferent career. And he thinks I can give him one. Someone must go to jail or before the Debt Recovery Tribunal . . .'

Reddy wondered if there was a message for his ears in this rambling diatribe. The cynicism disturbed him and he wanted to change the subject. Before he could intervene Mahesh was staring fixedly at Arvind and whispering:

'What, Arvind? What do you think people in love can do? That story I told you re-invented life. But love can also deny it and the possibilities in between are limitless.'

His fingers were playing along the rim of his teacup.

'Another Alok Vats? Out with it! We need a ripping, blood and gore yarn. Look at The Banker! He looks like he's swallowed a snake—'

'But please make it short.' Reddy had other things on his mind.

Mahesh smiled weakly his right eyelid twitching. Ranjan ordered a fresh round of tea. The Inn was now entering its somnolent phase, when customers are few and most waiters retreat to the kitchen. One surly waiter took their orders. The poets were dozing off in their corner, the remnants of beers and chicken forgotten.

'Something bothers me about this story; the lines between right and wrong blurred each passing day.'

'All's fair in love . . . now you've got us, Mahesh!' exclaimed Arvind.

'I want to tell it—like it happened; as I remember it. You ask me what it is about, I could simply tell you; a story of a married couple I knew . . . and their brief lives that left so many questions unanswered.'

'Come on, Mahesh, get to it! You are not telling us a story of a world war, are you! Everyone loses in a war.' Arvind looked pleased with this.

Reddy's impatience was mounting. Angrily, he turned to Arvind. 'We all know that.'

The waiter had brought the tea. Softly, Ranjan asked him for buttered toasts and biscuits. He was wary and he kept his eyes on Mahesh, waiting.

'What would you do when you have to take sides, apportion blame? You want to cry for the innocent but you cannot decide who is guilty.'

Arvind was impatient now.

'What was it, murder? For God's sake, what you were a cop or something?'

'Abhijeet, the surname's unimportant; a young man I got to know in 1992. My mother had died and I moved from Colaba, to Dadar. I rented a flat on the third floor of an old apartment block. For six months I kept to myself and probably would have continued that way but for Abhijeet'

'Our introduction seemed almost stage-managed. One night I found a young man, unsteady on his feet, at my door, his finger glued to the bell. I had heard it ringing riding the lift and I had wondered if the thing were stuck.'

'I tapped him on the shoulder, he turned slowly and I stared into a flushed face, bloodshot eyes squinting. He was startled to see me just as I was intrigued. He apologised, stared at the number above the doorframe shook my hand, apologised again, smiled, and lurched towards the staircase. I heard the doorbell below ring; someone shouted in Tamil and then the voices died as the door was shut violently.'

'What a way to start a friendship! So you found yourself a drinking buddy?!' Arvind laughed aloud, nodding in approbation.

'Something like that. One evening, I returned from my office rather late. Barely had I entered that the doorbell rang. He had a bright smile on a fresh face, clean firm jaw, a neatly trimmed moustache coal black, like his hair, soft eyes, of middling height. He introduced himself and walked in, assuming, I suppose, that a single male could do with the company of another male. At first I was irritated. "Sorry about that evening. I went to sleep on your doorbell". He smiled an apology again. I was going to ask him to leave, but he was so disarming I did not have the heart to tell him that the last thing I wanted was company that night. He asked me for a drink. Several rums later we had become friends. He told me all about his aspirations at that first encounter with a nervous energy; his hands would flee up to his thick crop of hair ever so often as if to take refuge there: the picture of worried youth.'

'He wouldn't stop talking. His father, he said, was a retired army officer, a Brigadier. Came from a long line of service officers. "Very disciplined guy, you should see his jaw line. You could slice bread on it." Without my asking he told me that the old man did yoga for an hour in the morning and walked five miles around the Five Gardens at night, before dinner. He watched me slyly, waiting for me to ask the obvious question. When I did not, he gulped his drink in one long pull, set the glass down and said, "He doesn't drink anything stronger than black tea with mint leaves, no sugar." Then he shook his head. "That's how he fights the dreariness of domesticity".'

The Inn was now virtually empty. The poets had shuffled out, Wilfred scratching his backside very vigorously. Arvind, waved and shouted jocularly.

'Better luck next time, Willy. Hope she's there!'

He turned to the other two and said, 'This army type. Must be a tyrant. Thank god they don't run our country. Give me those politicians from the boondocks any day!'

'Okay, this place closes in half an hour, Mahesh, are you getting anywhere with this story tonight?'

'Relax, Reddy, stories need build-up. How many more climaxes do you want in a day?'

Arvind snickered.

'We began to meet every Friday evening, a routine that I recoiled from initially. Abhijeet would wait for me in the foyer of the building, outside my door once . . . I was in no hurry to acquire a social life; my work was enough for me. But then I had never met anyone as insistent as Abhijeet or someone with that infectious and nervous energy. Soon I began to enjoy the evenings. We'd drink, order up some food or saunter down to a nearby restaurant. And he'd talk. I have never known anyone talk as much about himself as Abhijeet. He was not bragging. He was using me as sounding board for his worries, anxieties. He did not waste any time over pleasantries, formal courtesies. He came straight to the point with a candour that embarrassed me initially. I was hearing the roar of roiling anxieties, sometimes the silence of numbed hopes within that slim frame. He asked me about myself, my parents. He appeared to docket the information in some kind of mental cabinet "Writer?" he once asked, "Your father was a writer? It must have been fun . . . all those bedtime stories to help you dream." He smiled wryly, and with a slight trace of bitterness said, "My father told me stories of bravery, in war and death." Most of the time, in bars, in my living room, even in the brothels, he did the talking and I let him, because I found his frankness refreshing. He told me about his job . . .'

'*Brothels?*' Arvind's eyes behind his glasses were like saucers.

Even Ranjan was at a loss for words. He had half shut his eyes his face inscrutable, though an uncertain smile hovered around his pink lips. Reddy stared at Mahesh.

'He was twenty-four, two years younger than me but we were both virgins. When we discovered that one night at a bar in Mahim, we both laughed bashfully and decided to end our innocence sooner than later.'

Reddy was astounded. He stared at Mahesh as if he were crazed. But he was curious.

Mahesh smiled a shy smile that lit up his eyes. He pushed back his greying hair and stared at Reddy.

'I could edit this part. I would not like to upset you. But it is necessary.'

'Go on, Mahesh, Reddy is not a virgin.'

'One day, Abhijeet suggested we visit Pune over the weekend. The brothels there in Budhwar Peth, he had heard were cleaner, the women nicer and younger. Besides, in this city someone might recognise him. So the next weekend we packed off for the city, hiring a taxi all to ourselves for the three hour run.'

'So, what happened? You need to hurry, it's closing time.' Arvind was beside himself with excitement.

'It was a fiasco for Abhijeet. I lost my virginity in a room with a stout woman who told me she would teach me tricks to make my wife happy.' Mahesh smiled ruefully. 'Fifteen minutes later I was waiting for him in the small foyer. He was preoccupied and we left in silence after I had settled the payment. "We talked, Mahesh. That's it. I paid a whore to hear her story." She was from Bihar, brought to Pune by her pimp, who had "purchased' her from her poor parents in some village near Muzaffernagar. She hated the work, she was well looked after and she liked the rains. Abhijeet had not touched her. At one point, he said, she lay down and pulled up her sari, spread her legs and prised herself open, shut her eyes and told him to be quick. Abhijeet was horrified. "Like an old wound, Mahesh, a gash, God!" He made her sit up and offered to get her a job in Mumbai. Now it was my turn to be horrified. I asked him if she had agreed. He shook his head miserably. "No, she laughed called me a sweet but mad boy, looked at the clock on the wall, asked for another hundred rupees."'

They watched him cross the car park to the Army and Navy building, his shoulders hunched against an imaginary wind, his hands in his pocket. Reddy spoke first, 'I can't believe this! Can you imagine telling anyone how you lost your . . . Is he mad? Why is he telling us all this rubbish, Ranjan?'

'Reddy, sit back and enjoy the view. Look I have to go . . .'

'No. Ranjan I need to talk with you. The eviction, do you realise *The Last Frontier* is homeless? I am bereft of . . . And you have ignored me all week.'

'I have it all planned, Reddy. We are settled for life; let's talk on Monday, I have to go now.'

'Where to? Where do you have to go? Home is where you should be going and we should be heading for the station. We can talk on the train. Or let's go to that bar Drumbeat or whatever—.'

'Reddy . . . Grow up! Do you see this place? It's almost deserted. The restaurants are filling up. It's Saturday, time to relax . . . even Marx rested on weekends. Give your brains a break.'

'You don't understand, do you? I am talking of my life; I need it back! Okay, if the office has gone so be it; but you have to listen to what I have on Gandhi. We can make history, don't you see? Listen Ranjan, my report, I know, by inference at least, where the money is . . .'

'You do? Well don't tell anyone. Keep it for Monday, we'll see. Now you go on home, take Rajani out to dinner, your son Sripad, him too. Life's good. It will get better, trust me.'

'Listen, we can send him to jail. The Economic Offences Wing, my report. The Central Bureau of Investigation. They'll lap it up.'

'Reddy, please!. You are overwrought. Mahesh's story has got you all worked up . . . Do nothing, you hear? You have no idea . . . I'll get lodgings for your rag, I mean mag, but next week. Now, goodbye and love to Rajani.'

'Don't . . . forsake me!'

He had never felt this sort of exhilaration before: almost painful and nearly unbearable as he rode the elevator to the apartment. He did not know the name of the girl but he had made the contact and Bahadur picked him up. He had the money in his pocket; an hour was all but that was enough. This time he felt no trepidation; with a bounce in his step he rode the elevator.

The girl was waiting for him; she picked the room in the empty flat. He drew the curtains, opened a window and peered down at the street ten stories below; a sulphurous odour rushed in and he hastily pulled the curtains just she stepped out from the bathroom. Suddenly the curtain lifted, the rank hot breeze mingled with her fruity fragrance. He felt dizzy, the room now hot, now cold, till she realised the window was open and shut it firmly.

She sat at the foot of the bed, her grave eyes and unsmiling face, almost gamin-like, embarrassing him. He walked up to her, cupped a small but firm breast, kneading the nipple like a piece of bread. As if on cue, she unzipped his trousers and pulled his boxer shorts down to his heels, her hair brushing against his heated groin. She began stroking his soft buttocks, tracing a thin finger under his crotch. He almost collapsed. Her slip parted, he glimpsed her . . . g*ash! Like a wound!* God! She pulled him next to her then pushed him gently on his back. This time as she put his aching cock in her mouth, he shut his eyes, whimpering unintelligently. Then he burst in a frenzy of concentrated pain, his massive body convulsing like a beached whale in the last throes of death.

With mounting anger and frustration Reddy watched Ranjan waddle across the car park. He turned towards Churchgate station with heavy feet, dragging his frail body forward.

Wading through this sea of humanity, he felt he recognised the loneliness of commitment. The working class, the peasant had a community of suffering no doubt, but it was a fraternity nonetheless. Does a peasant feel lonely? He had never asked this question, but now he felt that knowledge and intellect carried the affliction of loneliness. Ideas and words separated him from the 'wretched and the unwashed', and the gulf was unbridgeable. All his life he had fought ephemeral battles for an imagined people. From now on, he would fight for himself.

Arvind returned to The Konarak bookstall in a state. God! A gash! That Mahesh! With such a deadpan expression he had slipped it in. Not a trace of awkwardness.

His salesmen had left. But he was reluctant to close up. He had to meet Poornima in an hour at Gaylord. He could walk there but he preferred to bide his time here. He stared morosely at the entwined bodies in the downloads he pulled out of a drawer but his mind was elsewhere. Poornima! What had got into her? After four meetings at public places and long conversations, he was still at sea. Something was missing. She hadn't told him everything. But her look that Monday evening, the first time they met on their own; so beautiful she appeared to him, so calm and yet . . .

'Arvind, isn't it lovely? All by ourselves?' Her voice had been slightly high pitched and her hands shook. 'So what should we have . . . a club sandwich, what is that the girl having there? Looks like mud.'

She had walked up to her and come back with a knowing smile.

'Temptation. I like that. Heaps of chocolate and ice cream. Should we have it? Come on Arvind!.'

He had said nothing, simply staring at her tucking in, a thin line of chocolate forming on her upper lip. She met his gaze, smiled and hurried to finish the ice cream.

'I . . . I have always wanted to do this—' She had laughed nervously. 'Aren't you going to say something?'

'Poornima, what is the matter?' He leant forward. 'Why are we meeting here? We could have ordered ice cream from Patel Stores and shared it with the others at home.'

'Oh, look at that couple there in the corner, Arvind! He has his hands on her lap. Isn't it romantic? I think they are going to kiss . . .'

'Poornima, I have had a bad day, an Australian couple was very rude at the shop, wanting discounts that would have ruined me. I haven't sold a single volume, my stomach is rumbling and I want to sleep.'

'Oh, Arvind, I am so sorry. Why didn't you tell me?'

He caught the mocking note. She reached out for his hand. He pulled it away violently.

'What's got into you, woman?'

'Nothing.' She smiled at him her eyebrows arching. 'Husbands and wives do hold hands sometimes even in public.' She gawked at the crowd of students gorging on cakes and milk shakes. 'I love this place, don't you? Everybody minding their own business. Look at that fellow, my God! Arvind! He's going to chew her ear off!' She giggled.

'Poornima what's happened? Did you quarrel with Sheetal, did Papa shout at you? *What's the matter!?*' He hissed at her furiously.

'Actually it was nothing like that. Just that old Broomsticks, I mean Parvatiji and I, we had a . . . long talk and, and she convinced me, yes, in a sort of unintended way, that, you know, we had to meet outside, where we could talk without someone overhearing. I just wanted to be with you . . . all by ourselves . . .'

Unable to grasp anything more than the fact that she was so different from the Poornima he had known all this while, he just stared at her mutely She had finished her chocolate, he asked for the bill. As they left the coffee shop, she slipped her moist hand into his and held it firmly. He did not resist.

That night, in his striped pyjama and vest on their narrow double bed, Arvind came alive as never before, to every sound from the bathroom. She emerged in a kaftan he had never seen her in. It had been a wedding gift that she had simply tucked away in the cupboard, wailing. 'This stuff is not for me, Arvind, it's like wearing a tent.' He had looked at her with astonishment, his wife of two years who usually slept in an old cotton sari and blouse. She gave him an uncertain smile, unclipped her hair, shook it loose, the thick black mane flouncing about her oval face. She smelt soapy as she lay by his side facing him, her eyes locking his in a flickering play of flirtation and pleading. He had looked for hidden meaning in the obvious and come away even more confused.

'How do I look?' Her voice was meek and muffled as she spoke into her pillow. She raised her eyes once again and stared at him, waiting. He muttered, 'Yes . . . good, I mean nice.' His confusion began to give way to suspicion. They had always made love in the dark. He would hitch her sari and petticoat up, climb onto her and thrust deep till he had spent himself. She would walk to the bathroom silently, wash and they would fall asleep in their corners without a word. But that night!

R anjan woke late on Sunday morning to the sounds of heated argument. For the first time the voices did not grate on his ear. He did not grunt in sleepy frustration. Instead he smiled, and stared at the ceiling fan whirring slowly. He thought of his little tryst the previous night with contentment. She remained in his consciousness as a source of never-ending delights. Ranjan felt his life had entered that phase in which he would have to take some very important decisions about his 'earning potential'. He must accept Gandhi's offer of blue-chip shares: in Deepika's name or in Madhavi's? He must check with his chartered accountant. Why load Gandhi's generosity onto his income? This was just the beginning. Bala would have to pay and he would pay well to stay out of the reach of the law.

He frowned. Reddy! He had sensed desperation in the old man and a determination to be heard. He felt uneasy. Must stop him from doing anything rash. Could he convince him to set aside the digging? Ranjan doubted it.

He yawned hugely, got off the bed with a sigh and scratched his crotch vigorously. He yawned again, shook his head and walked toward the kitchen and the raised voices. The argument was reaching its height; he knew Deepika would win. She always did.

'Did you hear that, Ranjan? Our daughter was playing waitress at a party last night. I don't suppose you noticed that she wasn't in when you staggered home?' His wife was trembling with fury. 'Yes, a waitress.'

'Mummy! How you vulgarise! Daddy, it wasn't like that! This place I went to? Aditya my friend had hosted a party for a Japanese trade delegation at The Fairfield Rooms, you know the place, they are rented out for parties, press conferences. A couple of us friends were asked to pitch in.'

Ranjan waited, his heart fluttering for reasons he did not like.

'Dad! Come on! Tell Mummy, will you! It's nothing. Aditya said the waiters there are country bumpkins so he arranged for a couple of his friends like me to help out. Its part of the hospitality thing I am doing, remember?'

Ranjan's mouth had gone dry. 'No.'

Deepika looked at him in dismay.

'You remember the talk we had last Sunday? I asked you about college and all that? Well, you left the choice to me so I decided to take up an offer to learn tourism and catering . . . a beginner's course . . . for free okay?' Deepika broke into tears, her chest heaving. Ranjan walked up to her.

'There, beta, don't cry!' He stroked her hair and wiped her tears. 'I understand. Of course Mummy is right to feel the way she does. So what did you have to do?'

'Nothing like what you think, Papa! It was self-service. They fixed their own drinks. We, five college students and I, spent most of our time chatting with the delegates. The idea was to show them how hospitable we Indians are. Okay, once one elderly Jap asked me to fetch him a drink.

That's all. And it was so . . . so educative.' She broke into a sob again.

Ranjan did not probe for details an average Indian middle class father would have been curious about. Not because he was uncaring but because he was still riding on the fantasy of fortune and pleasure. Had he been a little more inquisitive, he would have discovered some facets of Deepika's first experience with the hospitality business that would have fouled his sunny mood.

For her part, Deepika kept to half-truths, aware that as long as she played the little girl with her father she was safe. She feared his keen intelligence more than her mother's anguished admonishments. Imagine telling her father that the elderly Japanese had asked her up to his hotel room that she had been very flattered by all the attention those little men in black suits drinking scotch whisky and eating raw fish had showered on her at Col. Biswas's riotous party!

The prospect of eviction from his fortress had turned Reddy into something of a realist, or so he thought. He sat at his table asking himself over and over again: *Can I do it?* He heard Rajani in the kitchen, the fragrances of her cooking wafting out to him. He rose, feeling a sudden urge to talk to her. She had her back to the entrance, a thin ascetic woman, her white hair falling over her frail shoulders. Sunday oil bath, he remembered. He smelt the *shikakai* shampoo she used, and for the first time in years he wanted to hold her, to tell her that everything was going to be fine because he had found a way to make his life, no, their life, more meaningful.

'Rajani . . .' He stood at the threshold, a hand holding the wooden doorknob. She turned to him, still stirring the pot of onion Sambhar. 'Rajani, I, unh, I have to tell you something. You know that office . . . the Lalbagh place? Well, *The Last Frontier,* actually . . . it's over.'

She smiled a tired smile, walked up to him, wiping her hands on the edge of her sari.

'Comrade husband . . .'. Her smile stayed but her tone had changed. 'Comrade, do you know what your son has done. Sripad . . . I wanted to tell you yesterday but you were so preoccupied.' She held his forearm. 'Are you alright? You look very tense.'

'No, no. I am alright. What, what is it?'

'You know we haven't paid the instalment for the loan on this house for two months? Sripad has settled it. Isn't that sweet?'

She stared up at him, her head cocked to one side, her thin eyebrows raised.

'Yes, our son, the estate manager . . .'

'He has paid? I mean why didn't you tell me that it was due?'

'Would it have made a difference? You and that Frontier cannot pay our bills. You know that, I know that. Why do you think I give private tuitions to the kids of these . . . these petite bourgeois families?' Her anger was laced with bitterness.

'What security have you given us, my comrade husband? I am not complaining, just asking. Your Marxist friends have deserted you for the World Bank and university chairs and while you denounce them every evening, their families live comfortably. No working class or peasant has come to our rescue. I am damned if I am going to live like a peasant.' She looked at him with a contempt that startled him.

'Why don't you thank your son for 'protecting private property'? When do you want to eat . . . ?'

Reddy stared at her stiff back as she turned to the cooking range. The kitchen was very clean but very stuffy and Reddy felt breathless. He walked back to his table. *Money?* He heard his son under the shower, bawling out *O Sole Mio*, at the top of his voice, only one verse, over and over again. Why couldn't he sing something else? Or better still, bathe silently?

He looked around the cheerless flat; nausea seeped into his stomach at the prospect of spending the rest of his life here after the journal had been evicted. Incarcerated for life; parole on Saturday afternoons for the Gang of Four meetings and then back again to time ticking away, memories fading and then, oblivion.

Sripad emerged from the bathroom, his glistening hair brushed back from a wide forehead, his youthful body clad in red shorts and a black T-shirt with the words "*Up Against The Wall!*" emblazoned in gold letters across the front.

'What ho, Captain, still at the helm?'

Reddy stared at his son's smiling face, full of morning cheer, in complete incomprehension.

Lolling in bed, Arvind sniffed her pillow, his fingers, and smiled to himself. Life was good. Her behaviour with the rest of the family disturbed him sometimes; she was far too chatty with the old patriarch, she refused kitchen work if she found it demeaning. 'What? Peel potatoes and wash the rice? Me? A graduate in Home Science?'

His face suddenly clouded over; she won't stop at bucking the Purohit family hierarchy. He was scared to reflect on that prospect because he knew that he would have to jump right in.

That evening, when Devendra pulled him aside, Arvind believed he had the gift of prophecy.

'Arvind, I . . . unh . . . can I have a word or two with you? Let's go to my room." He clasped him by his forearm and led him away from the others. Without preamble he began.

'Arvind, I have been meaning to talk with you all of last week. But work and children's studies, quite a handful for anyone. Well, here we are. It's about your wife . . .'

He shrugged his shoulders, lowered his voice, and sat next to Arvind.

'I don't mean to interfere. Your wife is, of course, your wife. But she is a member of our household too so I am worried. You know what I mean?'

Devendra's hooded eyes narrowed. He laid a hand on Arvind's bony knee.

'She is young, so are you. So what is she doing all dressing up and all that, hunh? She talks so much, boring Bapu with all those silly jokes.'

He shook his head and waved dismissively. 'No, that's okay; she is young. But let me ask you; Is everything okay between you two?'

Arvind had lost his tongue; he nodded.

Devendra paused; the silence grew. 'Yes? So everything is fine? You know that she has gone out so many evenings over the last fortnight, all dressed in fine saris, *perfume-sherfume,* without telling anyone, and once when Parvatiji asked her, she just ignored her? You know that, yes? And where she goes?' Devendra smiled thinly, trying to sound his most fearsome, 'To meet someone?'

Arvind would have time later to regret his evasiveness. At the moment all he wanted to do was get away from this man who had got him in such an agitated state. He stammered. 'She, unh, okay, bhaisahab, I'll ask her; I am sure it's nothing. Okay, I'm hungry.'

'Wait a minute, Arvind. I know she met you once. A friend saw you and her at Gaylord the other night, sitting side by side. What's the matter with our house, one wants to know? You have your room. Frolic there, in bed.' He snickered. Then he rearranged his expression, sighed and a beat later, shook his head.

'No, the fact of the matter is, I know that she did go out, when was it? Yes, Thursday evening to meet someone that was not you. Don't ask what, who, I don't know; but it wasn't you. Get me? Just thought I'd mention it.'

He paused, and with his hands folded behind him, walked to the small window, peered out and nodded, as if he had just learnt the answer to his own question.

'Okay, I also know that you met with an attractive lady, again Parvatiji's friend recognised you but not the girl. I know men are men and these things happen. But what is the reason? Clearly you are not happy, she is upsetting you; so you wander a little on the side. No problem. We are responsible husbands; but she . . . ? She is so young, attractive and I suppose bored, she has fire in her loins, sorry, I don't mean to be rude . . . but the family's reputation . . .'

Arvind was stunned. He wondered if he should laugh or cry at this brother towering over him, the hooded eyes, the thin smile, stooping shoulders. Once again, he did not answer. He was too scared to take any chances with this man.

Devendra patted him on the head.

'You are balding, *Chottu*, get some vitamins. Women don't like baldies so early in their marriage. Okay, let's go; No, you go first. I'll wash up . . ." His bleak smile frozen into place, he watched Arvind lurch out of the room.

He walked to the bathroom and looked into the mirror, into a face ravaged with bitterness and lost love. He felt a contemptuous pity for his youngest brother, but also an envy that brought tears to his eyes.

It was that envy and yearning for the exuberance of youth that prompted him to invite Poornima the morning after Parvati had expressed her suspicions. To The Oberoi Towers—just a chat and cakes, he had said. They met in the lobby, his heart beating rapidly when he looked into that fresh, unlined face. Barely had she sat opposite him than he rose, and told her about having to meet a business colleague and that she could come along. They would have tea later; there was a family matter he wanted to discuss with her. She followed him meekly, a little surprised at this new familiarity. They rode a taxi in silence and her curiosity turned to apprehension when they got off at a residential block off Colaba Causeway. She hesitated at the elevator but Devendra smiled, assuring her it would not take a minute. He had barely walked in, ahead of her when she sensed the flat was empty. At the threshold, calmly she told her brother-in-law she was going home. Just then a neighbour's door opened and Devendra, in helpless fury watched her leave. Poornima never mentioned this incident to anyone. But she never forgot it.

Arvind was not to know all of it ever except through a maturing instinct that distilled suspicions, innuendos and the hostile attitudes of Devendra and Parvati. But right now, he was confronted with a new torment: Poornima unfaithful? She was beautiful. And if he, her husband of two years was succumbing to her charms, why not some stranger, possibly someone with thick black hair, muscles and a deep voice, someone like John Abraham, the star or someone older, like Amitabh Bachchan? This city had any number of rich old men with failing libidos that needed young women like, yes, like Poornima to rev them up. What was happening? What should he do? He did not dare confront Poornima because he wasn't sure that Parvatiji hadn't told her about him meeting some strange lady. Lies!! Had his brother gone mad?

He should have laughed it off. But he had been caught by surprise and all he knew at this moment was that the most important crisis of his life was shaping up right before him. He rose to call Poornima. Then he sat back. He had no idea how he was to confront this problem; a stray remark could snowball into a ugly quarrel, tears, door-banging, loud wailing, maybe a suicide. Who knew what women might not do!

Words! God, they could create a huge mess, he muttered to himself; best to keep silent. Better still, stay out of the house. Sunday seemed to stretch forever.

When Mahesh met 'The Gang' the following Saturday, he felt a sudden panic. Had he lost their attention? The day was unusually hot even for October and the lazily whirring fans of The Wayside Inn gave little relief. Outside, a shimmering heat blurred his vision of the car park and the Art Gallery. Not far from them, the pavement-dwelling family indulged its daily routines, the children running after tourists and Inn customers, the patriarch sleeping off his hooch and the wife picking lice off a girl's matted hair.

Ranjan sweated copiously, and Arvind felt irritable. He wanted to run back to his air-conditioned bookstore; his restlessness showed. Reddy was grumpy, he felt exhausted. But the heat was only part of the reason for the Gang's tetchiness. Each one of them had had a difficult week, five days of strange emotions brought on by unexpected desires and events. Ranjan brought the subject up.

'I think I can speak for all of us when I say that this seems like a perfect day to sit back and hear the rest of your story, Mahesh.' He smiled indulgently, a faint line of sweat glistening on his upper lip.

'Poor Abhijeet: money down the drain, so to speak.' He smiled dryly.

Reddy groaned silently. He would have preferred to talk of something else, but he was grateful to Ranjan for a long meeting the previous Thursday when he had finally briefed The Banker on Gandhi. Arvind felt 'traumatised'; that is how he described himself to his wife as he left home. Before she could reply, he had shut the door on her; that act had lifted his spirits somewhat. He smiled generously at Mahesh.

'What gives? Forgot the rest, is it?"

Mahesh gulped some water.

'After that trip to Pune, Abhijeet did not meet me for several days. I felt he was embarrassed, all the more so because he had been so candid about his time in that room. He hadn't stopped talking about that 'unfortunate victim', all the way back to Mumbai. He wanted to save her, indeed rescue all the whores in the brothels from "slavery" but he had no idea of how. Not once did he ask me about my experience and I did not tell him. At the time I thought he was masking some inadequacy of his own under all that ranting about the "unjust system". Till, one day, he burst into my flat in a drunken state, muttering incoherently, waving a sheaf of booklets under my nose.'

"Look at these buddy. You know what they are? Reports by NGOs and newspaper clippings on prostitution in this fucking city. It makes you want to cry." And he began to cry. I was embarrassed, I must admit. Then he grew silent rather abruptly, asked me for coffee. He told me he had requested an NGO working among the prostitutes in the city's red light areas if he could accompany its activists on their next visit to the area. The person he walked with into those warren-like rooms in Falkland Road had been cynical, he said. He had a knowing air behind thick glasses and a beard, hair pasted down with coconut oil, Abhijeet remarked with some disdain, and his attitude toward the whores, so Abhijeet felt, was almost brutal in its contempt He simply distributed leaflets about hygiene and protection against AIDs and was ready to leave. "I asked him if I could spend some time with a few girls. He agreed with a smirk. I sat back with some and you know what, Mahesh? They began laughing when I asked them why they did what they did." 'One of them then asked him a question in reply to his. "Do you work, *Saab*?" Abhijeet nodded. "For a boss?" Yes, he muttered. "For pay? Like commission?" Abhijeet said nothing. "Then what's the difference between you and us?" And they laughed till tears were rolling down their blotchy faces. Abhijeet had finished his coffee, then walked up to the cabinet and poured himself a drink. "So I left to the sound of their merriment. Funny, isn't it? They think I need help."'

Reddy perked up for the first time. 'Well, I wouldn't put it quite like that, but if you work for the capitalist system, then you have mortgaged your body, isn't it? Slavery, that's what it is. Like those . . . prostitutes, I mean women.'

'That's ridiculous Reddy and you know it. Everyone works for someone. And soon it becomes an addiction. Those women . . . why do they run back? Yes they do . . . The world's a market, has always been; every god is selling something including yours, my friend, ideology or religion. Why should sex be different?' Arvind was nodding vigorously.

'In fact, I think it's the most important thing in the world! Look at the Internet. The hottest selling number . . . sex.'

'Attaboy, *Shabash*, Arvind. You have something there for Reddy to think about; though that's all he can do now, poor chap. You don't need a theory of production, as Marx would have it, but a theory of reproduction. The development of society from feudalism to capitalism, more than anything else, is a movement from the palace courtesan to the Falkland Road whore, with payment now monetised. Commoditification; isn't that the word? But let's not interrupt Mahesh. He more likely than not will sink into his deep silences and then we are done for. So Mahesh, Vats next?' Arvind snickered.

'It was evident in the weeks that followed that he had taken the jibes thrown at him very seriously.' Mahesh gave a cold smile. 'Just as you gentlemen have.' He shook his head. 'No, no I don't mean that. Anyway, it was as if that taunt had struck some part of his nervous system and rattled it.'

'One night, he claimed that he had been sent to back-office operations. "This whore is of no use to anyone, Mahesh. Those guys with the American accents, boy, they are climbing all over me with their Florsheim brogues. One crab with bad breath is from Thunderbird College? You have heard of it or what, Mahesh?"'

Ranjan shook his head disdainfully. 'What's the problem? At least he wouldn't have had to trudge all over to Thane-Belapur on hot afternoons with a briefcase of bad debt portfolios! He was lucky.'

'But look at the young man Abhijeet! Why should he be discriminated against just because he isn't out of some American business school?'

Everyone looked at Reddy with astonishment. Ranjan had a twinkle in his eyes.

'Well, well, now you seem to be getting into the spirit of things! How does Mahesh answer that question?'

'That was exactly what Abhijeet agonized over. I was never sure of the facts of the situation. I just had his word for it but he swore that he worked twice as hard at whatever task he was assigned. At any rate, I wasn't really interested in discovering how good he was at work. What was worrying me was his capacity to cope with the workplace. You remember management experts from American universities flooding public forums with their glib talk on productivity and global competition. From Abhijeet I learnt of a hostile office atmosphere; the old bonhomie had given way to a crabby space.' That's what he called it; "space." He was beginning to feel isolated, lonely and afraid. And he was drinking far too much.'

'Then one day, I met his father in the lobby of the building as I waited for the company car to pick me up. He came straight to the point after a brief but pleasant nod at me.'

"Look here," he said, "I want to talk with you about Abhijeet." He noticed my hesitation. "It won't take long. Your driver can wait." 'He didn't take no for an answer. Brigadier Thiagarajan, Infantry, retired. Glad to meet you. Tea or coffee?" His sentences came out in bursts, but his voice was surprisingly pleasant, not the typical parade-ground type. "My son is very fond of you." His moustache quivered "I ought to tell you that he is a very excitable fellow . . . Drink brings out the worst in him."'

'He wasn't expecting any response for he carried on, "He may give you the impression that we force a way of life on him. Not true. He must do whatever he wants well, with conviction and with discipline and courage." The thick brush over his upper lip quivered with suppressed fury; he pursed his lips. "A man has to have courage. Duck when the bullets fly: but take the blows and move on. He cannot live like a rat!"'

'I was speechless. He had spat those words out, like an incontestable verdict. Then he asked me if I were married knowing fully well that I wasn't. He shook his head, a huge shiny dome ringed with white curls that fell coyly over his shoulders. "A man should marry only if he is willing to learn how to keep a woman happy. The man should be a—positive thinker!"'

'The last sentence was uttered with oracular emphasis. He glanced at his watch and fell silent. I took the hint and left, completely mystified by his pronouncement. It was only later that I understood what he was trying to tell me.'

His listeners had fallen into a deep silence. Reddy seemed to be dozing, Arvind stared at him, open-mouthed. Ranjan smiled and spoke softly.

'It makes sense doesn't it? If you don't believe in your own worth . . .' He shifted his huge body in his chair, grunted and reached for his tea. 'You are what you think of yourself. Wake up feeling like a rat and you will behave like one. Imagine yourself a lion and the world treats you with respect. It's all so, *ah-h-h* rational.'

Reddy felt Ranjan was talking drivel. He felt for the first time a sympathetic bonding with Abhijeet. A rat is cornered . . . so he felt cornered. *Positive thinking?* His life had been suffused with positive thoughts! And now he knew it was all a fake, a prop without the play, an actor without a script, if there was no one to test it upon; the spirit soon wearied. He felt a profound sadness, despair for all the . . . rats in their corners cowering before life's dreadful caprices.

Had Arvind been a mind reader he would have hugged Reddy for feeling the way he did. What was the difference between Brigadier Thiagarajan and his eldest brother, Devendra? Both could make you feel like a rat.

'One morning, a high-pitched wail rend the silence and suddenly stopped. I ran down to their floor and to my horror I saw Abhijeet slumped against the doorjamb. A foul odour of whisky and cigarettes bore witness to the manner he had spent the night. His mother saw me, clapped her fist to her mouth. Strangely the Brigadier was nowhere to be seen then he shuffled to the door behind her, his face immobile, his quivering moustache the only indication of a rage that could burst through any minute. He gestured and we carried Abhijeet into his bedroom. His mother stood off to one corner weeping, while the father stared at his son's pallid face. His cold brown eyes, said it all: a loser. Then I saw the old man's expression harden, his lips pursed; he had a plan. And I knew it would succeed.'

'Let me guess.' Reddy looked at Mahesh with a knowing smile. 'It is something I would have done; he packs him off to his home town for an immersion in humility.'

'No way! You got it all wrong! The father will find him a bride. Best thing for a guy like Abhijeet: a wife to stabilise his life, change his urges. Ask me, I know.'

Mahesh's dark eyes fixed onto the other's face. He nodded, more to himself.

'The third proposal seemed suitable; horoscopes matched. So a pleased Abhijeet told me. The girl looked pretty enough, he remarked between pulls on his cigarette, when he came up one late Sunday morning, waving the photograph as if it were his passport to a new life. We set about to celebrate the end of 'celibacy', as he put it, a nervous giggle matching his restless excitement. Meenakshi was her name. She came from a town near Chennai, a product of Madras Christian College.'

'She was not a modern girl, Abhijeet muttered, but, he assured me—as if I needed assuring!—that he would take care of that once they were married. I must admit I did not pay much attention to him after he had shown me the photograph. I felt piqued, a wistful regret too, at the thought that our own relationship would soon change forever.'

Reddy peered over his thick glasses, palms down on the table as if he were at a board meeting.

'But it never did, did it?'

'Well, no. But how was I to know that? As the evening wore on his mood changed; so did mine. He was sinking into gloom, muttering darkly about bondage and I was hopeful. Only later did I recall the terror in his eyes.'

Arvind shook Mahesh's hand heartily.

'Great chapter Vats! So what if it's an arranged marriage. They work! I can tell you, a man with two years experience!'

'Sure they do, Arvind and we have a thirty year testimonial to that, don't we?' In the dull wash of the halogen lights, Ranjan looked jaundiced. The heavy jowls, puffy eyelids and the bulbous nose held Mahesh spellbound. Arvind left with a cheerful wave; none responded. Reddy stood under the awning of a cigarette stall, watching them. Ranjan smiled at Mahesh, his face a death mask.

'The fun begins now doesn't it? See you next weekend.' He walked towards Lion's Gate. Reddy scurried after him.

'You're not off to your jaunts again, are you Ranjan . . . because I am coming with you!'

Ranjan burst out laughing.

'Reddy, my good friend,' he clapped him on the back. 'Mahesh has put us in good spirits hasn't he? But, I am tired, and I need some rest. I need something else; I don't know what . . . perhaps a life less replete with memories of . . .' Ranjan gulped.

'Such a painful thing . . . to be saddled with ancient hatreds, futile nostalgia.'

Reddy had never heard Ranjan speak like this, he of all people, so, so *positive!* Suddenly Reddy felt a shiver even though it was hot and humid. They shuffled along uprooted pavements, skirting mounds of garbage and shit, over darkened rivulets of piss, in the shadowed arcades of Edwardian stone buildings with nameplates pock-marking dimly-lit corridors in which naked electrical wiring hung slack along grimy walls, like blackened guts of unknown beasts. Ranjan was panting; a thin sliver of saliva glittering in the pale wash of the streetlights trickled down his various chins.

'You should be thankful . . . born a south Indian, away from the horrors of abrupt loss. A man takes generations to dig roots and claim the fruits. And you have done that Reddy, even the peasant in that fucking revolution you blabber so much about. You know why?' He did not wait for an answer; Reddy had none.

'They fought for stable geography not an arbitrary one. No tectonic shifts like the Partition, all we children of those miserable refugees uprooted from their *watan*, homelands, left with treacherous memory and all for what? Derelict in humanity and their landscapes, brimming with bitterness . . . what could they pass on but hatred posing as folk tales?' He wheezed like a leaky pipe.

'But I fought; I found humanity in . . . *Money!* The great agent of inversion! Marx was right, my friend Reddy, but not for the reasons you think. He understood the power of commerce. But you know what? You cannot force your dream down people's throats. They have to suffer despair, monumental loss . . . to start dreaming . . . their own dream.'

Ranjan almost fell into a half-open drain; he had not seen the black ooze so much as smelt its foul stench. He grunted, rested a heavy paw on Reddy's thin shoulder. The dull blue of the solitary fluorescent bulb, dangling precariously above the arched entrance illuminated their faces. They were just a short distance from the brightly lit and busy Shahid Bhagat Singh Road.

'Partition, my friend! Division! Genocide! That is what I am talking of, in case your fucking dimwit mind hadn't understood! Loss; recovery! Not revolution! Not the airy-fairy yearning for collective orgasms by lonely masturbators like you; as for me, it's hatred for the haters, understand? Self-Interest! Watch your back! No Credit without Commission! The three weapons of democracy!'

Frightened yet unwilling to leave him, Reddy nudged his friend along.

'That's your third beer, *madharchod*, and you know the rules; pay as you order! I should throw you out!' Vispy's eyebrows danced as he glowered at Sripad.

'Money! That's all you can think of, you Shylock! Look at me . . . The Face of Love—that's what you are staring at! Vispy my friend, oh my friend! I spoke to her this afternoon!'

Vispy's eyebrows met in the middle of his forehead. 'Who? Your mother?'

'No, you prick! That girl I told you about. You know the one that needed rescuing? Well, this afternoon, no, early evening . . . You want to hear it all? Waiter? One more please!' Vispy snorted but said nothing.

'Okay, this is how it happened. There I am in my small office in Pyramid Heights thinking deep thoughts about nothing . . . working, you know. A hot afternoon, fan whirring but I am so hot! Then the lift doors part and out she steps. Now listen to this, my old bachelor friend. I look up from my ledger and mine eyes register . . . open flounced hair, loose salwaar kameez of pale yellow with soft pink dupatta across slender shoulders, white thin-strapped sandals face free of make-up just faint lip gloss: very nice and summery. She looks my way and in a flash of inspiration that comes only once to people in love—so sorry Vispy old chap, you'll just have to hear about it—I have it! I dash toward exit, take deep breath and: "Excuse me, ma'am". She turns, her hair flying behind her, like Farah Fawcett's in those ads you know? "Madam," I say, "you have forgotten to sign the Visitors' Book." She is puzzled, I know for sure; she pushes her sunshades up. "Visitors Book? What is that?" I smile, bow and, "if you would follow me, won't take a second." To my surprise, she nods. I sit behind my desk pull the book out. She comes round, bends over to sign and her hair brushes my cheek I could put my hands round her slender waist. *Vispy! Such yearning! Tchah!* What would you know, an old spinster like you?'

Sripad took a long swig. He was starting to slur. Vispy flicked some change on the glass-top counter for a customer, without taking his eyes off Sripad.

'Okay, Bogart, then what? You asked her to run off to Shanghai?'

Sripad did not reply; he was peering into his French fries as if searching for an answer in the heap of soggy and over-fried slivers.

'Time for that, Vispy. Anyway, I read her name and her address: Well, well, I say to myself: Deepika, from Bandra . . . a film producer's daughter? Of course, I had run out of things to say by then. She was walking toward the door. Then she stopped. "What's that music playing? I've heard that song before." I looked at my portable player and it was an old U2 number, I couldn't remember the fucking name. Then Vispy old friend, another flash of inspiration: "*The music is you, while the music lasts*," I whispered. Isn't that great? Of course I whispered it but she caught on and glared. "'Nothing, just a line from another song.'"

Vispy shook his head. "Bastard, that's Eliot and you got it wrong.'

'Is it? I thought it was my creation. Anyway,' she softened. "Mrs Biswas told me about you; estate manager . . . with attitude." Then she was gone. No goodbye. But you know what Vispy? she loves me, I can tell; an old hand like me? I . . . can . . . tell!'

Both father and daughter were surprised to find each other home so early. At one of those rare dinners the Kapoors ate together, Madhavi talked incessantly with a nervous excitement, sometimes incoherently. Neither Ranjan nor Deepika paid her much attention, apart from an occasional nod.

Deepika's thoughts were occupied by the elderly Japanese who had slipped his hand around her waist as she handed his whisky-and-soda at the first of her "exposures to the fine art of hostessing." She had been surprised not shocked; she had simply smiled at him and with a flick of her hips slipped away from his limp grip. She had mentioned this to no one, not even to Aditya and the other hostesses that gathered for their post-party treat not even Mrs. Biswas. But she never forgot the sensation of his dry hand tremulous and tentative yet inviting, his whisky breath so close for that moment when her nipples tightened and her pulse raced.

That night she thought of Sripad just as much as much as Mr. Tamasaki. His ploy with that 'Visitors Book' had been laughable and he would have been passed off as those countless men with little more than self-regard in their asset books. But she was intrigued; behind the granny glasses perched firmly on the bridge of a thin nose, she saw alertness to her every move and gesture; it was unsettling. Like that old Japanese, Sripad had been alive to her presence, all the world blacked out, just the two of them. *"You are the music . . . ?"*

Soon she had fallen into deep slumber. She remained blissfully unaware of the storm brewing outside her door. Much later, she would recall the dinner, the incessant chatter that she had not bothered with, her mother's unexpected clumsiness with serving bowls . . .

'Ranjan . . .' He looked up from the financial daily and grunted.

'Did you hear what I said? Are you going to do something?' Madhavi's looked cross.

'Do what Madhu?' Ranjan picked up the afternoon tabloid. He noticed Deepika's bedroom door firmly shut.

'What was I saying at the dinner table? Why don't you listen to me, do you understand the dangers we face every day? Do you know what can happen to your daughter when she passes by the slums? All those dark-bodied men in dirty vests, lungis and lust in their eyes? Today she was wearing that yellow kameez, so thin, her bra showed, it would be so easy to tear it off, like this . . .' Madhavi, picked up a newspaper and tore it in two. Startled, Ranjan looked up. Madhavi held the pieces in her hands as if waiting for the applause to break. Her hair had come untied and fell unruly about her thin shoulders.

'Madhu? My God, you frightened me. Keep your voice down, Deepika's fast asleep.'

She scurried to the open window that looked on to the building barely thirty feet away. She pulled the curtains together with such decisiveness that Ranjan gaped at her in astonishment. She looked back conspiratorially, then turned and drew one of them aside, peering into the black night. A lone light shone from one of the apartments. She let the curtain fall and walked to a wicker chair opposite Ranjan. Her hands shook.

'Do you know? Some terrible things are going on here, and you don't even care! No! You listen to me!' Her voice dropped to an urgent whisper, the words tumbling into one another.

'They are filming me in the nude, maybe Deepika too. Don't speak; just listen! The cassette is circulating! We have to stop them!' And with a hiss as Ranjan reached the window:

'Don't draw the curtains, you madman! They can hear what I am saying. Ranjan! *Please!*'

He couldn't believe his ears. He looked at her in angry bewilderment He let the curtains fall together, his ears tingling. All he could say was, 'Madhu, let's go to sleep. It's late and you look tired.'

She ran to him, shook his shoulder with a force that surprised him. Strands of grey hair fell about her thin face. She sat beside him, shaking her head.

'I knew he was up to no good. He must have told those people across from us in that building.' She wiped her mouth with an edge of her sari and began braiding it nervously.

'Ranjan, today that dhobi—'

'Lakhan? The chap who irons our clothes? What does he have to do with all this . . . nonsense? Have you had something to drink? My whisky? Let me see . . .' He sprang to his feet.

'Are you mad, Ranjan? I hate the stuff!. God knows you have tried to get me to drink. On top of what they say about my being a fast woman that's all I'd need . . . to be known as an alcoholic! *Hey Ram!* Ranjan, how will we find a decent boy for our darling daughter? I am so worried and you sit there like a fat Buddha?!'

He stared at his wife with disbelief alternating with horror; she seemed the same except for a gleam in her eye and a level of energy he had not witnessed in years. He saw a thin face with traces of the chiselled beauty that had beguiled him thirty years ago. She was still full in the breasts, her general thinness accentuating them though they drooped. *Dhobi?* Surprised by his own timidity, he asked:

'What was that about Lakhan, my dear?'

She eyed him suspiciously.

'Lakhan, what do you mean? It was nothing. Last Monday morning someone forgot to shut the front door Lakhan, you know he comes around then, he walked in just as I came out of the bath, a towel around my hair and nothing else, and he stared, and I squealed and he retreated, saying sorry but he had seen me just as you could if you . . .' She turned away. Ranjan could only stare and wonder if he was imagining all this. But Madhavi hadn't finished. She sniffed and turned her glistening face to him. She reached out her hand, pulled it back, clasping both on her lap. She spoke to a shelf on the far wall.

'I was so depressed and worried and I must have told Venkat, you know the regular at Joggers' Park and—and at a bend in the track, no one was there, he pulled me close and, Oh! Ranjan! On the mouth once, twice, holding me, whispering . . . . God! Madness! But I forgot it . . .'

Ranjan's blood froze.

"*Whar!* What are you saying? In a park . . . ? On your lips?? God! Oh God! What is happening to us?'

He slumped on the sofa, slack-jawed, his heart pummelling his rib cage, his head desperately summoning his life's organizing tenets, the belief in the limpid lucidity of reason. He thought he would faint. He rose with a heavy grunt, pulled her up, and held her. She started, whispered his name and he squeezed her breasts viciously, she whimpered, and broke loose.

'What are you doing, you oaf? Don't you see the house is bugged? They are filming us! While you . . . you play with me?' She was wild-eyed now, a dribble of saliva had frothed on her thin lips; she wiped it off with the back of her hand. 'It was nothing, Ranjan, just a—'

His hand swung back with a life of its own and ended on her cheek with a thunderclap. Suddenly, a door opened and Deepika stood there in her nightgown, her face puffy with sleep.

'Daddy! What? What are you doing? You hit her? Mama!' And she rushed up held her close and began to cry. Madhavi stroked her head.

'*Beta,* it's nothing; go back to sleep. And don't raise your voice, dear, they can hear . . .' Deepika tore free from her and turned on her father who stood off in a corner, staring at his huge hands as if he had never seen them before.

'Nothing, Deepu darling, go back to your room . . . just a quarrel . . . that's all—' Deepika's wailed. 'And you hit her for that . . . ? Why did you slap Mummy?'

She ran to her mother, arms outstretched but Madhavi broke loose toward Ranjan who stood looking out the window. She pulled the curtains and whispered urgently but Deepika did not catch the words. She just stared at her parents, behind a wall of shocked grief and angry incomprehension. Through her tears, she saw them as if from a vast distance; her anguish turned to puzzled rage and she ran to her room, banging the door behind her. They could hear her muffled sobs.

At four that morning, exhausted by her relentless pursuits of a world he could never have thought existed, Ranjan laced the coffee he insisted upon, with one of his sleeping pills. Within minutes Madhavi felt drowsy, her voice dropped and soon she was snoring on the sofa. With a tenderness that amazed him, Ranajn carried his wife to their bedroom, wishing Deepika could have seen him. At seven the next morning, he called Dr. Karmarkar, their family doctor, who visited them later that day.

She continued to surprise Ranjan. At the clinic of a famous psychiatrist, to whom Ranjan took an instant dislike, she was coy. She told him of the plot to 'destroy the family' and that she could see things her husband could not. He listened patiently but detachedly, as if he were hearing a recorded voice, his thick fingers flying over the computer keyboard. Then, speaking to the monitor: 'Nothing to worry about, Madam'. As they were leaving, she turned and said in a low but clear voice, 'Doctor, I did not imagine these things. My husband is a good man. I am . . . responsible.'

Had Arvind known what his Saturday tryst would lead to, he would probably have called it off; so it was just as well that he remained blissfully unaware of the dark clouds gathering above his idyllic world. He cast a loving eye over the shelves and the books he had not read. His ears were cocked for the swish of a sari, clicking of high heels, the snap of a handbag. She was late; the wall clock's ticking was irritating him. Then the backdoor creaked and she peered in, her face radiantly impish.

'What . . . what . . . Arvind . . . why are you looking at me like that?' She laughed nervously, brushing back her open hair. 'So this is your office . . . hmm. Very small isn't it? But okay.' She flashed her smile again, whispered into his ear.

'I like it here . . .' She straightened, sat lightly on the sofa at the far end, leaned back and crossed her legs, her sari riding up.

'Come here Arvind.' He obeyed mutely, his senses gathering on some cataclysmic event about to unfold.

Without a word, she hitched up her blouse sat on his lap awkwardly, her arms around his head, pressing his face to her breast and the puckered nipple. Then she lifted his head and kissed him hard and he tasted her sour sweet breath, faint traces of mouthwash and broke free gasping. She stood up, hitched her sari to her waist and without warning took his hand and placed it firmly on her warm and wet crotch and he felt giddy, his cock straining against his trousers. A sharp intake of breath later, she moved away to the edge of the table, yanked her panties down over her small feet now shorn of her high heels, bent over and he saw for the first time in his life, for the first time in the harsh dazzle of overhead tube lights, her—*gash*! More like a zipless pouch, he thought. Open-mouthed, he gazed at her most intimate part revealed to him with no trace of shame or embarrassment, her invitation never to be so daring and breathtaking. Stumbling over files on the floor, he lurched toward the dark summit's musky bouquet, his mobile rang as he bent over her, burying his head in her hair, as she guided his limp hands to her breasts and the mobile wouldn't stop ringing. But he heard it no more, as the roar of thunder in his ears and her keening, low-decibel cry carried them up mountains and down valleys and up again, till they burst at the top of their own summits in a synchronous flash of a million stars. The mobile trilled again, as he lay inert over her, his face in her soft hair, panting between bursts of exhausted sobs that could not drown the banging on the door.

'Purohit *saab*, is everything okay? Are you there, Sir?'

For months afterwards that stocky Nepali watchman of indeterminate age, thirty years in that building, father of seven children would vary his version of that evening when for the first and last time, Arvind *saab* had had a 'woman in his office'.

They rode home in silence, Poornima humming softly her hand clasping his tightly. He felt exhausted; his legs turned to jelly, his senses still locked into the wondrous mystery beside him, grateful for her turbulent urges and those she kindled in him yet fearing them.

The mobile had sounded like a tocsin. His slim body shuddered spasmodically and he slumped against the damp and grimy seat, his hand limp in hers. A faint nausea rose in his throat and he did not know why but he wanted to throw up.

The house was silent and Poornima still hummed tonelessly. Slowly he disengaged his shaking hand from hers, worked the key in the latch and opened the door with growing unease. The hallway was dark and quiet. Then a light came on at the far end with Devendra and Parvati in tow.

'So! Where have you two been? No don't say anything!' To Poornima with a frown: 'Why don't you run along to your room, I need to talk to your . . . husband. Just for a few minutes.'

Poornima returned Devendra's stare coolly, smiled and left. Parvati hurried after her.

'*Chottu* . . .'. Once again that hated nickname! Arvind winced, his heart racing.

Huddled in each other's arms but unable to sleep, both Arvind and Poornima sought comfort in evasion and silence. He recounted little beyond the self-evident. Devendra had been angry at their "irresponsibility"; tonight they had celebrated Bapu's birthday at a favourite restaurant, how could they have forgotten this family outing? But Arvind kept a lot to himself; Devendra's naked aggression, his suspicions about motives and, his own first act of free will. He lay in the dark and thought of that fateful moment, the words flashing over and over.

'I was at the office all this while.'

Devendra had stopped pacing, turned and glared.

'Office? And Poornima? Meeting her . . . friend is it?'

Arvind shook his head. 'She was with me.' He had spoken slowly, his voice clear and strong.

'With you . . . all this while? What was she doing there? Brushing up on temple art? So why didn't one of you answer my calls?'

Arvind had met his eldest brother's contemptuous gaze and then, a glow of remembered joy half-shut his eyes and he brought his fingers to his nose. Devendra had looked into his brother's face, his lips contorting with a puzzled fury at this unexpected challenge. Then he had stepped back, his head spinning with helpless rage at the message in that serendipity, He unclenched his fists, pointed to the door and hissed;

'Get out of my sight, you . . . you . . . dog shit!'

F or the Gang of Three the weekend had been profoundly portentous and each was forced into a grudging recognition of those events as numbing blows to their self-perception.

Ranjan's nerves responded to Madhavi's altering states of self-esteem all of which seemed no less mysterious to him through the week and two visits to the family doctor later than on the first fateful night. Deepika's behaviour was inexplicable as well; she shunned him all week, shutting off her smile whenever they ran into each other. For the first time, he felt emotions he would have condemned in others; hurt alternated with anger ending in a sense of rejection. At times he almost envied Madhavi her condition for the sympathy it drew from Deepika.

It was in the privacy of his office that he felt reassured. A visit by Gandhi's accountant who informed him with an unctuous smirk that 'his boss' had transferred a fresh bunch of shares to the newly opened account of 'Miss Deepika', appeared to him a balm for his domestic headaches. An invitation to lunch with Nasreen Treasurywalla was like a shot of adrenaline in an ageing athlete. He almost accepted, but demurred for reasons he could not explain. And for the first time in years, his sleep was fitful; images of his daughter's selective affections clashed with those of Nasreen's pale cleavage to the rhythm of a thumping heart.

Reddy's week was spent in reluctant self-reckoning that left him exhausted rather than enlightened. All through the week Ranjan had been evasive.

'Let it wait, my friend, *Diwali* is coming up; besides I don't feel too well. In any case we'll meet on Saturday.' That prospect held little cheer for Reddy because the days stretched before him like the plains of north India, flat, bleached by an unrelenting sun into a shimmering emptiness. His panic at the commuter rush on the Virar-Churchgate local was no longer assuaged; only death could release him from these hellish journeys.

That prospect made him consider his fellow passengers with compassion—an emotion he had detested all his life; the cripple huddled at the exit between a thousand pairs of legs; shopkeepers, salesmen, petty traders, playing cards, singing *Bhajans* at the top of their voices, the steady tinkling drone of tiny cymbals that, much to his astonishment, calmed his heated nerves. He stared at the unlined face of a college student squeezed between swarthy men, a cell phone to his ear, even teeth flashing in the harsh light streaming through the barred windows.

And Mahesh and Abhijeet? Aimless lives, wasted energy. He felt sorry for them; he was willing to give them a chance. He looked forward to Saturday. He had to know if Mr. Mahesh had goals. A goal—and who said that it should be epochal?—anchored dreams.

Arvind could not escape the feeling of a gathering crisis. Some mornings he felt reluctant to leave bed, his inertia feeding upon self-recriminations about the words not uttered, an initiative not taken and a growing dread of an unpleasant family drama in the making.

Poornima was almost sure the retribution for their truancy from Papa's birthday would have more shadow than substance. In Devendra's bullying she read more than Arvind but like him she felt confident of the old patriarch's protection from the eldest brother's predatory instincts. Untutored in familial politics, she had only her own instincts to fall back upon but she learnt quickly the unwritten and unspoken truth that family bonds that tie can also strangle.

Her lessons came from the petty humiliations Parvati had hinted at; closer monitoring of their movements, interdictions on dressing, additional chores to pin her down, in short less time for herself and Arvind. But nothing prepared her for the old patriarch's words when they were summoned to his room one late evening after dinner.

The following day, at a very distraught wife's insistence, the youngest Purohit couple met at The Hanging Gardens. They watched the sun set over the slate-grey sea in silence. Crowds milled all around them, on pathways, over the lawns. Children played with hysterical delight; a group of four ran around the bench they sat on; Poornima glowered at them. Arvind remembered a phrase an old schoolmaster used to throw at him: lost at sea. That is what he felt now. Not just lost but abandoned, left to the sharks by an uncaring father.

What had he meant . . . have children? They had barely been married a few years; he had just started on the most exciting journey of his life! Discovering heady smells and lubricious warmth: his own heated responses.

Grandchildren? Give me a couple or the shop? That was blackmail!

He shook his head as if to clear it of such thoughts and a new one crept in. He smiled to himself as it grew into an idea and a desire. Yes! Why not? What had Bapu said? *Fatherhood restores balance in your life!*

He turned to Poornima who exclaimed.

'Look Arvind, the sun! On its way to death!'

Something in him snapped.

'Have you gone mad? First you bring this calamity on us and now you talk shit about death? Hunh? Poornima, tell me, have you lost your head?'

Her eyes blazed and she replied in like fashion. 'Don't shout at me! You should have raised your voice yesterday. Yes! I am mad at you, at your family and its superior airs; that Devendra is such a rascal! Hypocrite! But you? Why are you such a *bhikari?* A beggar! Their poodle!' And she began to cry. Arvind gaped, alarmed.

'I don't know what you mean, Poornima, but I think, I mean, don't you think it's time for us to have . . .'

'No!'. Her vehemence was like a thunderclap. 'No! No, no, a hundred times . . . *No!*' She rose suddenly, dabbed her eyes and blew her nose and flung the tissue over the low wall. She retraced her steps, huddled close and whispered:

'Hold me, Arvind. Put your arm round me and hold me close. It's getting dark. Yes, tomorrow the sun shall rise . . .'

The Wayside Inn was packed to capacity. The 'dead poets' eyed the 'Gang of Four', with open hostility; they needed one more chair. A waiter brought over a stool for the fifth poet while Wilfred ordered another round of beers and glared at Arvind who quickly ordered a round of tea. Lunch had been a silent and hurried affair, each member too preoccupied to make casual conversation. Michael was called to clear the table The Banker burped, Reddy tried to look indifferent while Arvind smiled wickedly and offered Wilfred a friendly wave. Mahesh stared at Ranjan's silent expression, taken aback by his pallor, limp jowls quivering ever so often. Reddy's lips were puckered in thought or disapproval Mahesh wasn't sure.

'The day the parents told me of the proposed wedding of Abhijeet their son, my relationship with them changed. Much against my will, I was drawn into the network of confidences peculiar to a family. Perhaps it was inevitable: they saw me as Abhijeet's closest friend; I lived on the floor above and appeared to them a stable, if withdrawn collaborator in this enterprise.'

'The same day I got a call from Abhijeet at the office asking me to meet him for dinner at a new bar in Andheri. I was confused; the prospect of bringing home a drunk Abhijeet wasn't a very happy one . . . and yet. Why not a place nearby, I asked. No, no, this is really good, I read about it in the afternoon papers; one free drink for every two. He pleaded: "Grant a dying man his last wish". "Dying?" I laughed and agreed.

'At the restaurant, a dark cavernous hall, with low air-conditioning and far too many waiters, Abhijeet insisted on a table near the small bandstand on which three guitar players and a drummer uncomfortably perched. Their music was listless perhaps because the night was still young. A fawning steward obliged, pen and pad at the ready. As usual Abhijeet ordered the drinks; his face was flushed, sweat beaded his upper lip and his right hand, never free of cigarette, trembled. I thought the place inappropriate for an intimate chat. Perhaps he read my mind because he got more restless, turned away when our eyes caught and was visibly relieved when the hall filled up fast.'

'The evening was a disaster. Abhijeet talked incessantly and incoherently, I turned away exasperatedly, Then to my horror, Abhijeet staggered to his feet and before I could stop him, lurched towards a couple that had been occasionally eyeing us. He bent over the girl unsteadily, the man glared, rose but the waiter got to him in time and ferried him back to the table.

'To their credit the stewards arranged a cab for us without much fuss and mercifully we were on our way home. I helped Abhijeet alight; he appeared reluctant to enter the building swaying on his feet, head bowed as if in contrition. He looked up and I saw his tears of wordless pain, perhaps self-loathing. I held him close to me, my arms around his slender frame, long after he had stopped trembling.'

Ranjan had dozed off, his chins folding on his chest, lips slightly parted. A faint wheeze escaped from between them. Arvind spoke in an urgent whisper, his brow knitted in concentration.

'Mahesh, you know, arranged marriages work as well as love marriages. Look at me! And if it gets you home sober. Well, what's wrong with a photograph?'

Reddy yawned and shook his head. He gestured to Arvind.

'What, what? Hang on! It makes no difference, young man, love marriage, marriages of similar minds, whatever. A decade into the relationship it won't make any difference; if it lasts that long.'

Ranjan woke with s start, bestowed Reddy with a sickly smile.

'Why Reddy, that is profound! And from a man who only thought of unwashed peasants! *Shabash!*'

Reddy ignored him.

'Tell me, Mahesh, did you ever think of asking him, did you ever find . . . what drove him? No, I do not mean fat salaries, a new jacket or a wife. Did he ask himself— why am I here in these immoral times?'

'If you mean: did he want to behead a *zamindar,* a landlord or blow up a police station, Reddy, forget it. Immoral? What do you mean, immoral? Trying times yes, but an age for decisiveness of purpose, of drive and the will to succeed! Some will fall by the wayside!'

An uneasy silence fell on them. Reddy glared at Ranjan who smiled crookedly and raised his eyebrows. Arvind still looked preoccupied but he also glanced warily at the Editor and Banker. Mahesh shook his head but said nothing. He had seen fear peeking through those boorish drives. His treacherous memory flashed forward to a wedding and Meenakshi, not yet a woman but no longer a girl. With a milk-white complexion, slightly taller than Abhijeet, her eyes had a startled deer's limpid mobility; they had captivated him. He shook his head and found three pairs of eyes on him.

'They were married one early morning at the local temple. I watched the rituals from the edge of the gathering and left before they ended. For me, the chapter was coming to a close and soon the memory of an intimacy holding out possibilities I should think, would fade. So I thought'.

'A fortnight later, just as I was about to leave for work, the doorbell rang. Abhijeeet's mother came up to invite me for a dinner that evening; a private celebration. Meenakshi and Abhijeet had returned from their honeymoon'

"The evening started off well enough. Meenakshi greeted me with her shy toothy smile; Abhijeet poured me a tall one without asking me. The Brigadier chatted for a while then disappeared into his room. Abhijeet took a

long pull on his rum and water and asked me if I wanted
to see their honeymoon photographs. I followed him to
his bedroom.'

'He handed me a thick envelope. The photographs
were snapshots of ill-matched moods. Against various
scenic backdrops, in picnic gear all by themselves,
Meenakshi's radiance is almost infectious. At hotel
revelries with like couples Abhijeet comes alive; a few
snapshots are without Meenakshi; did she capture her
husband on the dance floor? When she does appear, she
stares into the camera with sullen boredom.'

'The contrasts were so obvious I wondered if the
photographs were not some sort of prelude. Between
quick pulls on his cigarette, he launched into a diatribe;
she was clumsy, provincial, unable and unwilling to move
with the times. It was all so embarrassing.'"

'I found him theatrical and false; all the more so when
he burst out:

'"She doesn't even like my drinking, can't stand the
smell, says it's evil."'

'Just then Meenakshi came in with cashew nuts and
Abhijeet sank into silence. I offered her a chair but she
declined, smiling nervously. Her gaze wandered about the
room vacuously, resting finally on her husband's downcast
face, pursed lips. He jerked up, caught off guard, turned
to me and asked about my work, the office. He didn't
expect an answer because he began telling me about his
transfer to another department—Purchase. All the while
Meenakshi stood by a window, her edgy restlessness
now an immobile presence of wordless expectations.
Unnerving! She seemed a different woman from the one
I had seen at a wedding. She made no attempt to fill the
silence and her doe-like eyes that had held me captive
then with their limpid light, now stayed on her husband,
depthless yet measuring—him, us, perhaps the male

species. Abhijeet felt uneasy too; he seemed transfixed by his slip-ons. After an eternity, she turned and left.'

Michael walked over with the bill; Arvind grabbed it impatiently. He was late; he had to shut the shop, meet Poornima later. But he had to clear something with Mahesh. So he lingered as Reddy and Ranjan walked out together into the falling darkness and a humid heat. He held Mahesh back as the banker and editor got into a taxi.

'I think your friend was a very sad man but impatient perhaps? The beginning is awkward . . . People like me, no, I suppose people everywhere find the unfamiliar exotic; to wake up next to the same person every morning isn't the same thing is it? So people say; but I don't know. The grass is not always greener on the other side; you only have to look closer, you never can tell what lurks in your backyard. See you next Saturday. I want to know how this story ends!'

O utside The Connaught Café, one-way traffic roared past with manic speed; death-defying cyclists weaving through fume-spewing taxis battling Japanese and Korean sedans. The humidity was like some invisible sticky substance that had permeated the city's skin. Sripad was inured to the cloying density of the city's demography and climate. Like the 18 million who shat, fornicated and dreamt of the good life just round the corner, Sripad was in his own world.

He missed the gruff sympathy of his closest friend Vispy, who was immersed in his most devout pastime; watching films at Sam's place. The manager who substituted for Vispy liked Sripad and he had bent the house rules about paying for each beer as it was ordered.

Sripad was introspecting. He would stare into his beer then at his lanky frame refracted in the mirrors and run a thumb edge along his lower lip and crack his knuckles loudly. Love had imbued him with an exalted sense of life's purpose and an urge to live up to its awesomeness. He wanted to seduce his ladylove with a lofty self-image; versifier or film reviewer doubling as estate manager wouldn't do. What should he make his life's ambition? Scaling Mount Everest on one leg? Discovering new flora in Silent Valley? Perhaps tracking down the dreaded don— Dawood Ibrahim?

Sripad jerked his head up, kneaded his aching fingers. A sudden fear gripped him. He would have to support her and their children. He looked into the mirrored wall and saw an estate manager and a writer of third-rate film reviews with sad eyes, surrounded by taxi drivers and odd beer guzzlers, flinging soiled and crumpled paper napkins onto the dirty floor. He had to get another job; he would have to take a loan for a house, another for a car? He smacked his forehead. *God, why was life so contradictory? How could passion flower in this arid soil?*

The beer depressed him, it was giving him a headache, he had to get out of this place, he wanted to talk to someone, where was that fucker Vispy? Never around when you needed him most! He walked into the boiling heat, the blazing light and blue smoke bleaching his vision and he felt an urgent desire to head back to Pyramid Heights. He might see her again.

Deepika's days and nights melted into one another in confusion and nervous anticipation. Just a few days after the traumatic events at home Aditya had called, insisting upon a meeting that very evening.

"'Listen, *babes*, I got a great deal for you.' He rubbed his hands vigorously. He took a long gulp from his whisky and seemed to freeze, eyes popping. Deepika gaped in alarm. Then he burped. 'It's like this. A friend of mine he is a *fillum* producer, you know. Now he has got into television serials and is looking for a fresh and new face . . .' He spread his arms towards her palms out as if presenting her to an audience.

Deepika squealed. '*Fillum?* What do you mean? Films? TV? Me?'

Yes, *beta*, you! What a face! *What a base, no . . . grace!* I can already see you before the camera, Take Five! After I have negotiated for you of course, *babes*!! Okay, we have work to do. And I am not taking no for an answer. Okay? Come on! Stop laughing! First, some photo sessions; different roles you know; housewife, vamp, naughty schoolgirl, So this is the deal . . .'

'But Aditya, my mother would kill me!' Deepika wailed.

'Darling! One minute . . . Waiter! Large scotch, no make that double large. You sure you don't want a Bloody Marion? See, Deepu, don't talk like a villager!'

She enjoyed the shoot after an initial embarrassment. The image in the full-length mirror fascinated her; slim hips and long legs, small breasts that stood out in the padded bras. She couldn't help a shiver of excitement as the photographer adjusted a bra strap here, raised the hemline there, and the make up artists stared at her and she thought she was really in the movies and her head spun for a while and she blinked as the photographer caught her from below, her legs akimbo in a swimsuit that was so tight she could hardly breathe.

Late Monday morning she rode a taxi all the way to Mrs Biswas' who was expecting the composites and she did not wish to be late. Hurrying toward the bank of lifts, she glanced at the glass cubicle; it was empty of the estate manager. She frowned; perhaps he was doing his rounds.

'*Bete*, this is absolutely fantastic! My goodness, look at you! The bikini! *Beta*, you are going to be a big hit, I can see that! A Korean trade team is here next weekend then some gentlemen from Ludhiana. Colonel and I are very proud of you!'

At three thirty, Deepika left Mrs Biswas' house, exhausted and slightly embarrassed by the frankness with which she had admitted her ambitions and anxieties about her parents. As she was crossing the lobby Sripad waved to her. He walked out unsteadily; his speech was slightly slurred.

'Hello, hullo, there, what, what, so we meet again. *"Of all the gin joints in all the towns in all the world—"'* He stared through his granny glasses, and then very stiffly: 'Care to come into my parlour . . . ?'

She sniffed, then glared at the beaming estate manager who hurried past her, shouted something at a watchman and came back unsteadily, missing the first step, recovering his balance and composure quickly. She smiled.

'I hope you do not think me impertinent—Don't answer if you think I am intruding; what is a girl like you doing in a joint, I mean with someone like Mrs Biswas.' He squinted, his lips curling. 'No, I can see I have upset you. Don't bother. By the way have you seen *Casablanca,* the film not the city?' He shook his head. 'No don't answer. You couldn't have; much before your time . . . It's a classic—I can tell you the story if you wish while we wait for the tea, that way I won't ask you too many—'

'I am going to be an actress.' She had not meant to boast. Perhaps it was the urge to startle him, like he did with his odd quotes and formality that intrigued her in a pleasant way and sometimes irritated her.

'Films?' He did not say *fillums.* She liked that. She was also pleased by his reaction.

'What do you mean? That old Mrs Havisham, I mean Mrs Biswas . . . she is a casting agent?'

Deepika laughed. She felt light headed. 'No, silly, not her. What did you say your name was?'

He felt hurt and he slouched back to his office. She had forgotten.

'Rick . . .'.

Dev Reddy, the beleaguered editor-in-chief of the soon-to-be-evicted journal, *The Last Frontier*, finally had his way.

'Stop looking at your watch, Ranjan, I know your boss won't miss you for another hour. So listen carefully.'

Ranjan had readily agreed to meet the old campaigner because he was in a sunny mood; he had already secured for himself an arrangement of which he was very proud.

In a reckless mood on a late Monday morning, buoyed by his wife's recovery from her 'illness', Ranjan had called Nasreen at the BodyArt offices at the very moment Deepika was meeting Aditya.

That afternoon, they had driven to her apartment in a high-rise near Mumbai Central, a three bedroom apartment empty except for a maidservant who served them lunch and then quietly withdrew to the kitchen at the far end of a long dark corridor. The house had a lingering smell of fish and perfume.

She led him to her bedroom; neither spoke as they undressed and made frantic love. He found her energy astonishing and he had to admit that he barely lived up to her physical exertions. But he was taken aback when soon after, over coffee in the drawing room—

'Ranjit, this could be the start . . . that Baloo, really, God! I am so tired of that profligate!' She sought something more than sympathy from him, or so he thought. He waited.

'Of course he has a heart of gold, no doubt about that!' She sipped her coffee, shook her head, the bangles on her right hand jangling as she waved it in mild annoyance. 'But that doesn't get us far, does it? I mean, BodyArt has to grow; which it isn't; it is slipping, which it shouldn't.' Ranjan was astonished at this candour and he still said nothing. She hadn't finished.

'Of course, you too are generous; but you are made of steel!' Suddenly she giggled and looked away. Ranjan stared at her open-mouthed, fascinated by her audacious enterprise. Her sari slipped off her shoulder.

'Randhir, we could make a great team; Bala dreams the visions, you know, I handle manpower; you the money. So, what I am saying Ranjit is . . . join our board.'

He smiled. 'So when can I meet Mr Gandhi?'

She returned the smile a fraction too late, after getting her sari back in place. She sighed and nodded.

An hour later, Ranjan had come straight to the point.

'Bal, Nasreen came up with a proposal I find very interesting.' He stared with distaste at Gandhi's chipped, stained teeth peering out of the beard flecked with bread crumbs. 'Why don't you finish thst pizza. I'll have a whisky.'

'Sure, Ranjan anything, we're business partners now aren't we? I tell you; *Waiter!* One large scotch for the gentleman and be quick! I tell you, Ranjan, business is good; businessmen are better. So how do we go about this—'

'What?' Ranjan asked carelessly. .

'*Har . . . har!* You must be tired, my dear chap. What else? Your role . . .'

'Bal—' Ranjan lent forward, his eyes on Gandhi's hairy hand coaxing his beard to a sharp point. 'I'll join, but . . .'

'Say it and it's done, Ranjan!'

'Sack Nasreen.'

Ranjan smiled at this recollection, much to Reddy's irritation. 'Are you paying attention, Ranjan? Really! This is—' Ranjan patted his hand.

'Do go on. My friend. I am listening.'

But he wasn't. It had been a coup of sorts; the image of a sputtering Gandhi as he sorted out this imperative from a prospective accomplice was one Ranjan would not forget. Gandhi's discomfiture had been so acute, that he spilled his orange juice, screamed at the waiter, and finally, after a long defence of Nasreen, had fallen silent, staring at the corpulent face, beaming at him.

'I understand, Bal. Yes, of course; then in that case, I'll advise you on an informal basis and you pay me for the services. We can work out the modalities later.' Gandhi had accepted immediately and Ranjan had had three more whiskeys.

Reddy moistened his lips, puckered his mouth like a man about to speak decisively. 'I don't need to tell you do I that he got away with large credit lines from banks because they liked him; crony capitalism!'

'Hold it right there my fiery comrade! We do want our money back!'

'After the horse has bolted? You chaps could have prevented this fraud on public money!' Reddy fumed.

'Reddy, please! Have you called me here to tell me the obvious? He is not the only one; there are bigger sharks that have swallowed our money! We work on a clubby principle. Success breeds its own myths. We won't give your journal any money even though it is widely respected; but we will to *The Times of India* should they [propose to venture into an aqua-aerobics club because it is hugely successful! So tell me something new; how can my bank get its money back?'

Reddy tightened his mouth, pushed his lips out and slurped the scalding coffee. Then his face lit up with a manic glee and he shook his head. 'You cannot! It's gone! I think I know where, but I don't have proof. Neither do you.'

'Okay, my dear fellow, you have learnt something new this late in life. Congratulations! My question to you is: So what?'

Astonished, Reddy stared at his friend of more than two decades. Then he flicked his wrist.

'Never mind Ranjan. And you are right; Today, I have learnt something new. There are other ways to bell a cat. But let me tell you something that even you don't know.' He leaned forward, crossing his hands on the tabletop.

'I used to have a very smart assistant in Lalbaugh. She left me for reasons I haven't figured out and now writes copy for baby soap advertisements. Anyway, yesterday she visited me with a friend, a young journalist at a business magazine called *Corporate Inc*. Heard of it? Well, I hadn't but he had a story. Something that had fallen into his lap, quite accidentally; it concerns BodyArt.' Reddy leant back and looked expectantly at his friend. Ranjan stifled a yawn and glanced at his watch.

'One day an elderly lady came bustling into his office insisting on meeting an editor. Just as luck would have it, he was the only one around. She pulled out a sheaf of foolscap sheets with names and numbers set against them. She told him they were the depositors in a chit fund called Lakshmi Prudent Savings. Ninety nine per cent low middle class backgrounds, many pensioners who had placed their life earnings in the hands of a very successful businessman with an impeccable background, whose agents promised them higher than market returns. Lakshmi has vanished; no one answers the phones and the boss, the very successful pioneer of bodybuilding advises them to wait for the economy to improve, that their money is safe. The last time a delegation of those depositors were told that was nine months ago; he has not met them since. Luke was very embarrassed not because the old crone sounded so miserable, but because he knew a scoop when he saw one and he could do nothing. His publisher was a golfing friend, a drinking buddy; crony journalism. Luke is a good boy with a conscience; so, he came to me.'

'So run the story, Dev, you don't play golf or drink. Besides, it'll be a change from those hungry peasants.' Ranjan glanced at his watch again and gave Reddy a distant smile. 'I should be going now—'

'That chit fund was founded by Gandhi and has two of his flagship company directors on the board; one of them is a lady, I forget the name.' He stared at Ranjan fiercely. 'Did you know that, my friend? BodyArt has milked ordinary people of their life savings and you can sit there and say it's all part of the economic *cycle!?*'

'Hold it, Reddy, I never said that. Of course it's awful—if true. As a banker, a public servant, I can only feel sorry.'

'Tell me, Ranjan, you know I value your capacity to read between the lines, to find organizing principles in the commonplace; why is Mahesh telling us that story? Such a banal story about a stupid aimless boy and his stupider wife? Why do we look forward to his monologues? Probably fictions if anything' Reddy's lips were quivering. He waited. 'You won't say or you don't know why? Should I tell you? We sit there, my friend—'

Reddy crooked his index finger and tapped it on the table. 'We spend our time there because we know that Mahesh is looking for something below the ordinariness of that stupid chap. He is searching for something, perhaps some answers and he thinks we can give them to him. You remember what you said the first time we met him? "He has a story in his heart" He is looking perhaps for some code of conduct and that is what I am looking for in this case of a recklessly self-indulgent swindler!'

Ranjan doffed an imaginary hat. 'I salute you, Reddy. You have turned philosopher in an age of raucous materialism. What will Marx think? Listen, the only code of behaviour that I see in Mahesh's story is in that old cliché, "God only helps them that help themselves". Substitute the economy for God and you have our world in a nutshell. There are no moral codes beneath Mahesh's story! The story is its own morality! Means are now their own ends. Don't you see that? We bankers lend money to earn more of it; so we love the sound of money, the smell of success! Dreamers like you protest; but, no *handouts please!* Look, we could argue for hours but I have to get back.'

Reddy watched a plump hand wave as the taxi sped away; his hands curled into fists he stared vacuously at the traffic swishing past, furious; saddled with so much knowledge and so little power.

As the weekend drew closer Mahesh Vatsayana felt as if the story he had begun so involuntarily and perhaps impulsively, had assumed a life of its own. Abhijeet and Meenakshi were no longer restless spirits stalking his memory; they acquired flesh and blood tones, their torments and desires had once again become palpable. The silence that fell when Abhijeet asked her to leave them was almost pulsating, as he, the participant-narrator, victim of memory's treacherous reach, remembered her exit. He recalled most of all his own desire; for the first time, but not the last, he had wanted her in his arms.

'I had intended to maintain a distance from Abhijeet's crude drives; his behaviour had been obnoxious and I hadn't forgotten Meenaskhi's anguish. Yet I accompanied him to our favourite watering hole. I was intrigued by his high excitement and flattered, as I always had been, by his enthusiasm for my company.'

'Barely had the waiter left our table than he leaned forward. He had a story to tell, of passion discovered, of an ardour that threatened to burst him with its intensity. It was only gradually that I realised he had in mind not

Meenakshi; "Assistant to Selvaraj, my boss you know; beautiful and cultured lady.'"

'I couldn't believe my ears. Then his earnestness began to depress me. The dimly lit, smoke filled hall, the men with their brassy self-confidence, the trill of cell phones and the slurred voices toting up the pickings of the day added to my sense of sordid desolation. But I also felt a deep, sadness for this young man, his restless passions and enervating self-doubts.'

Ranjan looked around him. From where he sat, back to the bay window, his vision was limited to the Gang and the doors leading to the steamy kitchen. Tetchily, he burst in.

'Self-doubts? *Tchah*! Nonsense!'

Mahesh was stung. So was Reddy, but he let Mahesh take the floor.

'But don't you see, he was not sure of anything except his doubts? Nothing he believed in had the ring of infallibility. To me, that was his humanity!'

Arvind had to have his say.

'I know this for sure: a man wanders but he comes back you know . . . and why? Because his woman makes him; she is the tough one. Isn't that true, Mahesh? She brought him back!'

Confused, he kept silent. That revelation had sounded dramatic and appalling; Abhijeet also knew that. He had slumped back and leered. He had nodded to himself, then pushed forward, palms flat on the table, and whispered heavily that Meenakshi had accused him of "impotence".

But he couldn't get himself to give them this detail of Abhijeet's anxiety partly because of his own ambivalence that evening. The rum had begun to cloud his thoughts and this intimacy confused him even more. He felt a desperate urge to confess to the leery face in front, his hopes, his own passions, but he hadn't. He felt a rage at a perfidy he had been exposed to with this mad confession which he desperately wished Abhijeet had cooked up. In the taxi, he had put his arm around Abhijeet.

He looked up from his reverie to find his audience of three waiting impatiently. Michael was hovering; they were the only customers. The Inn wore a desolate look; a forty-watt bulb and a fly-specked tube light the only illumination. The manager, an elderly member of the owner-family, was too courteous to disturb his regular customers, especially The Banker whom he had known for thirty years. But he too was restless.

'One morning I noticed a van parked on our side of the curb, into which men were loading furniture that looked familiar. I rushed down and ran into Abhijeet's mother supervising the men. She smiled a sad smile and told me that she and her husband had decided to return to their ancestral home near Chennai. I was surprised but said nothing as the last of the baggage was loaded, the men paid. The father invited me in with a nod, said little. Abhijeet was at work and Meenakshi had helped them pack'

'Two days later we were at Dadar TT railway station. Just before boarding the Madras Express, the mother burst into tears; Abhijeet had not showed up and the train was to leave any minute. She hugged Meenakshi. The father looked down at his feet his mouth drawn together as if to prevent any words or sound tumbling out. I shook his hand and told them I would do all I could to help. My words sounded hollow but they seemed to perk the mother up. As the train streamed out of the station, I saw a tearful face leaning out of a window, eyes on Meenakshi and a wave before the train rounded the first bend. Meenakshi just stood there immobile, staring at the spot where the train had disappeared from sight.'

'I drove her back to the empty house, and as I was about to leave she asked me in for tea. I accompanied her to the kitchen, lit a cigarette and watched her put the water to boil, her back to me, head bowed. Then she turned and I saw she had been crying. I ground my cigarette but did not say anything; I did not know how to console her .Her face had drained of colour, the whiteness accented by the dark shadows under those luminous eyes.'

'"What should I do?" she whispered. I said nothing but reached out and to my surprise she rushed towards me clenching my shirtfront with both hands, her body racked by sobs. A pervasive smell emanated from her, the odour of fright, of an animal aware of its helplessness. Then she backed off, turned to the tea, her shoulders shuddering once or twice. She poured the brew, added milk and sugar. Without a word or gesture, she moved to the drawing room. I waited a while then sat across from her, amazed at the change; that effulgent beauty had given way to a more sombre one; in it you could see the ravages of turbulent emotions, wilfully suppressed. Eyes clenched shut she sat before me, blood-drained fingers intertwined on her lap as if in silent prayer. Then her large eyes scanned my face with a quizzical and intense expression, as if searching for something; not consolation or kindness. I would like to assume it to be dignity. Perhaps she found it or maybe she had reached the end of her tether; her face cleared. Then she spoke; at first a trickle, then the torrent.'

'It was a cathartic outburst of terrifying nights with a man whose drunken behaviour ranged from violent threats to vicarious taunts about his affair, as he termed it with Selvaraj's young executive assistant. He often humiliated her before his friends. With painful candour, she admitted she was not modern, that she hated office parties. Then the surprise; she was even willing to 'share' him with that 'girl', if only he would treat her with respect, and some affection. Then she stopped, aware of what her self-pity had driven her to—before a stranger; then she shook her head as if in self-rebuke.'

'After a brief silence, she changed track, throwing me completely off guard.'

'"He's lying you know, there is no one . . ." 'She sniffed, blew her nose into a small handkerchief folded it carefully.'

'"It's not me; he is terrified of women.' It was her moment; I said nothing though I was shocked at the bluntness of the charge. She had said it with such wearied detachment.'

'"He hates women actually, it's a pretence, all this—' She said it defiantly. Then with some heat: "But that does not matter. Behind that boor is a little boy, soft at heart, afraid of the dark."'

'The metaphor was apt. Then she sighed, a bit melodramatically. "Anyway we are on our own. He will need me now, for sure." She gulped the rest of her tea, her expression challenging me to contradict her. I nodded, thanked her for the tea and left.'

At the kerb, they stood in embarrassed silence, aware that a lot had been left unsaid. Each waited for the other to make the move. Then Arvind excused himself and left. Ranjan let out a huge yawn and signalled a taxi that drove up with speedy flourish. He looked at Reddy. 'Coming? I am off to the station.' He was surprised when Reddy shook his head and waved him away. Ranjan stared at his old friend, nodded and left. Mahesh and Reddy stood in silence looking across at the car park; swarms of people shuffled past them with determined aimlessness. Suddenly, Reddy felt a tug at his trouser leg. He started, looked down at a beggar, so deformed that he could only move on all four crippled limbs. In the dark, it was difficult for them not to imagine some grotesque alien had shuffled up to them. Reddy took Mahesh by his arm and hurried him across to Jehangir Art gallery.

'I, er, you have a few minutes? There is something I would like to talk with you about. Should we sit here? I am in no mood for another cup of tea or coffee and I do not drink. So . . .' Mahesh nodded and they found space in a far corner at the top of the shallow steps. Young couples and tourists sat near and around them in groups, chatting animatedly, smoking, self-engrossed. The Kala Ghoda had a festive air.

'Er, see, I want to ask you something. What are you looking for? You are a young man . . . I mean, where do you go from here?' He felt acutely embarrassed; he was surprised at the quick answer.

'To love again.' Mahesh turned to him, his dark face inscrutable, thick hair blowing away from a wide forehead.

'What? Yes, you mean to find someone. I think that woman, Meenakshi . . . you were . . . No, don't answer. See, I am an old man, well not very old, fifty-eight, though mornings I feel ninety-two. You wouldn't think it looking at me but I . . . I, too loved a woman. See, I do not have such cherished memories; in my case it is nostalgia, flickering to life fortuitously with a tiny detail recalled. In a few years, if I live long enough, the recollection shall atrophy into absurdity and before that happens . . .' They watched a soiled paper napkin lifted by a sudden wind that died as it had come. Then a strong gust in the opposite direction carried it toward the car park where it lost steam between a Honda City and a motorcycle.

'I have no place to go but to bed, alone. I have all the time in the world.'

'Thank you. Her name is unimportant. She was the wife of a very frustrated academic, a teacher of Sociology in a local college who had, at one time been an active member of a splinter group of Marxists. He had lived in the Dharavi slums preaching revolution to the migrants that flocked to the city and made their way to relatives, landlords, touts, anyone that could give them shelter and hope of a better life. He offered them the biggest hope, but they would have none of it; they heard him but they followed the man in the polyester safari suit with a tight smile and a gold ring on his third finger. That is what he told me when we met a few years later, when I went to interview him for our journal. He had a bitter smile, and would say that his stint in Dharavi gave him a swollen liver and got him the job teaching in a suburban college courtesy the principal who had, at some time been a member of the Communist Party of India.'

'His wife wanted to write children's stories. She invited me for dinner and I kept going back to their house in Bandra, to interview the man for his experiences; but his savage hatred of the poor and his yearning for the good life soon began to bore me.' Reddy broke off and shook his head. 'I almost lost my faith in Marxism. To see so much resentment! As if he had been abandoned by parents. Sometimes, I too feel that way, but after having travelled a longer distance. He was still in his mid-thirties, they had no children, she wanted to be a mother, he wanted her to formalise a pact of celibacy. I think he was mad, and she was persistent and I kept going back even though I never published much of his interviews after his resentment had begun to acquire a life of its own, you know what I mean, he was that way for its own sake, it was his life. She served him well but I think she hated him for having denied her motherhood. She thought I would; and I did. It was so quick.' Reddy's voice had dropped and Mahesh shifted closer. A young couple watched them and giggled running down the steps.

'I had just moved in with a young lady, she was a feminist a fiery radical and we broke the mould by not marrying for three years; her family disowned her. We lived in Antop Hill, in a room with a small kitchen and common toilets. I thought I was happy but that college teacher's wife . . . I found her disturbing and irresistible. In her I saw mystery that I had seen only once very briefly by a riverbank in West Bengal when I was younger. I had failed to exploit the advantages of youth when one is not a child anymore nor adult burdened with responsibilities. What could I do now in mature age? I was living with a woman who shared my ideals; I married her and she is the mother of my two children. But till a little before we married, I kept going back to the professor's wife. He was so indifferent, perhaps he knew, but he lived for his rage and his bottle. He would drink himself to silence, falling into a stupor at the end of an evening that began very loquaciously. We were his audience, me more than her. Then she would help him to his bed and return to wash the plates and . . .'

'Then one night he had a stroke from which he never recovered. The widow, she must have felt relief, I do not know for she vanished, to return a year later. One day she called me at the office, something she had never done before. She told me that her relatives in Vidharbha in eastern Maharashtra had treated her shabbily. She came from a well-to-do Brahmin family, solicitors, professors and they had disapproved of her marriage to a radical from Tamil Nadu, dark complexioned, sullen and ill-mannered even when hopeful. She had found work with an NGO in Madhya Pradesh. I spent two weeks with her in that desolate countryside, a mining area with shanty towns and pervasive violence, sharing her silent grief and pain, watching her teach the women of mine workers to read and write. I . . . I tiptoed round my choices. And then I returned to Mumbai never to go back.'

'You came back to your wife . . .' Mahesh whispered in the dark the dull yellow of the streetlights on his face. Reddy turned to him.

'Yes, I came back, no, more to the point; I fled from that place in Madhya Pradesh. She had an infant with her that was being raised by a woman who lived with them. I found that disconcerting when I went visiting but she was unfazed. She demanded nothing but I was sure if I had shown initiative—. She needed someone I was certain, she liked me I was sure, but she asked for no pity, no commitments. Left to myself, I never came to terms with my feelings and dreading a reckoning I fled, never sure of the reason; perhaps the fear of becoming another frustrated radical with a swollen liver; of living in that remote part of the country with the silences, the mine workers and the murderous violence; and the burden of that enterprise, parenthood, that she had knowingly imposed on herself. Perhaps I failed myself, fearing emotional possibilities, seeking refuge in the simple belief that I was a man of the city, the sanctuary of ideological certainties. I do not know what I fled from most.'

'But you loved again,' Mahesh asked with a trace of irony.

'Yes, oh yes, I loved everything I wrote, every belief I renewed, my passion for revolution rekindled after my return.' He noticed the silence. 'Of course I loved my wife! She bore my children didn't she? One of them is an outstanding Marxist. He may become Prime Minister yet!' Mahesh got to his feet and brushed the back of his trousers. Reddy stared up at the dark figure silhouetted against the streetlights.

'Goodnight, Mr Reddy.' He walked down the steps briskly.

'I loved her, I always did! She was my comrade-in-arms! She is my wife; I have someone to go back to!' Reddy watched him cross the road to Elphinstone College. 'Yes, I have someone to go back to . . .' he whispered as people turned to stare at him.

'Are you mad? *Salsa?* What the hell, Poorni, what the hell is *Salsa* and *Tango?* And who do you dance with?' Arvind wailed. 'Here I am in the middle of my accounts for Diwali, God, what a mess! And you have to add to my troubles by this, this crap about dancing? Aren't we already in shit here? That's all that Devendra*bhiaya* will want to know. Salsa! Next thing we are Salsa-*ing* out, bags and baggage!' He paced the room agitatedly, his thinning hair fluttering every time he passed under the whirring fan, his widening forehead, now beaded with sweat. Poornima sat on the bed examining her fingernails.

'Not a bad idea . . .'

'What? What! What did you say?' He was convinced his wife was cracking up. 'You know, Poorni, you need to occupy yourself. Learn shopping. Take Sheetal with you, or Parvatiji.' Poornima looked at him as a teacher would a slow-witted student. She was disappointed; God had gifted her husband with a high forehead, sensitive mouth, clear vision behind those frames—all signs of wisdom and foresight, and then forgotten him. She sighed.

'Don't you want to know why Salsa or working in a call center? I don't know what either is but *MidDay* carries ads for both. I could earn Rs 20,000 a month. What's wrong with that? At least I know I am doing something with my life and time.' She ran to the bedside table and shoved a copy of the *MidDay* under his nose. 'Read that! And tell me more about call centers.'

'Listen, Poorni, this is not for you, okay? This is for those kids that support alcoholic parents, who plan to migrate to America, who do not mind being cursed and shouted at, called black monkeys and God knows what else? You want to be a telephone operator? Then you want to go dancing with some Feni-drinking Goan who'll run his hands down your backside? Forget it! Not my wife?' He was surprised at his vehemence. But when he saw Poornima weeping into her handkerchief he was confused, he apologised profusely. He put his arm around her heaving shoulders, brushed her hair back but she would not stop. Then impatiently, 'Stop crying, Poorni, you're not a child anymore. Come on, stop it!'

She walked stiffly to the bathroom and bolted the door. A few minutes later, a wan smile on her pale face she wanted chocolate ice cream.

At the pastry shop, scooping dollops of the ice cream with apparent relish she startled him:

'I don't want children right now.' He gaped at her. She shook her head, staring into the empty ice cream bowl. 'No, I am not going to be a mother just to please your father, okay? And . . . I want to find something to do, anything to get out of that house with the greedy eyes, those groping hands and grasping minds. Do you need a salesman?'

'Salesman? Oh, you mean salesgirl. No, why? You mean . . . ? *No!*

'Yes, I'll learn. I am a graduate, I have some English but I'll pick up. I want to be paid.' She arched her eyebrows. 'What? You don't want me?'

As the festive season approached, Ranjan's moods alternated between sunny optimism and dark foreboding. His stratagem of acquiring increasingly faster instalments of 'assurance fees" by pressuring Bal Gandhi with the threat of criminal proceedings by the bank brought on a warm glow that not even the quickest promotion ever did. He could now call himself a rich man, and soon, would count himself among the wealthy. He took pleasure from that prospect, not the least for the doors it would open to a wealthy son-in-law and, for himself and his wife a peaceful and comfortable retirement.

His sexual appetite was robust, fed by that young woman-child who brought him to tears with her boundless capacity to speed him to exploding climaxes. He had been lavish in return. But she was getting irksome of late. She had begun to mistake his unquestioning surrender in bed to complete dependence and accordingly had begun to ramp up her demands, the latest being a two-bedroom apartment in Andheri, for herself and her sister "to set up our own business," as she put it when he was surfacing from near-death.

He had to find new pastures and that prospect buoyed him.

Then slowly but surely and with intimations of death by asphyxiation, his moods darkened whenever he saw or thought of his wife who still mystified and often terrorised him. His breath shortened with the smell of sulphur on it, his pulse quickened and he was painfully reminded of the medicines he often overlooked

Desperately, he sought refuge in the healing power of money; once he had a sizeable fortune, Madhavi too would find happiness. In the meantime he vowed to display affection for his wife, perhaps they could have an evening together, take in that new restaurant in Bandra with the live band. Suddenly he thought of Abhijeet and Mahesh sitting out a drunken evening at a similar spot. He felt a wave of hope wash over him. Yes, he inspired confidences, people viewed him as a man of wisdom, for hadn't he the gift of evaluation? That was why Mahesh was so candid, he told himself, not because that old editor and that young pup with the thinning hair gave him their slack-jawed attention but because Ranjan Kapoor presided!

Then one morning he picked up the financial papers and read the front page. Bal Gandhi the well-known owner of the immensely popular chain of body-tuning outlets had been charged with fraud under Section 138 of the Indian Penal Code: a warrant of arrest had been issued by a metropolitan court. The item was far too brief and left Ranjan terribly fearful. On reaching the office, he asked to be connected to Nasreen Treasurywalla. Punctuating her incoherent account with nervous giggles, she told him about three constables and a sub-inspector visiting them the previous afternoon.

'Oh, Rohan, you ought to have seen those pigs eating out of our manager's hand! Just a few crisp ones in a brown envelope and coffee with cheese sandwiches and they were thanking us! I tell you, Ranjit, corruption in our police force is crazy! What is this city coming to?'

He knew that it would not end here. Now his managing director would want to know why he hadn't thrown the book at Gandhi yet! Gandhi could panic and cast around for other benefactors to shield him from the law; he had to act fast. He asked for an appointment with his MD and rang Reddy at his Lalbagh office.

'If there is anything you know about this, tell me right now, my friend.' He heard a silence at the other end. 'Er, Reddy? Dev?'

'What Ranjan? What are you talking about?' Ranjan snorted.

'Look here, Dev, I know you know what I am talking about: the raid on BodyArt. Did you, do you know anything that you should be telling me?'

'Ranjan, comrade friend, I know this much: it is high time the police came a-calling. And that surely you know too? But apart from that . . .' Reddy's voice trailed and now Ranjan was fuming. He banged the phone and stared at it, biting his lower lip in helpless fury. His buzzer sounded and he sprang to his feet and walked briskly toward his managing director's office.

For Reddy it was Day One of the revolution, the first volley against the bourgeoisie. He gloated at the confusion he had created in his old friend, happy to find himself so disingenuous. His plan had worked! Serves him right for prevaricating!

Ranjan's dilly-dallying had stirred Reddy into action, so he should have thanked the wily fox for inspiring him to action.

He had persuaded Luke Pinto, the business journalist from *Corporate Inc.* to organise a meeting with some of the aggrieved depositors of Laxmi Prudent Savings, at the office of the *Last Frontier*. The elderly depositors happily went along with the plan. His writing skills drafted the brief for the lawyer Reddy found: a brief-less advocate who had helped retrenched textile workers file compensation claims decades ago and who was still waiting for the outcome; naturally that worthy viewed the depositors as his last chance to prevent a frightening slide into poverty and alcoholism.

The case was filed and the warrant issued. Ranjan called in panic. Reddy triumphantly waited to visit Gandhi in Phalton Road police station; he waited in vain. For a man who had written reams about the ruling class and a 'collusive' police force, his disappointment ran deep, far too deep.

It made him reckless. He reached for the second plan, a venture he had merely toyed with in idle moments of personal vanity. Now it acquired a force of its own. He had no idea how he would do it but he would find a way. In the meantime tomorrow was Saturday and he looked forward to meeting Ranjan and that kindred soul Mahesh.

15

They ordered to ease the tension. Arvind was still angry with Ranjan for having offered little counsel in dealing with his crisis.

He looked across the food-laden table at Ranjan with a vague bitterness that he could not understand. He needed a respite desperately. If only Mahesh would come.

Reddy too felt the chasm widening; he had a feeling that his friendship with Ranjan had run its course. How could he, a man of action keep truck with this indolent sybarite?

Ranjan seemed unaware or perhaps indifferent to the shifts in attitudes. He was preoccupied and he had nothing to say. They waited in silence.

'Sorry for being late. A business meeting took unusually long. Let me order something too though I am not particularly hungry.' They stared at his profile as he beckoned Michael with a slight nod. Arvind broke out in a smile and slapped him on the shoulder.

'You better wrap up that story; that dead poet staring into his future, I mean beer, says this place is shutting soon. I cannot imagine meeting under some swanky ceiling with air-conditioning and unfriendly waiters . . .

Can you, Reddy?' He ignored Ranjan. Reddy did not reply; he too smiled at Mahesh.

'The end is near I think? They are on their own I believe you said the last time?'

'I met Meenakshi more often than Abhijeet after the parents had left town. One afternoon, I ran into her in the lift; after an awkward silence, I inquired after Abhijeet, she stared at me and without a word, got off on her floor. A few minutes later, my doorbell rang; she stood there, an uncertain smile on her pale lips and a cup in her hand. She refused to come in and after I had given her the sugar, she asked me to join her for tea. She had re-arranged things. Flowers on a side table, the upholstery and curtains had brighter shades. Who had removed the photographs of Abhijeet's parents on the shelf near the three-seat sofa in the living room? There were some reprints I had not seen before. "Amrita Sher Gill", she remarked shyly. She had read about a retrospective and bought a collection she had got framed. She saw the question in my eyes and nodded shyly; she had given Abhijeet a small lecture on that painter. I was surprisedL *Tea and idle talk at eight? Happy hours with tea?* She smiled. I was confused. With a spring in her step she carried away the cups.'

'We met frequently in that empty flat. Sometimes she would wave from her balcony as I came into view. At times I surprised her mid-afternoon. I got the feeling she was rehearsing for some impending ordeal; was she practicing her lines, a pitch, an emotion on me? Often I was irritated, furious too, but what could I say? At other times she would say nothing for hours and I would hope.'

Mahesh stirred the remains of his tea. The others watched him.

'I, unh, I had never met anyone like her. I felt at ease; next minute her presence unsettled me. She could withdraw into a deep inner world yet leave the gates open. I had no maps; just contrary clues—disdain and a wondrous perplexity, gay abandon and studied tranquility. I believed in her and asked myself: why? I couldn't care. Every evening, every occasion with her, is etched in memory; nostalgia you might say, but no less painful for that.' He stared at Reddy, his right eye twitching. Then his face softened.

'I wanted very much to hate him; sometimes I did but I did not envy him.'

'One night he called me, said we had to meet; something he had to discuss and it couldn't wait. He surprised me; his hand was trembling but he asked for a fresh lime soda so did I. He stared at the fizz, then looked up and told me of a mess-up in his office, a problem that could get out of control very fast.'

'His cosy relationship with Selvaraj his boss had come to an end over differences on certain purchases of steel components for the company's manufacturing plants. Selvaraj was keen on a Korean supplier Abhijeet insisted a company in Pune run by an old college buddy offered scored on quality but the imported steel products were marginally cheaper. Abhijeet held that the Korean firm was 'dumping' its products, selling below costs and for that reason alone he favoured the local firm. He sipped his soda, refused a cigarette. He was furious. "You know, Mahesh", he said, his voice trembling, "Selvaraj has been wined and dined by the Korean company; his assistant told me. Kickbacks for sure, the fucking bastard."'

'We ordered dinner. I asked him to call Meenakshi and tell her not to wait up but he stared blankly. Selvaraj had him by the short and curly, he said bitterly. He wanted Abhijeet to sign the initial approval of the Korean bid; Selvaraj would endorse that decision.

'What? And Abhijeet was not willing?' Reddy asked excitedly. 'He was in favour of the national bourgeoisie; a patriot!'

Arvind squinted at Mahesh. 'Tell me, Mahesh, he was the only dissenter? What about that dame, I mean, Selvaraj's assistant, that lady Abhijeet . . . ?'

'I asked him about her as we drove home. He was evasive. He simply told me that she did not understand these things.'

'Of course the Korean company won the contract. Abhijeet called me a couple of days later to tell me: "Price wins over quality friendship". These are his words and the pun was probably intended. I never learnt what transpired because Abhijeet never discussed the matter again. But I could see the results of that struggle. Or should I say, capitulation, and the probable bad blood between him and his boss when we met once in a while. He seemed to have aged; gaunt frame, dark shadows under red-rimmed eyes; his hands shook constantly he muttered about quitting, his career was over, words to that effect. Once he talked of going back to a management school but that required money and as a single earner it was difficult. Meenakshi had expensive tastes and she wasn't skilled for a well paying job. All this he uttered without any rancour or bitterness, very matter of fact.'

'I felt dissatisfied with our brief encounter, I wanted him to share with me more . . . but, pleading tiredness, a bad stomach, stuff like that, he avoided me. I knew he was not always home till late. So where did he go? Had he found someone . . . more entertaining, more tuned into his anxiety frequencies? I felt immeasurably sad. And I sought Meenakshi's company even more.'

'But now her mysteries became playful where they had once been enigmatic. I desired answers; and she? She had been so forthcoming in her search for self-assurance; now she didn't seem to care.'

'That chiaroscuro of meanings was replaced by the glitter of the commonplace: the dinner she had cooked, his praise for her housekeeping. The house was as usual squeaky clean but it looked unlived in; that interested me. I should have been pleased by the possibility that he was treating her well, but—'

'—I wanted something else: to penetrate that arch behaviour, that shield of voluble coyness. We had come a long way since that afternoon after seeing off Abhijeet's parents and, and, she owed me—explanations. I think she sensed my churlishness and often I caught her staring at me from vast distances, as if placing me in some grand scheme. Flustered, I would rise and leave without a goodbye, only to return.'

'One morning she called me on the building intercom at around ten thirty. I ran down the steps to find her at the door. Her face was puffy and free of makeup. But she had dressed as if to receive a guest; she smelt of sandalwood, her hair in a tight knot. Silently, she took me by the hand and shut the door. I followed her, heart in my mouth, mind aflame.'

Ranjan's heavy breathing had become noticeable. He leaned forward, palms on the table. Their teacups rattled.

'You know, two lonely people . . . the most powerful aphrodisiac; all those afternoons and evenings; yes. So moving.'

He stared glassily at Mahesh, his tongue flickering between pink lips.

'*Aaahhh . . .*'

'That is disgusting, Ranjan, are you blind? Ridiculous! Compassion, my friend, not passion!' Reddy glared at Ranjan, his pursed lips disappearing into his mouth. His eyes blazed behind his thick glasses. Arvind was shaking his head in vehement approval.

'Yes, boss. I think you are completely missing the point. Mahesh is trying to save the marriage. That guy Abhijeet, he doesn't know a good woman when he sees one, eh? All alone in that flat. God! I tell you, sometimes an extended family has its merits, really!'

An embarrassing silence descended. Around them snatches of conversation floated like confetti. They wondered if Mahesh, head bowed, hands on the table, tightly clasped was begging forgiveness or praying. Then he looked up, his right eye twitching noticeably.

'She told me of a fight the previous night. She had tried to make light of his fears of losing his job, talking of options, moving to Chennai maybe, to her parents' till they found something better. He had flared up at this and screamed, ranting against her expensive habits, her unwillingness to contribute.'

'In her eyes I saw the pain of humiliation, of worthlessness. She had stalked out of the bedroom, intending to sleep out on the sofa; he dragged her back, tied her hair to the bedpost. Shocked, I rose with a start. I walked up to her, scowling and whispered furiously, *'Pack your bags and leave this house . . . now!'* I was in a white rage; I wanted to kill him. She looked up and smiled. 'Sit down and don't get so dramatic. I let him. He cannot do without me—he wouldn't let me leave.'

'I was doubly horrified. I asked her if he had been drunk. She shook her head. 'He smelt of chicken *pullao.*' She smiled once again. 'He wet—the bed. But he slept soundly. I dozed off when I heard the milkman's clatter. I could have reached behind and untied the knots . . . but I didn't. When I awoke around nine, he had already left.' She stared at me with such chilling fixity that I turned away in utter confusion. I wanted to stay, to be near her and I wanted to flee from that house with its forlorn tidiness, plastic flowers and the Sher-Gill reprints and a madness that seemed to have overtaken her. She held me back, her presence magnetic yet menacing in its tranquillity. I sat back, limp with nervous exhaustion, unable to think or move.'

'Then she spoke with a formality that surprised me, a directness that was no longer playful but purposeful and distant. "I would like you to help me find a job." I was thunderstruck. I gaped at her like an idiot. Her smile was bleak but ironic, with an undertone of despair.

'"I . . . I . . . have a B.A. In commerce and I have trained in Carnatic music. What else? Yes, I can stitch ladies stuff, blouses, salwar kameez; I could try trousers, tops—"'

'She rose and walked to the window, looking out at the almost barren tree that partly blocked the view of the busy road below. Then she turned, kneading her fingers. Her eyes had a dull sheen as she cast about as if searching for her other talents. I sat dumbfounded, desperate to comfort her, at a loss of ways to do it. Then, I rose and held her close to me . . . not for the first time. That day I did not go to office.'

Ranjan let out an audible sigh. He cast a sly glance round the table. Reddy retorted with a furious shake of the head. Arvind's horsy face mirrored perplexity: Meenakshi and Poornima his wife—*they could have been sisters!*

'My work kept me busy for a month; barring a few calls from Meenakshi, an odd visit, I barely met them. She never mentioned that bit about a job again. I think I was happy for them; I counted my own blessings. Occasionally I would feel the urge to run down, ring the bell but I desisted.'

'Three months later, Abhijeet called me at the office; He was celebrating his birthday over the weekend, at home. Just the four of us, he told me . . .'

"*Four?* Why four . . . ?' asked Arvind excitedly, a gleam in his eye. Even Reddy looked puzzled. Ranjan appeared to be asleep and wheezed noisily; no one paid him any attention. He opened his eyes, smiled and shut them again.

'That evening I ran down two steps at a time humming to myself. Abhijeet opened the door almost immediately. I was appalled at his appearance; his face had lost colour, his eyes were an unhealthy yellow, darting till they rested on some piece of furniture only to start wandering again, and his hands shook. Meenakshi had dressed for the occasion; her tall and heavy figure clad in a gold-bordered maroon sari. Her smile was strained. She excused herself, arranged the flowers I had brought, and went back to the kitchen.'

'Abhijeet and I sat with our drinks at the dining table, in silence. But I felt in the house an air of suspense, as if the two of them were holding their breaths and I was a bit puzzled by that—till the doorbell rang. For a second we stared at each other then all of us sprang to our feet; Abhijeet made it to the door first and flung it open. A young, hesitant voice; then I saw her with a boy of eight who looked as if he would have liked to be elsewhere. I knew who she was and I turned to a transfixed Meenakshi. Her large eyes, trained on the boy mirrored puzzlement, disappointment and anger as a high colour rose on her pale face.'

'What a change in the man! A smile threatened to split his face as he opened Smruti's gift. He came alive in a way that sent Meenakshi scurrying into the kitchen. He played charming host, fetching a soft drink for the boy, another for her. I noticed he barely touched his rum, the fizz dying on the nearly full glass.'

'At first embarrassed, Smruti began to enjoy the attention he showered on her, occasionally casting an anxious glance toward the kitchen from which Meenakshi did not stir. I sat a while longer, watching Smruti's mobile face; every feature, her full lips that looked swollen, surprisingly free of any lip-gloss, close set eyes. She responded to Abhijeet's fawning devotion with a seductive coyness. I was distinctly uncomfortable. The boy's inquisitive stare followed me to the kitchen where Meenakshi sat on a stool her head bowed. I walked up to her, staring at the untidily daubed red powder in her thick black hair's parting, a rather pathetic symbol, under the circumstances. I felt sorry for her then hated myself for it; to feel pity was to demean her, myself, both.'

'Around midnight, I staggered up to my flat, feeling on top of the world. Abhijeet had volunteered to escort Smruti and her son to their home across in Bhandup. A light flickered in the enveloping fog of sleep closing in as I undressed but I couldn't help a silly smile.'

Ranjan let out a lugubrious yawn stretched his arms behind his back as far as they would go. He was still breathing heavily.

'Phooey! So little said about so much water under the bridge!' His face was getting flushed. Reddy burst in.

'Go on Ranjan! Is that all you can think of—? Cannot a man and woman meet socially without getting into bed? That's the problem with people like you! No goals, just fun and games!' He was working himself into a fight. Ranjan looked at him with half closed eyes.

'That's so touching! Behind those crude clichés lurks an utter romantic. There's hope for you yet, Reddy!'

'No thanks to you Ranjan! Money is all you—' He was seething. Alarmed, Arvind raised a hand to quieten them. Ranjan ignored him.

'And why not? Money turns the world. Some are frank enough to admit it and wise enough to let money work for them! You deride it but need it to keep your clichés alive and kicking, my friend. Money rules you, not me." He slumped against his chair. His breathing was getting shallower. Mahesh looked at him with alarm.

'Hey Ranjan! Are you okay?" He rose and walked to his side. He wiped the beads of sweat, felt his pulse. His dark face showed some panic. "Quick, Arvind, get a taxi! We have to rush him to a hospital!"

He insisted his wife and daughter not be informed. In the Out Patient Department, he was stretched out like a beached whale on a stained sheet thrown over a thin mattress. A young resident doctor checked his blood pressure, frowned and prescribed some extra tablets in addition to the ones he was taking. She would have preferred Ranjan to register into a ward for a day but he was adamant about going home. she insisted he stay a couple of hours for the sedation to take effect. His mobile trilled frequently and Reddy was keen to answer but Mahesh refused. They knew it was his wife.

At ten-thirty Ranjan opened his eyes. A weak smile played around his ashen face but his voice carried well. He felt a bit woozy but he got to his feet with Arvind and Mahesh's help. They saw him off in a taxi around eleven that night. Reddy accompanied him up to Bandra station in silence. Reddy was still fuming; he could not get over a suspicion that Ranjan was faking it. He had reached a point in his relationship with his old friend that made him mistrustful of almost anything Ranjan said or did.

Arvind's returned home in high spirits. The evening had offered him a new insight into his own association with Ranjan. He felt that ill-formed superiority most healthy people feel toward the ill; in his case that feeling was compounded by an idea that Ranjan's sudden illness was a kind of divine penalty for his unwillingness to help him in his hour of need. He would have a lot to tell Poornima.

A faint light spilled through the half-closed bedroom door. Was Poornima awake? His mood changed. He pushed open the door gently; it creaked on its hinges. Hunched over a glossy magazine in bed Poornima looked up ran to him and tried to kiss him. He pushed her aside. She looked at him, bewildered. His anger had a life of its own.

'You have been in that stupid kaftan all evening? You look naked! Lift your arm. Shit, I can see your breast!. What's the matter with you? Did Devendraji and Amol see you like that? God, what will they think what will they tell Bapu, that their youngest sister-in-law is a . . .' He was very agitated now and his voice trailed into confusion.

'What Arvind, what will they say, that they have not said before?'

Arvind raised his hand like a traffic policeman.

'Don't shout okay? This is not a fish market . . .'

Poornima stared as if he were sprouting a third leg. She clutched his forearm.

'He's told you . . . something?'

Unsettled by her quiet fury, Arvind pushed her away and strode to the window.

'You know Poorni, I have had a bad day, Mr Ranjan had a stroke and I have just come from the hospital. But that is the not the worst part. You know what is? A feeling that your wife is well . . .' He shook his head and turned to her. 'Why are you dressing so sharp these days?

Sleeveless blouses, perfumes, untied hair . . . why are you so restless? What is it our family cannot give you?' His tangled rage made him incoherent but she had begun to fathom it.

'Arvind . . . ! What . . . did he tell you?'

She wiped the sweat from his brow with the edge of her kaftan. He saw her firm and rounded thighs, and pushed her away.

'You can't be too careful anymore. I don't know if some fucking stud bull isn't waiting to pounce on you. Don't talk to strangers on the phone; somebody wants some sugar . . .' He pressed his temples, bewildered and furious.

'This city is full of *langot kachas,* men with pricks on their foreheads. I mean, sorry for talking this way, but you are so beautiful and that dress makes you so—*Put your hands down, I can see your chest!* Shit! What's happening to me?' He pulled at his thinning hair then brushed it down slowly, as if the move calmed him.

'Listen we should be grateful; such a big family here, brothers and sisters-in-law, Bapu my father. They care, you know? What, what if we were . . . just us . . . me in the shop and you all dressed up, restless and someone rings the bell, some dark handsome guy with a twitch, lonely, hungry for other people's wives . . . ?' He stared at the mosaic floor, shielding his eyes from that piercing light.

Poornima felt her blood run cold; she watched him with the fury rising like a tidal wave. Suddenly she felt calm, her limbs slackened. She shook her head, smiled and held his arm.

'You know someone like that?' She said in mock innocence and wide-eyed curiosity that rocked him back. It was his turn to ask in wonder.

'You know him . . . ?' He walked toward her slowly, his fists clenching.

'Who?' She asked, her smile still in place, scanning his face for some clue, hints of whispered half-truths. 'Never mind . . .' Arvind's fists unclenched.

Poornima had to get to the bottom of her brother-in-law's intent. She pressed her forehead and asked nonchalantly.

'But someone told you something . . .'

'Who? What are you talking about?'

Poornima turned to the bathroom, came back with a wet towel and wiped his face.

'Devendraji has your welfare at heart doesn't he? He doesn't want us to go our ways does he?' She wiped his face all the while whispering in his ear. 'He wants us here right? To share . . . of course as the eldest he has rights.'

Puzzled even more so by her babbling he tried to speak but she put the wet towel to his mouth; pressed it firmly as muffled sounds came through.

'No, don't answer. I am so stupid, you know? I forgot the most important thing. Bapu and he want to meet you tomorrow. He peeped into the room, without knocking of course but then he is entitled to that privilege, isn't he? Yes, Arvind, he was so worried; you can tell him you were at the hospital. So let's sleep now, my king, tomorrow is a big day for you!'

She walked around to her side of the bed, curled up and in an instant was gently snoring.

"Ah-h-hah! Feeling weary after a late night, *Chottu*? Hmmm?" Devendra with the smirk and hooded eyes welcomed him thus. His father had not greeted him as yet. He walked round to touch Bapu's feet in greeting, felt a dry hand lightly fall on his thinning hair, in blessing.

His heart was in his mouth and he regretted ranting at Poornima; he should have sought her advice.

'Chottu, we are very . . .' Devendra ploughed in. Bapu cut him off.

'Let me handle this Dev.' After a pause, 'So, Arvind *betey*, how have you been?. Last night you were at a party? Poornima would not tell Devendra . . . did she?' He turned his ancient head toward his eldest who sat a little in the shadows, next to the TV.

'No, no, she said nothing . . .' Hoarsely. He cleared his throat softly.

'Anyway, Arvind, I will be frank with you. See, a rich businessman from Kolkata, deals in books, has all the international brands and he wants to expand and is willing to put up seventy per cent. Modernise the shop, completely turn it into an American bookstore, he called it, what? Devendra? Yes—a bookmall. Of course he wanted more space but getting anything in south Mumbai is something to feel grateful for and the price we quoted—? He jumped.' He squinted at Arvind, head tilted inquiringly. Arvind found his tongue knotted and his brain turned to porridge.

"*Whar . . . what . . . ?*' Devendra was examining his fingernails and shaking his head. A thin flame of anger lit in the pit of his stomach.

'I, hunh—I see. Yes, Bapu. Oh? A-a-ah! It's hot in here. Can I run the fan faster?' He walked briskly to the panel returned slowly, the two watching him silently, exchanging glances. The old man sat forward with a noisy grunt, his forearms resting heavily on the padded arms of his high-backed chair. His head sank into the hollow of his neck and he squinted as if staring into bright sunlight.

'Son, you like the idea? See, I will not do anything you do not want. You are my darling boy.'

Arvind tried to answer but the old patriarch was just getting into his stride.

'But you must think this through as a grown up now. The world is changing, our stock business is facing competition; American firms with vast funds . . .'

'We have to flow with the tide . . .' Devendra chipped in from his dark corner. The patriarch quickly raised his hand like a traffic policeman. But Arvind was startled. *"Flow with the tide?"* Hadn't Ranjan used those words yesterday?

'Yes, Dev, I too know that phrase and I have followed it all my life . . . So, as I was saying . . .'

Arvind felt his head breaking loose from his body like a hot air balloon. He looked up at the ceiling as if expecting to find it there. He lowered his gaze and stared almost tearfully at his father. Betrayed! Cornered . . . stripped to the bone. Phrases approximating his turbulent feelings came popping into his head like bubbles on a pond. He kneaded his fingers. This was a historic moment and anything he said would affect his future . . . and Poornima's.

Where the hell was she? She should have been listening to this claptrap so she could understand the mess she had landed him in. What would Mahesh have done. *Bhah! That arsehole!* What does he know of life and its tortures? What to say? Could he ask for time? Take a break as in that fucking soap opera this Devendra prick, watches every night, his eyes glued on the actress's chest? He could run up to consult Poornima. His tongue broke free.

'But what about me?'

'Yes, what about you . . . ?' Devendra smirked. Bapu examined his youngest son with mild exasperation.

"My dear boy, of course I told our partners my son will run the place.' Bapu stopped to glare at Devendra who had snorted loudly. Arvind felt the ground rising up to meet him. His head was spinning so fast he would have fallen had he not held the arms of his chair. He wanted Poornima desperately to be here.

'Run the shop. I am already doing that!'

Bapu and Devendra clicked their tongue simultaneously. Then Bapu spoke with a sigh.

'Yes, but now you will do it on a salary. We bear thirty per cent of it as the junior partners; he pitches in the rest. Good, isn't it? Our man in the organisation . . . someone we can trust. Isn't that better than working with Devendra? That of course is the other option. What do you say? No, discuss with your wife; she is very smart and I am sure she will advise you well.' He slumped against the padded backrest, peering short-sightedly at his youngest son.

Reddy felt like singing but checked himself; he did not want his son to hear him belt out the *Internationale*. He washed himself vigorously, humming the battle tune, savouring the growing contempt he felt for Ranjan: serves him right! Had he climbed onto Reddy's bandwagon, why, he might not have had that stroke! Physical health . . . is *what*? he asked himself aloud. *Hunh*? *What*? It is, he told his image in the clouded mirror, the reflection of *mental* health. And *that*, my comrades, comes from service to humanity!

'Okay, dada, come on out I want to shit!' *Sripad!*

'So, dada, what's happening? How's the red rag, I mean *The Last Frontier*? Want me to write book reviews, film reviews? Got all the time and now—the inspiration.' Sripad wolfed down his roti and daal and nodded affectionately at his father focussed on his mushy rice and curd. Reddy did not reply. Rajani hesitated before reaching out for her son's arm.

'Tell him . . . go on' She prodded her son gently. Reddy looked up with alarm.

'You think I should, mama? Does he know what it means? Okay, ok, just kidding. Here goes. Daddy . . . What kind of person do you see in front of you, enjoying this delicious meal by this very elegant lady who, I am proud to say is my mother?' A beaming Sripad nodded at both as if acknowledging applause.

'Come on, Dada, what do you see here?' .

'I see an idiot. That's what.'

Sripad shook an admonishing finger

'Close, but not there.' He felt vulnerable. He rushed in before Reddy could speak again.

'I am in love. That's what you see, father dear, a man in love—comprehensively!' Reddy continued chewing. Sripad's confidence was ebbing.

'She, she is very pretty, but what of that? She is, ah-h-h, intelligent, well mannered—no, who cares shit about that either. She is witty and—I like being with her.' He nodded at his beaming mother who was just about to speak when Reddy muttered without looking up;

'She does—what?'

'She, unh, wants to be an actress.' Sripad was now fidgeting.

'I want to live forever. But what am I—now? That is what I am asking you, my son. What does she do as . . . of . . . now . . . ?'

He did not know. What *did* she do? He knew she frequented Mrs Biswas' but he couldn't tell his father that; it would make no sense. So he told him the truth.

'I don't know/' He wished he hadn't raised the subject. The old editor lifted his head slowly, almost reluctantly.

'You don't know? My son doesn't know what the girl he is in love with, does? Fine. I said you were a moron.'

Sripad was now agitated and slightly fearful. His father wasn't through with him.

'What does her father do?' With firmness this time, an icy peremptory tone. Sripad blinked rapidly and blurted.

'But I am not marrying her father.' He hadn't meant to say that.

'That is why you are a moron.'

'Because I am not marrying her father?' He was furious and ignored his mother's urgent pleas to quieten down.

Reddy brushed his shirt-front and said to no one in particular.

'I find this ridiculous. First, my son is an estate manager then he wants to marry a girl whose father he does not know anything about; a girl who does not know what she wants to be if she wants to an actress. Great! That is so good that I need to make a phone call. Please help mama with the dishes. And maybe . . .' he blinked angrily behind his thick glasses, 'maybe, you ought to learn cooking, and to stitch.' He stormed out of the house.

Blinded by disappointment and a heightened self-pride, Reddy acted impulsively. He almost ran to the nearest phone booth, three buildings away and called Luke Pinto, the business journalist from *Corporate Inc.* He was consumed by a powerful urge to act.

'Mr Pinto, Luke . . . ?' He could hear laughter, music, clatter of plates.

'Yes, yeah, ya? Who that is . . . ?' Luke Pinto sounded drunk. He giggled into the phone. 'Boss, is that Pankaj . . . ? Say something my friend, you sound angry. Sorry, okay! You'll have the story first thing tomorrow night . . .'

Reddy heard a huge yawn, a sigh and a pause later: 'Who's this—?'

'Mr Pinto, this is . . . *ahh!* . . . Reddy, you know, *ye—aas*! That old editor; yes, anything happened to that Gandhi warrant? Is he in jail? I, unh, the papers say nothing? He threw a party? Everybody attended? Businessmen? Financial institution heads? Why? No, there isn't any echo, I can hear you well enough. Speak louder, you are muttering. The police have done nothing? He is flying to USA tomorrow? No, no, there is no echo, my friend, but there is dismay in my heart, can you hear it? Those poor souls; what are they going to do? What do you mean, carry on? Carry on with what? They are the dispossessed . . . no, I am not a preacher. What is that? You just returned from Sunday Mass, yes okay, you've heard enough—What? What did you call me, you *scoundrel!*

He glowered at the handset as if it had bitten him. What humiliation! He staggered homewards, his fury ebbed. Sripad! He had dealt him an unfair blow. The lad was groping! Maybe he was not gifted enough. Maybe he, Reddy, would have to live with his son's utterly middle class, hole-in-the-head kind of contentment. History, he consoled himself, is a choosy picker!

T he Gang of Four did not meet that Saturday or the next. Neither Reddy nor Arvind could have explained it but The Wayside Inn lunch without Ranjan was not the same.

Mahesh didn't show up either. Travel and work took him to cities and hotels he would forget the instance he left them. He ploughed through meetings, conferences and reports with brooding ennui, his brain dead to everything but shifting memories and the need to wrap up his story. He felt incomplete, like a marathon runner stopped a kilometre from the finishing line by a traffic snarl. At times he felt like completing the chapter, the reckoning after one of those casual encounters the hotel or his office would arrange for him. But his post-coital self-contempt never gave him a chance to consider that option seriously and all he was left with was a faint wish he were dead.

In that fortnight the city of Mumbai geared itself for Diwali and the Hindu New Year. A spirit of gaiety weaved uneasily through the city's foul stench worsened by relentless heat. Festive lights and lamps were lit in high rises, slums, tenements; a people that had never felt the horrors of war lit fuses to unsafe sometimes lethal fire-crackers in residential blocks, on narrow streets and alleyways, in pocket-sized compounds of high rises, rejoicing in the noise and sulphurous smoke that hung in the air long after the explosion.

Divali was an occasion for the most ostentatious exhibition of jewellery and brocade saris and the women of the Purohit clan adhered to tradition with extreme discomfort in the sweltering heat that drove one or the other to sudden bursts of fury at the slightest provocation.

For the first time in her life Poornima hated the festive season and all the "fuss" it involved. But dress she did, out of a churlish aim to outdo the other sisters-in-law. She was the most beautiful even if she panted in the heat and sweated "like a pig". Not once did Devendra's desperate yearning escape her hawk-eye attention. In him, Poornima saw passion she had never seen before in any man, certainly not in her husband. It muddied the purity of the rage she felt at his manipulation of the family's hierarchical strings.

In her intense distaste for the cloying intimacy of the celebratory season, she found Devendra's mute passion so stark that at times she wanted to scream at him: *"Okay! Take me, but let's get out of here!"* She felt horrified at such thoughts flashing across her heated brain like streaks of lightning in a clouded sky and she would seek refuge in her husband who was rediscovering this season Sheetal's lusty charms. On one such occasion, he was gawking at her breasts as she bent to pour dal on his plate and taking time to straighten up, her eyes never leaving his. He barely heard Poornima's furious whisper from the threshold.

'Keep your eyes on the food, *Arvind!* You want to turn blind or what!'

For Arvind, that would have been a small price to pay for an escape from the ordeal of Diwali's hothouse atmosphere and the frazzled tempers of the elders. He was sometimes tempted to dare the impossible but he was given little time to act because his father and Devendra had scoured the Konarak books-of-accounts and neither was pleased. This time however his father spoke to him in private. It made no difference to his sense of impending doom because Bapu raised the subject of "issues".

'Arvind beta, we have made losses, The Konarak is costing me dear and you know we are businessmen first and book lovers after that. No, let me finish . . . We will go ahead with the collaboration and you must decide: family business or the salaried manager of the bookshop? No, don't answer, because if I were you, I would choose the latter, dress American, home early evenings, Saturday Sunday off you know, in these modern firms, and . . . have children. My friends ask me—Purshottam *bhai*, has that *putar* of yours got issues or not? No, don't answer, Arvind, just get down to it, this is a new beginning. At least three little ones—'

Frantically, he searched for Poornima.

'Poorni, I need to talk with you.' He dragged her to the bedroom. She was irritated because she had been building an ally in Sheetal. It paid to get close to a rival.

'I can't take this shit anymore, darling!'

'Good, my boy, give it to them!'. Poornima boxed him on the arm. He stared.

'It's my shop, our home, my life at stake. What is the fucking matter with you, you stupid cow? Why you shaking your head? Should I run out and adopt a few? Stop those pills from tonight! Where are they? I'll throw them out.' He ranted; Poornima listened quietly.

'Tell me Arvind, no honestly, do you think you . . . at least I am not ready. Honest. A few years from now . . . ? Perhaps.'

'What! You stupid woman? You think couples sit down and analyse their ability for parenthood? They just fuck, the woman splashes out three and then . . . how do you think India has one billion . . . ?'

'I don't even want one! Right now, I want a life! Look at you! What have you done? Children? That's easy! No, don't answer! You want children? No, wait, let me finish!. Okay! On one condition . . .'

'Condition? What fuckin' condition? Are you my father? You are talking like him already—"*No, don't answer*"'

He was furious at her for being right. She stared at him silently. He sighed.

'Okay, what is it you want?'

'Our own home!. Our children must have that, we must have that . . . I want to be in our own home.'

A bitter anger welled up in him, a fury at the betrayal by loved ones; first that old man with a brain poisoned by that bastard of a brother; then this stupid wife infected with hare-brained ideas! He wanted to scream, whack some sense into that pretty head. *What did you know about the world and its treacheries? We have it good here! You can be a mother and work at what you like only with help from the family!* To live all alone with three screaming brats . . . ! Did she not understand!

He had to talk to someone. A stranger, a person who did not know him as well as Ranjan and that old windbag Reddy did, a man he could unburden his sorrows to and seek directions to a safe shelter. Mahesh . . . yes, he wished they could meet, just the two of them, perhaps in the bookshop, man to man. He had no one else to turn to.

Neither did Reddy. He spent the week and the next simply relishing the plan, marvelling at its simplicity. But first he had to confront his quarry, see the face of the public enemy. So one afternoon in Dalal Street, he climbed the rickety steps to the third floor of an old building that didn't look like it would survive the next monsoon.

He pushed open the glass door and broke out in a shiver at the fierce air-conditioning. The young lady at the reception was talking into a headphone and pressing keys on a switchboard simultaneously; she did not notice him. Then she took off the headgear, sighed, and blew her nose in a tissue that she yanked fiercely out of a box.

'Yes!' She barked. Reddy was startled.

'This, hunh, BodyArt?' He peered anxiously at her and tried to work up a smile. It came out as a smirk.

'If you need muscle toning.' She snickered and blew her nose again.

'Ah, aanhh, I want to meet Balchand . . . Gandhi, Mr Gandhi.'

She looked up in sharp disapproval.

"You got appointment. No? He's very busy—leave your card, What you want to see him about? Your son wants discounts? Arrey, Lakhan! *Mera chai kidar hai?* These *chokra* boys! I am dying for tea—where is your card?'

She did not wait for a reply but got busy on a call. He could hear snatches of conversation from behind a glass fronted room with blinds. A voice was raised, then a woman's husky response.

'Bala, I can't convince . . . the advertisers are saying . . . court warrants . . . the bankers . . . God I am so tired . . .' Then a male, high pitched whine, "But seriously, Nasreen . . . a call to friends, we are round the corner . . .' Reddy froze. Was that the voice of Public Enemy Number

One? A third voice chimed in timidly. 'Ahh . . . it seems to me that we need to take a broader view—' 'Oh, please Aman, spare me . . . exhausted . . .' The thin voice again, plaintively ' . . . Ranjan should . . . call . . . ideas . . . Nasreen . . . where is . . . Now! . . . No! Do it right now.'

A door pulled open; louder voices soon faded away.

Ranjan? The bank was trying to get their money back; Ranjan would be involved. Was there something else? Suddenly he wanted to run, his bowels rumbled. He had to think this through.

'Hellow, uncle, still here? Give me a visiting card and we'll call you, okay?'

He nodded, turned briskly and tottered down the rickety steps into the blazing mid-afternoon heat. *Ranjan!* Was that why he was being fobbed off? *'Running dog' of this capitalist fraud!* But what if it's not true? Give it time, he told himself, but watch your back! Reddy nodded into his coffee and scribbled a number.

'Ah-h-h! Boiled eggs and toasted bread. Getting younger are we, Reddy?' A thinner, somewhat pale-faced Ranjan stood before them, his frame still huge enough to mask the rest of the diners from Reddy's view.

He ordered a soup and dry toast. 'Ah, that steak your friend Wilfred is having smells so good. Anyway, this is only for a couple of weeks. My doctor says I can get back to the good life very soon.'

'As if you haven't had enough of it already, Ranjan!' Reddy smiled at him through a mouth full.

'No Reddy. You can never get enough of it. But I'll admit—nothing like a trip to death's door to give meaning to life, eh? What do you say, Mahesh, love and death, two sides of life right? Oh I am so glad to be here. So much work this week the bank almost collapsed without me! Just kidding Reddy don't glare like that. So young man, how's the book business, Diwali must have been fun? Oh-h-h! All those *gulab jamuns, boondi ladoos!* Of course, I don't miss the firecrackers. Really . . . there . . . there goes another one—now in the afternoons too.'

Arvind gaped. Ranjan was still beaming.

'It's so . . . good to be blessed with this . . .' he spread his arms as if readying to embrace them all. He was unstoppable.

'Yes. So, Mahesh, are we done with that story or is there some . . . more? That lady, Meenakshi—you were saying if I remember. Here's my food! So damn good—soup and dry bread. Hmmm!'

He set aside the spoon, lifted the soup bowl to his lips and slurped. All eyes were on him. They probably thought his brain had softened with the attack but he did not care. A new chapter had opened; he needed new friends like this dark brooding fellow perhaps, not that old bag of bones or this *hijda!* Eunuch! Can't handle his wife leave alone a bookshop! Time to move on; Long live BodyArt! He beamed at Mahesh.

'If I remember, you left the party in a rather happy mood. Entertained by that fellow's lady friend, Smruti was it?'

'You remembered! Thank you. Perhaps the story should have ended that evening. The end was near but I never expected it to be so—unusual. You trust your judgement and expect loved ones to behave like you would want them to. Then you realise . . .'

'When I returned to my flat that night after a very enjoyable evening, I did feel regret because I knew that our relationship, mine with them, together and singly, had changed forever. I assumed, like so many of us do, that it takes a threat of imminent rupture to clear the air. Her dancing eyes and seductive charms, yes Smruti was very alluring, those were the mirrors they both had looked into and seen each other. That is the way I thought, for quite a while after that evening. I had my own feelings for the two of them to contend with, yes both of them . . . I never felt confused as to my priorities or preferences. Both of them.'

No one spoke. Arvind gestured for tea.

'I tried to slip back into the solitude that I had lived with quite comfortably before I met them but it was difficult. I had travelled so many roads with him, with her, and I could not just erase them from my consciousness. I was surprised at this . . . weakness but accepted it; the distancing was painful. Often I thought to ring their doorbell on a Saturday afternoon and catch her at her playful self. I want no answers, nothing but to wind the clock back, I would tell her: so too with Abhijeet. He . . . I thought he would call, he never did. Once I rang his office to be told he was in conference. I did not leave my name or phone number.'

'One late morning, I ran into her, literally. She was climbing the narrow stairway with some shopping. She let out a small scream I insisted on helping her. The Sher Gill reprints had disappeared. She looked pale, her hair in a severe knot; nails chipped, she had grown more heavy and she panted at the slightest effort. But her smile was radiant and still awkward. I did not know how to begin . . . anything. She was not encouraging. Then I blurted:

"'I missed you. I mean are you okay? How is he treating . . . I mean . . .'"

'Her eyes had a strange and empty light that I had not seen before; bright yet stripped of tone. She spoke to the far wall.'

"'Do you like the tea? It's a new find. Orange Pekoe. I drink more than five cups every day. I love Hollywood films. Did you know TNT channel shows them daily? Do you watch? No, of course not. You have an office to attend. Yes, yes, fine. He has work, travel, Chennai, Bangalore with his team. He likes his work now. Good for him. You'd like some more biscuits? No? Okay come again. I'll tell him you came. Bye.'"

'Oh dear! The brush off . . .' Ranjan exclaimed, rolling his eyes. 'You should have persevered . . .'

'As usual Ranjan you only have sex on your brain. Good riddance I say. I think this should be the end of this story? So much to do—.' Reddy frowned into his tea.

'So you have tormented yourself over this ungrateful couple?' Arvind felt very superior.

'No, no. There has to be something else.' Ranjan cheerily interjected. 'This is life imitating fiction. So you need a dramatic ending. What eh, Mahesh? Give us our money's worth.' He chuckled.

'When I met Abhijeet little did I know it would be for the last time. He was his old self, expansive, full of high spirits; life's dealt a good hand, he said. He promised an evening like old times on his return from a short vacation he was planning the following fortnight. "I told her it would have to be after Chennai. Panchgani—where else? See you when we get back. Lots to tell."'

'The next morning I took the stairs, the lift door had been left open on a floor above me and I was impatient. I happened to glance at their door and to my surprise I found it padlocked with a note pinned below the peephole. Meenakshi's awkward and girlish scrawl in Hindi instructed the milkman and newspaper vendor to stop supplies for five days . . . What had happened to his Chennai trip? What had changed his mind? Had she insisted? That would explain the hurried note.'

'I felt peeved. They had sneaked out early morning for that hill resort and I hadn't heard them leave.'

'Time passed far too slowly. By the evening of the fifth day I was impatient. Perhaps they had decided to stay back another day. The next morning I found the milk and newspaper outside their door as I was leaving for office.

I took them to my flat, putting the milk in the fridge. I fretted all day. When I returned the padlock was still in place. I lay in bed, smoking one cigarette after another, my ears cocked. Midnight came and went in silence; all you could hear was the low growl of air-conditioning from neighbouring flats. Then I pulled out a collection of short stories, Poe I remember, read and waited. I must have dozed off because when I awoke the sun was streaming onto my face. I walked to the door picked up the milk bottle and the morning newspaper. I put the water and milk to boil, idly turning the pages.'

Mahesh's voice had dropped several decibels. Three heads craned forward.

'It was below the fold on the city page; a small news item. A couple had fallen off Tiger Point in Panchgani; death had been instantaneous. An ID card in the man's pocket helped. The police presumed the lady was his wife but they were not sure. The local authorities had the bodies sent to the city morgue where they were awaiting identification by his relatives.'

'Oh God! Now that's a twist I must say! Got rid of her! All for his lady love?' Ranjan was beaming. Reddy pitched in incredulously.

'What! Mahesh I say, what are you saying? How did he? I mean was he drunk?'

Arvind just stared at Mahesh, his mouth slack jawed, his eyes popping out of their sockets.

Mahesh did not say anything. His head was lowered and his right eyelid twitched furiously. He put a hand to it.

'An hour later I was at the Coroner's Court identifying myself as a family friend. The Sub-Inspector of police in charge of the case stared across a bare, ink stained desk after I had told him that the parents of the deceased would take some days to arrive. I would have to . . . to identify the . . . bodies . . . . to make sure before I informed them.

I would have to call his office to get their address. He stared at me a long time with red-rimmed eyes, his huge frame perched uneasily on a rubber tyre.'

"'Piles . . .'" he grunted, shrugging his massive shoulders. Then he told me the details. Tiger Point is a favourite with the tourists for its view of the valley. At that time of year, October, it was a bit deserted; the holiday season had yet to set in. A group of villagers walking across a hill flanking the Point had seen the couple sitting on one of the rocks close to the edge. Then the lady rose, walked to the brink looking out at the distance, a hand shielding her eyes from the late morning sun. After a while the man walked up to her, rather lurched toward her, perhaps he stumbled over the uneven ground; they were not sure. The couple seemed to be arguing, the farmers said. The local police had asked then how they knew that. They guessed because of the way the two gesticulated at each other; at one point the man smacked his forehead several times, at another time, she put the edge of her *dupatta* to her face and tried to walk away from him, the man grabbed her arm and shook her; she pulled away then abruptly ran to embrace him. All the farmers can say is that the couple teetered on the edge, arms flailing as they probably tried to regain balance, everything happened in seconds, almost a blur but they both fell. The villagers, they stood there helplessly, an unwitting audience to this silent mime of life's tangles and their resolution in death, a long tumble, locked for an instant in one final embrace, to the forested valley below.'

No one spoke, none moved a muscle; they could hear Ranjan wheezing. Mahesh thought he heard someone gasp, a roar sounded in his ears and time collapsed, an image flashed before him; a man reading a news item and knowing he was condemned to the shadows, to ponder which was an accident, life or death or both and if so, then were they meaningless?

All these years he had wanted to believe they were, but it hadn't been easy because love had haunted him with the question; *who was to blame?* The faces before him mirrored answers that he did not now want to hear. He did not care anymore. Those restless souls had moved into the ordinariness of the present and dissolved. As far as he was concerned the answer lay in the narration. And he had told his story.

Reddy had something on his mind. He pursed his lips. 'And the parents?'

'They came to the city a few days later, claimed the bodies. The old man lit the funeral pyre, his grey face a picture of immobile grief, his gaunt body moving around the pyre atop which the corpses crackled. Back at the flat, Abhijeet's mother made us some tea, her face twisted with a hysteria that threatened to tear her fail body apart. She stared at me with a a mad gleam in her eyes, her pupils dilated dangerously.'

'What could I say? Death by accident of course; the police inspector had to be roped in, he was a compassionate man; no law was broken by being— brief. They accepted that, a tragic twist of fate, but fate nevertheless. They stayed a few days packing things. As I saw them off at the railway station, I thought I saw in the old man's eyes a glimmer of doubt as he shook hands with me for the last time, but I wasn't sure. A month later he had died of a heart attack and the old lady was being looked after by some distant relatives.'

The manager of the Inn had abruptly switched off the main lights. The wash of the streetlights cast thin shadows on the walls. They settled the bill and trudged out of the restaurant, for the last time. No one had anything to say and strangely none wanted to leave. A passer-by would have found four men of varying ages and postures staring out at the lights of the art gallery as if expecting some important personage to emerge.

Arvind gently patted Mahesh's shoulder several times. He looked ghostly pale.

'Women! You never know with them. One minute this, another minute that. But what the fucks I say, they were one finally, right? He thought life could be rushed, she knew death would not wait. No difference.' He peered into Mahesh's astonished face, nodded as if in approval at what he found there and walked away purposefully. Ranjan turned to Reddy.

'So, my friend, getting late isn't it? The good wife must be waiting. Hurry along then.' He smiled, missing Reddy's hate filled stare in the darkness. Abruptly the old editor waved a finger at Mahesh.

'Suicide, accident murder, what does it matter? It's over; we have to think of the present. Listen—,' he whispered loud enough for Ranjan to hear. 'I need to talk, privately. An offer you will not refuse. History . . . listen, come along to the other side.' With surprising force he dragged Mahesh across the car park.

'Mahesh, ahh . . . . you are a man of principles; a man of honour really, is what you are. That greedy swine Ranjan, what does he know about humanity! Compassion is a dirty word for him . . . lust . . . an animal is what he is. We—you and I—we are made for the exalted life. Join me, I need a man of your silences, strength . . . I know, okay, listen, a man like you can help me destroy, no, bring to book a criminal! We are made for History!'

'Mr Reddy, I do not know what you are talking about . . . and frankly, I am not interested.' Mahesh's smile revealed little.

'You are not interested in justice? Then what was the story all about? Isn't that what you have been searching all these years? What I am suggesting is pretty much more straightforward; and socially more relevant!"

'Thank you for your verdict Mr Reddy but the judge hasn't been appointed yet and I am, as I said—sorry.' Reddy had started fuming.

'But there is a judge in this one and it is History! How can we let a criminal like Gandhi get away?'

Mahesh appeared nonplussed. He shook his head, looked up at the ashen-black sky.

'Gandhi . . . ? Mr Reddy, I do not know what you are talking about. I am perfectly willing to listen to your story if I do not have to develop it . . .' His face softened. 'Listen, it is the cycle of crime, someone once said; one goes the other steps in. Leave it to the police. They are paid to cope with this cycle. Not us . . . romantics. We can hardly deal with our own pain.'

'*Bhah!* What nonsense you talk. That is the problem with you! I had great expectations. I mean, listen . . .' Reddy was now holding his arm, almost pleading.

'*A shot at immortality!* A man has that choice. Don't you see that? Those two lives: Wasted! An accident that's all . . . anyone can fall off an overhanging rock, Mahesh . . . my son. But you—! Do not trade in your tomorrows for your yesterday—'

'Goodbye Mr Reddy, take care of yourself . . . and thank you for the patience and . . . offer.'

Reddy watched in disbelief and disappointed rage. He wanted to scream at him; what emerged was a croak.

'Stupid man! Then die with your memories . . . you . . . you nothing!'

He crossed the car park back toward the Inn thinking to walk home. He wanted the rush of commuters flowing like ceaseless rivers toward CST and Churchgate stations, the cheerful cacophony of street vendors hawking counterfeit CDs, handbags and T-shirts. He needed that dense humanity to anchor him to this moment, this reckoning with a fluid present. He felt a soft hand on his shoulder at the traffic crossing.

'It's not time Mahesh. At least not after a story like that'

He did not resist as Ranjan pulled him into an alley behind a fruit vendor screaming his wares in a thin reedy voice.

'I would like to ask you to join me for a drink at The Kandeel bar not far from here; but you would refuse. I don't blame you. You must feel drained after recalling that tragic end. And then to have an old man—Reddy . . . what did he want? I saw him waving his arms about—'

When Mahesh did not respond he yawned hugely.

'His jacked-up dreams can tire one—and on a Saturday night? After a story like yours a man needs comforting.' He smiled and shook his head. He seemed to be talking to himself.

'What could he have wanted? Surely not some detail of your afternoons with her? History . . . ? I overheard. That's the junk he lives with . . .' He stared at Mahesh with an intensity that forced that dark saturnine man to respond.

'Oh, just a chance you might say to find something . . . I never had . . .' He too smiled. Ranjan chuckled apparently satisfied with that answer. It appeared to him like a cue for what he had in mind.

'Reddy would offer that? No, no, my dear man, he hasn't the imagination and the . . . balls you might say. A man reconstructs his past to cope with his present. But how many times can you revisit your memories? They are fickle—leave then well alone, I say. Find flesh and blood, otherwise you become like . . . Reddy. Hah! Two blind men . . . what was it he wanted . . . help in some mad enterprise?'

He held Mahesh's arm in a tight grip.

'This world belongs to the living. Your story—I can understand why you kept it in your head all these years. Perhaps we, The Gang of Three were fortunate. But I, I mean, you and I . . . have desires and—a man like you . . . We cannot live with remembrances alone. Come with me. Your story was . . . stirring. I feel the need for some company and together we should explore this world of flesh and blood.'

Mahesh turned to him. 'You think you are a romantic? No, Reddy is, I was. I loved them both.'

'Yes, yes, that's all fine—' Ranjan said exasperatedly. 'You have the answers you wanted? Suicide? Murder? Is your search over? My father spent the best part of his life trying to understand genocide and he died in pain. Learn to live with your confusions. Even God has given up. We—you and I—we are the arbiters of our actions but there is no trial my friend and therefore . . . no punishment! I don't believe it's even necessary. How lovely it would be to die in the arms of a beautiful woman—' He raised his eyebrows, 'or a man if that is your preference.'

He smiled then glared at a passer-by who had brushed against him. 'Stupid bastard.' He felt his pockets for his wallet.

'Come with me. I have learnt of a delightful place that can help you . . . forget. Reddy—? *Tchah!*'

He walked briskly toward a taxi, put his hand on the door, paused and looked back. Mahesh had raised his arm in a half salute. Ranjan shouted above the shrillness of the street:

'You only live once!'

He signed in as Vinod Khatri. The security guard called a number on the intercom and in a minute he was escorted up the high rise by a simpering youth in black jeans and white shirt.

In exactly fifteen minutes Ranjan Kapoor's world was going to collapse round his ears but how could a man with such self-assurance have divined that fate? A doorbell was rung and another white-shirt-and-black-trousers with a pencil thin moustache welcomed him in. He was led to a drawing room where two men waited. For a minute he thought he had walked into a doctor's clinic. He smiled to himself: medicine to clean his soul! The two were startled upon seeing him, then bent to forage in their briefcases; both pulled out sheaves of paper and buried their noses in them.

He smiled. His "Good evening" got no answer and he laughed silently to himself. A tall, beak-nosed lady trailing a strong scent of jasmine greeted him.

'Ah, Mr Khatri, welcome, my name is . . . '. A phone rang somewhere and she turned to the white shirt and ordered him to answer the call.

'Yes, so—' she smiled at them. 'You gentlemen are a bit early. The party, well, let me introduce you to each other . . . Mr Vohra, Mr Benjamin and this is Mr Khatri. Two Europeans—or are they Greek? Anyway, they are expected any minute. Actually it is a cosy, intimate, you know, get-together; drinks, dinner, chit-chat and—*Arrey* Matthew *betey*, where are their welcome drinks? Get the trolley in here, you donkey! What a sweet boy, but today, I don't know. So, as I was saying . . . Yes, I'll be back in a minute. Just make yourself comfortable. Ahh, here are the drinks. Give them what they want, son.'

Ranjan sipped his scotch and eased his frame into a more comfortable position in the plush armchair. Soft music wafted through invisible speakers and the air-conditioning was just right . . . a hum and cool air. He shut his eyes for a minute, took another sip and noticed what appeared to be a photo album on a side table. He looked around and saw his fellow guests leafing through similar albums and whispering animatedly to each other. He opened the glossy album, gold lettering against a white background, turned the pages, sipped his drink and almost choked as he came upon a photograph. He rubbed his eyes and stared in disbelief. Then he flipped the pages with a hand that seemed to have filled with cement. His blood ran cold; his vision blurred then sharpened and locked with painful intensity: inches away, a pretty face on a slim frame in various attire from sari to swimsuit, a face hinting at a promise of fun with a nervous smile that made her so much more alluring. He saw her for the first and last time in photographs that had captured her fledgling sexuality; the mind rejects what the eye sees, then registers horror, a deep horror that rose like an evil monster from the depths of his bilious stomach clawing at his heart, squeezing it tighter till he thought he was going to choke.

His eyes burnt with a fire splintering his head; he wished he was born blind yet he saw with sharp clarity the room, the two men writing in a pad that had lain next to them, a similar pad next to him. He heard bells, a million bells peeling thunderously and he wondered which temple he was in and now he wished his brain would shut down his heart, send him into oblivion so that all traces of this horror were erased but he remained seated, his mind divorced from all other bodily functions, working out scenarios, one more horrendous than the other till it had reached the most devastating one of all, her appearance before him. That nightmare drove him to his feet, the echoing bells giving way to a resounding hum.

He walked to the door, the album slipping from his paralysed hand and he did not stop even as he heard voices from far off call out to a stranger, it had to be a stranger; who was *Khatri?*

He did not stop for the lift, tumbling down the six flights round a dark and deep stairwell, his knees buckling ever so often, sometimes stumbling on a step, his breathing shallower by the minute. He lurched into the cool night, the smell of jasmine in his nose and he wondered which garden he had walked into. His face felt flushed, his heart had a pain that was blackening his brain of all thought, then his knees gave way and he fell. In the distance, far away, perhaps in a dream, he heard shouting and men lifting him up and he saw the black starless sky and he wondered why his face was wet and why his heart would not stop and the earth swallow him and then his eyes rolled and he was sinking to the sound of that cursed deafening hum, his blood freezing and his brow hot as ice.

19

Like a knife, the trill of the telephone pierced the fog of sleep. Deepika sat up wild-eyed, wishing it would stop and then it did. She pulled her wristwatch with the same sense of dislocation that had woken her so rudely. The sun streamed in through the open window, outside the fish vendor was calling out, *"Po-o-mm-freyet!"* She walked barefoot to her parents' bedroom: empty. She gasped, gathered her nightgown at her throat as if it were going to fall off her shoulders and ran through the passage to the kitchen where she saw the note.

'Deepu,' it was her mother's scrawl, *"Don't get agitated, beta, but your father had a fall last night and he is at Bhatia Hospital. I tried to wake you up but you were sleeping like a baby. I'll call you in the morning. Don't worry, everything is fine. Mummy."* She ran to the bathroom and brushed her teeth, dialled her mother's mobile but it was switched off. She sat at the dining table holding her tea with quivering hands, her head woozy, staring at the telephone willing it to ring gain. Then she called Inquiry, got the number for the hospital. She was told the doctor was examining Mr Kapoor and that her message would be passed on.

She slumped on the sofa staring at a laminated print of a waterfall set in vivid green foliage, shivering in the early morning breeze that wafted in, dry but still sulphuric in an unpleasant way. She shut the windows, pulling the curtains together. She sipped her tea, a thin bead of sweat at her temples, her body drained of energy. Her sleep had been anything but restful. She had felt herself being pulled back from that abyss of slumber by sounds that jolted her into fretful wakefulness. She dreamt of the film producer and an ageing actor hoping for a comeback, chatting her up as she served drinks and then sat by their side.

Then abruptly the sequence would shift to an image, blurred at the edges of herself as a young girl, naked, being tossed up in the air by the famous actor of yesteryears, his thick mane of greying hair thrown back, his arms opened to catch her and then at the last minute he turns and she is falling. She heard a telephone ring, voices that broke into the silence of her nightmares and she thought that at one point her mother had entered the room and she had said something that she could not now recall. Just then the phone rang and she wrenched it off the cradle.

'Mama . . .'

'Mama . . .' She pulled herself together even as her mother went on about the doctor's visit and her father's sedation and she thanked God as we all do when we have no other recourse from overwhelming circumstances that we would rather not know about. Deepika heard it all. Then she asked her mother the questions that had been buzzing in her head.

'Mama . . . what happened? He fell? Fainted!! Where . . . no when . . . last night . . . Near Bhatia itself? Where? Chikalwadi?' Did a door slam somewhere? *Sleater Road!* The phone fell on her bare foot but she felt nothing. *Near a side entrance to Pyramid Apartments. Sleater Road!* That is all she could remember of all that her mother had said. Then with sudden impact another thought struck her, and another, like large raindrops against a windowpane. Mrs Biswas, Gauri Aunty! Sripad! Hospitality services! The party that she had attended at The Mayfair rooms, the hot hands on her bum, reaching out to slip a note into her coat pocket and on the way brushing against her breasts, the open offer to visit a hotel room, one too many of them, the world of film auditions in private offices.

With trembling fingers she dialled a number. An ebullient Mrs Biswas inquired about the previous night's party and wondered why she hadn't come around for the post-party party, 'it was so nice just a cosy thing, so intimate . . .' Her stomach had begun to churn and then she popped the question the answer to which would change her life: *had someone been sick? No, not sick, but a very polite gentleman, sipping my whisky, leaves abruptly, so rude, but seems he was in hospital having fainted, imagine! Without paying for the whisky, Deepika are you there? The line is bad; I can't hear you. Deepika?*

Her stomach rumbled, bile rose in her gorge and she ran to the bathroom, opened the tap frantically, held the sink with both hands and puked, tumultuous heaves that dredged up all the curdled dreams, raging lava from an angry volcano, in racking sobs that would not stop, gasping for air in that stifling space to fuel more retching, her feet one by one, rising involuntarily as dry racks followed the disgorging like painful echoes, the stomach willing to turn itself inside out.

Then the storm ceased and she opened her inflamed eyes to swirls of her regurgitation refusing to sink out of sight, her nostrils filling with the stench of her soured life and she put her hand into it, stirring the slime over the sinkhole, her sobs now like knife stabs in her parched throat, her mouth drained of all moisture, pain like a craw in her gullet piercing whenever she gulped. She tried scooping out the slime with a plastic mug and her stomach heaved yet again and strange sounds poured out of her mouth in a grotesque simulation of a retch. her hands shook so much that the near-full mug slipped, falling to the ground with a loud thud splashing her gown and floor. She screamed, tore it off and ran to her room and threw herself on the bed, her breath coming in short gasps, wishing she were someone else, or a child or dead.

She dreamt her head was being beaten with a sledgehammer and woke with a growling stomach. She helped herself to some orange juice and suddenly broke into tears as horrendous possibilities and crazed conjectures flew like screaming banshees in her head and she closed her ears, rushed to the bathroom yet again, the miasma of her eruptions hanging thick and heavy. She held her head close to the swirling water and wished she could drown in that sink, she wished she were unblessed with the knowledge of possibilities her body evoked. She yearned for a state of absolute ignorance but she knew that the period of innocence had died on her just a few minutes ago and that her life would be forever stained by the venality of passion. She felt orphaned.

She wailed at the ceiling, once, twice and then again and again, the empty flat echoing her lonely despair. She had an intense urge to flee, to be someplace, with someone who could make her laugh and forget this world of twisted longing. She dialled Sripad's mobile.

Two hours later she was at Vispy's café.

'Deepika! What is the matter!. Here's your Fanta. Drink up, you'll feel better. I know I shall, once that miserable rat, *Hussain!* My beer! Good . . . listen . . . *hunh* . . . I'm onto a screenplay okay, the idea's all here, in my head, down to the last shot, and it's about a girl like you, okay, and you will be . . .' He couldn't get his eyes off her devastated but beautiful, face.

'Paddy, tell me the story of *Casablanca* again will you. No better still, can we see the film? Can you arrange it? Today . . . right now. Can you?'

She felt grateful to her mother who kept her abreast of her father's condition; not once did Madhavi insist she visit the hospital. Deepika knew she would one day have to meet him; that eventuality brought on an uncontrollable and sudden shivering.

Left to her own devices, Deepika tried to exorcise the tumult in her life through physical exertion. She jogged for hours after restless nights. She browsed among the street bookstalls near Churchgate all morning under a blazing sun. She bought nothing; simply flipping the pages, staring at the words quietened the agitation that would surface without warning. Late afternoon, she would walk to Vispy's restaurant for hot buns and tea and his detached yet comforting presence. In the evening he would arrange for her another film from his vast DVD collection especially the Marx Brothers and Charlie Chaplin. She wanted to laugh and she did.

Just as she thought she had conquered her demons the trembling fit would seize her suddenly, her hand quivering like a tuning fork and she would want to cry but her teeth would chatter instead as if she were freezing to death, her head would ache and then just as suddenly she would be fine.

Eight days into an intense inwardness that brought her little comfort or wisdom, a chance event encouraged her to step outside herself. When Sripad called to say his father had met with a fatal accident the night before and his mother was inconsolable Deepika impulsively asked for directions to his home and much against his wishes, took the Virar fast from Marine Lines.

Her mother was expecting her to call that evening. She forgot. She would remember only the next evening but by then Madhavi, agitated beyond proportion, unable to restrain herself had poured her fears into Ranjan's ears. She did try calling Deepika but mobile services did not extend to Virar then; Deepika was inaccessible and Madhavi assumed the worst. She had no reason to expect her daughter to be visiting the Reddys.

She did what she had to; how could she have kept from him the suspicion that his darling daughter, free of restraining influences, had flown? Madhu spent only a few minutes reflecting how she should pitch it to this man in sedated repose, but tell him she must; twelve hours had lapsed and no word from Deepika.

She shook him awake and whispered to him her suspicions as accomplished fact and watched her husband, the pillar of rectitude, urbane author of the correct response, the measured word, sophistication personified, philosopher-friend of the lost and misguided, indifferent husband and distant but doting father, slide into chaos from which he would never recover. She recoiled in horror at the unexpected speed of his disintegration; his eyes bulged from their sockets, his body thrashed about on the wrought iron bed and he howled, a beast in the throes of mortal terror. And then just as suddenly, he collapsed into himself, whimpering over and over again, 'the sky has fallen'.

How could she have understood the terrifying journey he had just taken into insanity and enlightenment? As his mind crumbled, Ranjan Kapoor, The Banker, saw his life for what it had been; a monstrous affliction that torched every one close to him including himself. He saw his wife's delusions as the cry of despair, his closest friend Reddy's pleas for help as the wail of the innocent and Deepika's absence, the flight of the helpless victim. He wailed one last time for the knowledge that had evaded him in the prime of life and then felt oddly comforted after the light in his brain burst into a million shards and he saw the white plains of nothingness before him, beckoning him home. He had paid his dues; the sky had fallen. At last he was free.

Twenty-four hours after Madhavi had whispered those fatal words into her husband's ear, Deepika called from their home, and for a second Madhavi did not recognize her own daughter. Then she started screaming, a frightening cascade of despair and relief and accusation tumbling into incoherence and hysteria and uncontrollable weeping. An hour later Deepika walked into Bhatia hospital and shoved the copy of the paper with the obituary notice in her mother's hand, treading quietly up to her father, her right hand trembling violently. He was asleep, his mouth twisted in a smile or grimace she never knew and she could not help the tears, though she wondered once more, for what or whom she was crying; her coming of age or her father slipping out of one.

She felt her mother's hand on her shoulder, a pull and an attempt at a hug but she resisted; her grief was still too mysterious for her. She edged round the bed to the window, looking out on the traffic snarling up on either side of the road, hurt by her mother's insensitivity to her new found compassion for other people's loss, yet uncaring of her mother's.

Between daughter and mother, the chasm that had always existed widened but strangely, Madhavi felt no bitterness; just remorse at the way life had turned each Kapoor away from the other. She wanted to embrace her daughter but she lacked the emotional space to accommodate her at this moment when her heart and head were filled with the awesome responsibilities that loomed before her. Then Deepika turned away from the window and ran to her and threw her arms around her and she muttered her daughter's name over and over again, stroking her thick hair gently, as if in farewell.

She walked to the station along the main road past Nana Chowk rather than cutting through the Chikalwadi lane that would have taken her past Pyramid Heights. The trembling stopped as she approached Grant Road station and waited on the platform for a Virar fast.

She would never meet her father again she resolved. She wanted to remember him as he had been not as he was now. But it would never be easy for her; and till his death ten years later she would visit him, in their home in Bandra and then in Pune where Madhavi would take Ranjan to stay with her parents and close relatives. Deepika would sit at his bedside with pity, love and self-loathing, and a hand that trembled all the while.

A rvind felt triumphant at his aphorism. What had he said? *"He thought life could be rushed; she knew death would not wait."*

How could morbid Mahesh counsel someone capable of plumbing such depths of human folly? Bhah! But wait! Had he been thinking of Poornima and himself? She wanted to rush life, wasn't that so when she insisted they cut loose from the family? God! What a nitwit! To think that they could manage all on their own? In some God forsaken swampy, mosquito-infested estate in Bhandup or Mulund? *All because she did not want children?!* And what if she changed her mind once they were out there and they were saddled with two or three snotty-nosed kids? God! No! He will not be rushed! That would be worse than death!

His vaunting spirit crashed against this vision of life's drudgery. He was desperate to hold her hand and look into her eyes for the assurance that she would not rush life, to seek the conviction that to do so would be sillier than jumping off a cliff, hand in hand or locked in one final embrace . . . *Shit!*

Shoes in hand, he tiptoed across the narrow passageway to his bedroom. Below the shut door, a thin sliver of light peeped through; he pushed open the door and found his wife sleeping on her back, one leg bent at the knee, her kaftan having ridden up to reveal her strong calves and the round thighs. *That kaftan again!*

He stood at the threshold, hand on doorknob, spellbound by this spectacle of feminine form and frightened by its awesome power. He wanted to ravage that tranquil sensuality, to rip apart its waif-like innocence. He did not move.

'Arvin' . . . wharshappening . . . ?' She had sat up and he hadn't noticed. "Why are you looking like that? God, you are . . . have you drunk something . . . ?"

Mesmerized, he stared at his wife, her kaftan now gathered around her waist as she swung around to sit up, her parted legs pointing at him. He hurriedly shut he door and shot the bolt, terribly frightened by random possibilities in this huge and silent house with its power-laden hierarchies. In a flash of intuition he saw himself as their victim and understood now why motherhood in this household was another form of surrender and captivity.

'Why are you so quiet, Arvind! Have you had *some bhang* or what? No, with that you would have been laughing and singing like an idiot and sending me out to get you *laddoos* and *pedhas*. What is it, say something!' She ran to him and pulled him by his hand and threw him on the bed and fell on top of him and kissed him and bit his lip and he still said nothing just staring, till she got off him and sat on the edge of the bed, kneading her lower lip.

'You have found somebody else, hmm? Arvind! Have . . . you been with . . . that cow, Sheetal? Tell me, I know you watch her like you could bathe her in milk . . . Don't look so startled! I've been watching your tongue hanging out!' She sniffed his shirt, turned his head one way and then the other.

'Hmm . . . no traces, I would have known, she always smells of mustard oil. So . . . *What is happening, yaar! Say something!* She was getting frightened; black magic! The cow had cast a spell on him! His tremulous voice interrupted her burgeoning nightmare.

'Tell me Poorni, has someone, one of my brothers, or the servant, that Motiram, did anyone enter the room when you were asleep or in the bathroom? You mentioned once that Devendraji had peeped in . . . ?'

It was her turn to stare.

'Why are you asking me that? Has someone said anything to you?'

He wasn't listening; he was lost in a world of horrific possibilities.

'You wouldn't know would you? You are sleeping and someone comes in, or stands at the door watching you, imagining, getting close enough to . . .'

'Who? Who came in? Are you mad or what? I leave the door open only for you. Otherwise it is shut, when I go to toilet or have a bath . . .' She looked away and sniffed. He still wasn't listening. Calmly, he spoke.

'Poorni, if you are serious about finding a new house, moving out of here . . .' He held her hand and pressed it hard. She laughed nervously.

'Arvind, it is now getting close to midnight—have you eaten? Can I get that *chole* Parvatiji made? Oh, by the way, I almost forgot, Devendraji looked in to ask when you were returning. They want to talk, I think . . .'

Arvind gaped openmouthed.

'He came in here? When? And . . . and . . . where were you? In this dress?'

'Don't be silly Arvind, what is the matter with you tonight? Of course I was in this dress. I was reading

Filmfare when he walked in and told me that they, I suppose Bapu and he, wanted to discuss something. I didn't answer, just stood up and looked at a point over his head and nodded. He muttered something then, like, "Now you both can have fun . . ." I don't know what he meant and I never asked. Then . . . he went away. That's all. So meet the President and the Prime Minister of India tomorrow, okay? Come here, you beast!'

A post-coital depression kept him awake till he heard the crows cawing in the early morning dark. At eleven that same day he entered the drawing room, unsure of what surprises lay in store but resigned to the worst.

'My son, are you not well? You look pale, like someone had dry-cleaned you . . .' The old man peered from under thick white eyebrows at his youngest son with genuine worry. He turned to Devendra.

'I don't think this is a good time to bring up that business. He looks ill. Arvind, it's like this. You, I am sure will be happy to know that the deal with that Kolkata chap, is off. He has found some other party with more space and in Andheri. South Mumbai he says is old assets little spending power. The suburbs are where the money is. So . . . Konarak will stay as it is, in your hands—.' The old man held up a hand even though Arvind hadn't meant to speak.

'Of course, some changes are in order, son, you get my meaning?' Devendra looked down his beaked nose and sneered.

Something happened. He thought he saw a dam burst and waters flood a parched earth. He shivered and looked at his father.

'Thank you Bapu. But there is something I want to tell you. With all due respects, Poorni and I would like to set up our own home. Move somewhere cheap, in the suburbs—'

Devendra shot up from his chair.

'What! Are you mad? You want to leave! But what about your responsibility, your duty to . . . to Bapu . . . us? That wife of yours, I know she has put this reckless idea in your head!'

'Sit down Dev don't be silly. Let's hear all . . .' The patriarch grunted, made himself more comfortable and asked a bit mockingly.

'So you want to be independent. That's good. But how will you support your family, when, and if, it comes? You must work harder, the shop must generate revenue. Now it's a pastime. Not that I want rent or anything . . .'

'In fact, I was going to suggest that before I was interrupted. I shall give you rent plus a share of profits. By next Diwali . . . you'll see the results. But we want to move . . . soon.'

With apprehensive defiance, he looked his father in the eye; the old man returned his gaze with a new gleam in his rheumy eyes, his mouth puckered in thought. Arvind did not know if he was laughing and he didn't care.

'What will you both do all by yourselves in some poky smelly flat, hunh? What will your lovely wife do for company? At least here she has her sisters-in-law to advise, solace . . .'

Devendra voice had risen. He was shaking with a fury that left Arvind nonplussed. Then the penny dropped and for the first time in his life he saw the ugly side of unrequited desire. He walked up to his brother still ranting about familial responsibilities, placed a hand on his shoulder and whispered, "Give it time, you'll forget her."

He thanked his father who did not reply and walked back to his bedroom. Poorni was singing under the shower. He pushed open the door and watched his wife rinsing the shampoo off her hair, her nakedness a joy to his eyes. Suddenly she stopped, pushed wet hair aside, gave a start and then smiled, trying to cover her breasts. He walked under the shower held her close as she protested weakly, a laugh rising from far below her throat, a gurgle and she began to unbutton his shirt. He stopped her and whispered.

'Which suburb? West or east?' He saw the confusion in her eyes, a slow dawning as a huge smile creased her soft cheeks and he whispered again, 'Finish your bath. Wear that green sari with the yellow sleeveless blouse. Leave your hair open. And don't forget the lipstick, the high heels. We are going out to lunch, then a film, tea, shopping and dinner at Cream Centre.'

As if through a thick fog, Rajani Reddy, widow of The Editor, Dev Reddy saw her son Sripad and stranger in salwaar kameez come into view. She never got the name but she felt a gentle hand on her shoulder, a hand that shook but felt warm. She rested her cheek against it and sobbed quietly. She moaned his death but more so her sudden and inexplicable widowhood. She had been told it was heart failure, a natural enough reason for a life cut short; but she had no clue of the events that had led to a body and an empty briefcase in a wooded area near Powai lake.

So her bereavement was accompanied by a rage at her husband's callousness; she wanted to avenge her future loneliness by cremating him with all the Hindu rites; but she yielded to her sons who insisted on following their father's last wish brought to them by a lawyer from Lalbaugh a relapsed alcoholic who learnt of Reddy's death quite by accident and promptly turned up with a will and an invoice. The old editor exhorted the widow and sons to keep the "fires of revolt burning" and demanded his body be gifted to the JJ Hospital. Hemu, the eldest returned to Kolkatta pleading work; Rajani simply nodded, hiding her bitter rage behind a veil of grief as Sripad and Deepika handled all the arrangements.

As in life so in death, Reddy remained a stranger to his wife and sons. His overweening pride and insolent self-confidence prevented him from seeking allies in his household and isolated him in his illusions.

He never got a second chance to test Rajani's gift of introspection that would have helped his "campaign." Sripad, his younger son could have leavened the old man's morbid obsessions with a pinch of cynical urbaneness. Both introspection and mild skepticism could have kept the old warrior alive.

Reddy passed into oblivion like so many he despised: unknown by most, remembered by few dear ones with a remorse that quickly disappeared into the sands of their own troubled existence.

No one knew that Reddy had had intimations of death that had frightened him into nervous inaction for a week.

Mahesh's refusal to join him for a stab at 'History' had infected his resolve with doubt. Always a man of words and little action, Reddy found his task more intimidating by the hour. The more he procrastinated, the more indecisive he became. He slept all day while his son set off jauntily for his duties as estate manager. Rajani grew apprehensive at his moping about the small house, his grumpy presence unsettling her fragile tranquility.

Sometimes he would pour over his notes on BodyArt and curse his old friend Ranjan—that 'bandit with good manners', his elder son Hemu for having failed the revolution and Marx for having failed him.

On Sunday, exhausted by doubts and uncertainties, Reddy sat in a coffee shop near home at the same table his son had occupied seven days earlier when he had received Deepika's distressed call. He needed perspective and his cramped flat did not provide him one. He pulled from his briefcase a sheaf of single lined sheets and underlined in red, his son, Hemu Adhikari's designation and place in the echelons of the Marxist Party of India. He smiled to himself. So what if Hemu and he had not spoken to each other in ages? Gandhi could not know that! To tell the truth you must exaggerate or hide, Reddy thought, chuckling at the idea. Yes, Mr Gandhi, *are you in a soup now!*

His resolve stiffened when he saw Rajani hunched over the low cutting board, sniffling as she sliced onions with arthritic fingers. No! He had to do it for her. Her life too needed mending!

On Monday, he tidied up his work place. He shoved the BodyArt files into a small cupboard near his bed, locked it and hid the key in the bathroom loft. He had no use for them now, his briefcase contained all the information he needed to lure the wolf from his lair. He did not think Rajani would know what to make of his notes. He tried a smile on her as she served him lunch but she was preoccupied and he resisted; time for that later, he decided.

He muttered a farewell promising to return early and looked around the small flat with the square dining table that doubled as his writing space, the frayed and faded sofa covers, the black and white poster of Karl Marx still staring down balefully and inexplicably, he felt a hot swell of tears and a painful choking and he thought of Mahesh and the loneliness of memories and his own confession one Saturday night of a long lost love. He smiled as he shut the door and another opened in his overworked mind on a dusty countryside with wretched huts and shanties and the young lady with dreamy gray eyes living with a woman from Kerala who seemed to him more than just a companion. Reddy sighed at these memories. The past! *Bhah!*

He would not need the journal again. He was crossing the 'last frontier' into another territory, History no lessl the new owners of the tenement blocks could claim them for shopping malls, playgrounds for the rich and infamous or car parks for the brain-dead. Yes, the journal had served its purpose and it could now wither away. He would write from home; perhaps his memoirs?

He looked around the small cubbyholes that had been *The Last Frontier's* fortress, a small haven in this decaying textile district on this island-city of presumptuous greed. As he shut the door he saw behind it a thick envelope that had escaped his attention. He picked it up and sighed; the eviction notice hardly mattered now. He threw it onto his desk at the far corner and shut the door for the last time. He walked by screaming children playing in the bleaching, mid-afternoon heat, past old men with sunken cheeks, stubbly chins and empty eyes, relics of long-forgotten labour strikes. They watched him without a flicker of recognition even though they had seen him pass the same way for twenty years. They did not return his smile and he did not care.

He reached the main road and walked past showrooms displaying branded goods, brushing against happy couples and families hunting for discounts, past smokeless chimneys of deserted textile mills that rose into the sky like derelict totem poles of an extinct race, behind grimy, piss-caked brick walls.

He noticed nothing of the life and death around him; not the glittering shops nor the forlorn graveyards of an industrial age. He sat at a street-side tea stall to rest his weary feet; it had a phone booth: good. 3.00 pm. Time for the first call.

'BodyArt. Ye-e-es, how can we help?'

Suddenly he was frightened. He banged the phone down and searched his pockets. He dialed again.

'*Haalloww* . . .' A heavily accented male voice; must be his secretary, Reddy thought.

'Yes, hunh, I can speak to Mr. Gandhi?'

'You are . . . who?'

'Mathur.'

'Mathur who?'

'Mathur business man. I have a good proposal.'

'Send by courier. He will read and then respond. Do not forget to put your e-mail ID. He only replies by email, *whokay?*'

'You are who?'

'Raghavan, EA . . . Executive Assistant. How you got his number . . . ?'

'From very close friend of Bala's . . .'

Raghavan did some quick thinking before replying.

'Just *won* minute. I will check if he is free.'

Out of the corner of his eye, Reddy saw the tea stall owner pointing to the phone. Puzzled; he stared at the old man, shook his head and turned back; Raghavan had reappeared on the line.

'Mr. Mathur . . .' The phone went dead. Reddy looked at the instrument as if it were a strange animal he had caught by its tail. Then he heard the shopkeeper's assistant shout in his ear.

'*Kaka*, put one more coin and dial again. One minute, one rupee, okay?'

He dialed. Raghavan came on instantly.

'Yes? Ahh Mr Mathur, where you are, I say, saar? Hold on wokay?'

'Yeah, Bal here. Who is this?' To Reddy it sounded like a screech.

He felt calm. This is how he imagined the Voice of Authority would be: calm. He put his hand on his hip and struck a pose.

'Yes, Bala, Mr Gandhi, look, I have something to say to you.'

'So say it. By the way are you related to Chips Mathur? Cambridge in the seventies? . . . You don't know any Runty? From Karachi his father came, an advocate.'

'No, no I am from Telengana, Andhra Pradesh, a fiery sort of place, lot of blood flowed—' He smirked.

'I don't know what you mean . . . Anyway, what do . . . ?'

The line went dead. He looked at the phone as if it had bitten him. How dare the guy hang up on him! He dialed furiously, barking into the mouthpiece.

'Hallo!' Before he could play tough . . .

'I don't have the time Mr Mathur. State your business.'

'Mr. Gandhi, in a few moments you shall know all. Bear with me. I have a proposition to make you. It is this—'

'Proposition? What is this? Mathur! Speak to my sec . . . I mean my MD Nasreen. *Raghavan! Raghavan!* Transfer this call to Madam!'

Reddy shouted: 'No, wait! Your life depends—'

'What! Who are you?'

'I? Me? I am the—voice of the people. The game is up. Own up!'

The line snapped once again. Reddy blinked. The shopkeeper was shaking his head. Reddy found a coin and dialed again. On the other side Gandhi had begun to get a bit worried. Was this some crank, a creditor's thug?

He rushed to his door and shouted, 'Nasreen!' just as the phone buzzed. He ran back and yelled into it.

'Raghavan! Hold the line for a moment. No, okay, I'll take it!'

Some heavy breathing later, the voice came on, soft yet determined.

'You must believe me when I say your life depends on it. One minute—' Gandhi heard a rustling sound.

'Okay listen to this . . . I am quoting okay? "*BodyArt has borrowed recklessly from banks, ours included and if the third round of repayment is missed we may initiate proceedings . . .*"'

It was Reddy's turn to stare at the handset as if it were playing tricks on him. Gandhi had hung up.

How was he to know Bala had broken out in a sweat?

'Nasreen! *Raghavan!* Get Nasreen here? Quick! Nasreen!'

'What is it, Balooo? I am so tired!'

'You may be dead soon, Nasreen. I will be dead. This guy, he just read out something that Ranjan had sent us. You know that confidential note he did for his MD . . . the copy is in your file isn't it—the ones dealing with his bank? Get it!'

Nasreen stared, her mouth agape. A strong breath of tobacco escaped into the small room almost gagging Gandhi. He turned his head in disgust.

'Files . . . ?' she whispered hoarsely. 'You have them, don't you remember? You said you would take them home and put them in Mama's room. Your mother, you said would not let anyone steal files from under her nose . . . Oh, Balan! I can never forgive you for saying such nasty things! I never shut doors and we still do not know who stole our dossier on Sunita Singh.!'

'Stop blathering! Is that bastard Ranjan putting the squeeze through some gangster? God, is he blackmailing me for some more or what? Isn't he happy with what I've given him, the bastard! I tell you, Nasreen, never trust a Punjabi, my mother always said, Really if that fucker is double crossing me, I swear I'll kill him!'

Nasreen twittered.

'My husband says that about Gujaratis, so does my Punjabi boyfriend!' Gandhi wasn't listening.

'Talk to him and find out. Better still—'

'Okay, you wicked man! Not tonight though!'

'God, this Runty Mathur is going to call. I better humor him. Listen in will you. I'll put the call on speaker mode . . .'

'Yes, Mr. Gandhi—time to pay your debts. I have come collecting . . .'

Just then Raghavan walked in with Fatima the receptionist. Gandhi cupped the mouthpiece.

'What is it?' he snapped.

The receptionist was agitated.

'Sir, there are some . . . eunuchs outside. They want to meet you.'

Bal stared at her, openmouthed.

'Eunuchs? I don't know any eunuchs. Nasreen?'

'That is what I came to tell you before you started this gangster rubbish. Get off the phone and get rid of . . . of those creatures! At least get them out of the office! Jimmy sonny is coming and what will he think of his mother?'

'Eunuchs? Tell them—Eunuchs? Why have they come here?'

'Debt collectors on behalf of Raj Kamal Finance and Mutual, they are. We owe them twenty crore.'

'You talk to them. Fatima, tell them to meet Madam Nasreen. I am not in office for the next couple of weeks. Go. Yes, Mr Mathur . . . ?'

'This is costing me a lot of time and money *Mr. Gandhi*! Listen without interruption!. *Tchah*'

Once again the line went cold. All Gandhi heard was a hum. He was very irritable now but also intrigued and very apprehensive. The red light on his phone began blinking.

'Sorry, Mr Balan, I had an incoming call, you know, from the Central Bureau of Investigation. CBI . . . I am one of their advisors. Let me be quick As I was saying. I know all about you, in fact more than you know about yourself. History has peculiar ways of catching up and this is its voice speaking. Soon you will have to give yourself up . . . Actually—hullo, hullo? Are you there? Say something, no, just grunt. Okay, so I was saying, parasites like you—no, no don't get angry, nothing personal, you are part of that class that's all, anyway—parasites like you should be tried in a People's Court but then where is it, I ask? So for your crimes against the Indian people, you have to get your just dessert another way—'

Gandhi was appalled at the man's audacity. Give the devil his due he was a great showman . . . applied the heat and then switched off. Keep the guy at the other end sweating! He was sweating despite the fierce air-conditioning that blocked his nasal passages so that he kept his mouth open most of the time. He couldn't bear the heat. He stared at the phone with slack-jawed wonder.

How was he to know Reddy had run out of one-rupee coins and was frantically trying to find someone to give him change for a hundred-rupee note? Gandhi swore to himself he would ask Reddy for his number the next time he called. He rose suddenly dashed to the door and walked into Nasreen's cubicle where she was entertaining a mean-faced teenager.

'Nasreen. Listen in on this. I want to trace this call. Keep the guy talking and may be invite him over for a coffee. Perhaps offer him some shares of BodyArt. How much do we have left apart from the 51 per net we own?'

Nasreen groaned and rolled her eyes.

'The last ten per cent went to Ranjan, Baloo. We have just twenty one per cent.'

'Fuck him! He's behind this I am sure. We'll get those shares back from that swindler. Work on it will you . . . ? And stop pampering this idiot son of yours.' Just then the phone rang in his room. He heard a very irritable voice.

'Sorry to keep you waiting. It was the Enforcement Directorate on my mobile—.'

'What's the number Mr. Mathur, tell me, I'll call you.'

'Never mind! Don't waste my time, you . . . you . . . so and so . . . just listen! That's all . . . Now! Even a criminal like you needs options. The Dictatorship of the Proletariat is democratic. So! You will issue a public apology through the *Times of India* and *Corporate Inc.* agreeing to pay back to the depositors of your finance company what you swindled. If they do not agree to publish it then I wall arrange for an extended interview with you to appear in the people's journal, *The Last Frontier.* Needless to say, I, Devepulla Reddy, sorry, Mathur, will conduct the interview, so you should be ready with all the truthful answers.'

He heard a giggle that sounded like a horse neighing. Reddy was incensed.

'You find this funny? Wait a minute. My mobile is ringing . . .'

Nasreen had not stopped giggling. Bal stared at her silently, wondering what he had found in this singularly unattractive woman to have her for three decades at his side. He thought maybe it was time to put her out to pasture; send her back to her golfing, hard-drinking husband.

'Yes, Mathur, what is the second option? Report me to ED? The CBI? Ah, you have information? Tell me, I am just curious; where did you get those documents . . . ?

Okay, sorry, no harm in asking is there? Your son is in the present government? What portfolio he has? Ahh! Coalition party member. Is he from Cambridge also . . . I know some bureaucrats; they were with me . . . You know Tipple? No?'

Reddy felt the initiative slipping from his hands; he raised his voice.

'Listen, don't ask me so many stupid questions. Stop behaving like a child or else I'll have all these papers plus my jottings on the desk of every Commercial Editor of every paper first thing tomorrow morning. Is that clear? What? My son? Which one? No, he is from Presidency College, not Cambridge. Stop asking me more questions about my stupid son or I will get him to ask questions about you in Parliament, Zero Hour, Starred Question, whatever . . . You want that, hmm? No? What? You want to meet me? Why? Oh, for the interview, yes of course! What about that public apology? I see . . . after meeting me . . . Wait, my mobile is ringing. I think it is the finance ministry.'

Reddy put the phone back with a manic grin and paced the narrow sidewalk, visions of glory and immortality almost blinding him. He had done what the police could not; brought to heel that criminal dog!

"Gandhi? Me again. Okay so where do we meet? Oberoi. No, I cannot come there. You will pick me up. Okay, outside, hmm, Pritam's near Dadar T.T. Okay with you? In an hour? Gray Esteem, no. 6191. Right you are, sir.'

He was singing. His heart rose to the skies and he wanted to hug the beggar child who followed him across Tilak Bridge. Hordes of commuters and shoppers rushed past him; the gaggle of beggars reached emaciated arms out to him but he managed to avoid contact as he hurried toward *Pritam's*.

All his life he had harbored a secret desire to live where the air was clean, the sidewalks wide and gentlemen nodded polite greetings as you passed them by and the cafes were full of thinkers he could exchange notes on social ferment. But now the heat and the dust and the constant smell of dried urine and shit and rotting garbage did not bother him.

Forty minutes to go. He knew that they wouldn't come for another hour, what with the evening traffic rush, so he decided to pamper himself at the crowded restaurant. His stomach heaved a bit when the *Chole Bhaturey* came, a fluffy fried sour dough pancake and a side dish of chick peas floating in dark brown gravy. The heady aroma filled his nostrils and he took a deep breath and tucked in. Delicious, the first bite and he waited for his stomach to report; so far so good. He dipped a bigger piece of crusty bread in the gravy, scooped up the greasy chickpeas and lifted it to his waiting mouth and chewed slowly ever fearful of digestive tract mutiny. He ordered sweet buttermilk to douse the fire he felt must be building in his belly and sipped gratefully.

Ah-h-h, it was so simple! Why had he agonized over it so long? The man was a sensible fellow! The game was up and he wanted to make amends. An interview, a public apology and salvation for the hapless depositors who would get their precious savings back. What more could he do?

Just then his stomach began to rumble ominously and his bowels came to life with a suddenness that drove out all thoughts. He rose quickly, and locked himself in the small cubbyhole, holding his breath against the stench that the whirring exhaust fan above and behind him was unable to drive away.

A few minutes later, he hurried out to the brightly lit entrance, glancing at his watch with mounting anxiety. An hour and half had passed and the car still hadn't come. He belched, a noisy release of agony, that came from the pit of his volcanic stomach and he knew that his long dormant acidity was preparing to attack. He settled the bill, hurried into the dark night and the smells of car exhaust, looked right and left but saw no vehicle that matched the description he had been given. Suddenly, he felt a tap on his shoulder. Startled, he turned to stare at a dark face with a 'chin strap' beard, a thin frame in a checked shirt and dark trousers.

'You are waiting for Esteem car, uncle? Okay, come with me. Car is behind on that side street. No parking here, no?' Reddy hurried, his escort striding rapidly without looking back once. He stole a glance at his watch in the pale yellow wash of the streetlights. Nine thirty. Two and a half hours late; he must register a protest, assert his authority. A furious belch escaped and he felt the foul aftertaste of his indulgence. Yes, he must show resolve!

The check-shirted man stopped at a car, spoke to someone and then vanished into the night. Reddy approached the car and bent to peer shortsightedly.

'Mr Gandhi? Glad to meet you. Long time you took . . .'

The rear door opened, Reddy spun around to face a dark complexioned man with a huge stomach and indeterminate chin, faintly smelling of Pan Parag, the scented tobacco powder.

Gold-rimmed glasses perched on a small and flat nose. His voice sounded almost affectionate. But it was decisive.

'Mr Mathur? Name's Jadhav, call me John. Get in. Let me hold your briefcase.'

Reddy hesitated; the outstretched hand did not waver. Should he walk around to the other side of the car? Just then that door opened and a small-framed man with a shiny bald dome glared over the vehicle at Reddy. The editor handed over the briefcase.

'Thank you. Get in.'

Wedged between two strangers he had not bothered asking for identification, Reddy felt the first signs of foreboding just as the Esteem sprang to life and shot out the side street into the main road. Instead of turning south toward the Oberoi, the vehicle turned towards Matunga and Sion. Reddy felt he should ask some important questions. He couldn't because his bowels were threatening to open up. He shut his eyes, sat still for a few seconds and burst out.

'Where are we going? Gandhi had said—'

Velvet voice cut in.

'Eventually. By the way, these documents you have . . . ? I need to verify—'

Reddy bristled.

'What do you mean? Of course they are genuine! I got them from—an impeccable source.'

'Then kindly show them to me. Famous men cannot be too careful. Blackmailers . . . they are everywhere.' He reached out.

Reddy was in a quandary. Not to show them was to be considered a fake and who knows what they might do? On the other hand, they would draw the connection with Ranjan. He handed the briefcase back to Jadhav who did not open it, staring straight ahead at the highway they were traveling on at great speed.

'Lal Singh, take the Powai road yeah?. Okay, turn here.'

Reddy looked out the window at cars whizzing past, occasional glass fronted buildings between shanty type structures that seemed to lean on them, billboards with pretty and handsome faces showcasing the good life and he wondered, with mounting anxiety, which part of the city they were in. He knew little of the city's geography but he did know this much; they were very far from The Oberoi hotel at Nariman Point and were heading further away every minute. He stole a glance at the men on either side of him. Jadhav had still not opened the briefcase and Reddy had half a mind to ask him for it. He kept silent, holding his breath as the car moved gingerly over potholes, negotiating auto rickshaws, trucks scooters and motorcycles, past rows of residential blocks in varying stages of construction, mounds of cement, bricks, immobile cranes with their forklifts pointing skywards, shanty huts with single-fluorescent tube lighting. Then he glimpsed a shimmering body of water through black trees and heard the soft voice in the air-conditioned gloom.

'Lal Singh, okay, slow down, right, the gate comes up now, right turn here slowly . . . aah! Go on, don't stop.' He waved a hand, smiled at the security guards who looked away as the sedan coasted in confidently.

Reddy turned to Jadhav.

'This . . . this is not the Oberoi. Of course I haven't been there ever but these—.' He peered intensely at the low level buildings between trees. They looked like those semi-detached houses on a university campus he would have visited very often. Where were they? He opened his mouth to ask then heard that soft voice, 'Follow the road between the trees, Lal Singh, slowly, you are not on the highway, this is a place of learning . . .'

'But not of wisdom, yeah what Johnny?'. Reddy turned in surprise to the bald man. He had spoken for the first time. He peered at the pinched face, the pencil-thin moustache as it came into focus from the moonlight filtering through the trees.

'Er, what, what do you mean? This is the . . . ?'

'Okay, Lal Singh—'

The car came to a halt, the engine died and silence descended over them. Crickets and frogs croaked drunkenly, the trees whispered gently and a cool breeze washed into the car. Voices from a dimly lit house on a low grassy mound carried over the silence and the darkness and his fear mounted. In the icy-blue spill of the moonlight Reddy glimpsed a narrow track veering off into a thicket. Reddy's mind froze.

'Where . . . are we . . . '? He stammered, trying to peer at what appeared to be the sea, no a river or was it a lake. *Lake in Mumbai?* The thought chilled him to the bone. He thought he should scream; they should hear him in that house on the knoll.

'Where are we? This is not The Oberoi Hotel? Where is Gandhi?' His voice sounded like an echo in a deep well.

'Gandhi? Who? We don't know any Gandhi. Father of the Nation?. Come let's picnic. Lovely, isn't it?'

Shiny Pate had spoken. No one moved. Jadhav sighed and opened his door.

'Come Mr. Mathur, let us stretch a bit. It's a long way back to Dadar TT. You live there? Hindu Colony?'

As if on cue, the small man jauntily alighted. Reddy was alone in the car with the driver who sat staring ahead at the road that curved fifty yards ahead. He heard them calling out to him and as if in a trance he obeyed. His bowels had frozen, his mouth felt dry and his head was beginning to pound. He did not know what to think or say because he had no idea of what was happening.

'So, Mathur—that is your name, right?' Johnny shook his head and clicked his tongue. He stared up at the starlit sky. He let out a small cry of pure pleasure.

'Stars! There are no stars in south Mumbai! They are here, no? Lovely, no Mr Mathur? What is your real name? Never mind. See, he is a very big man, our children are getting good physicals and you want to send him—where . . . ?' He did not wait for an answer but opened the briefcase, yanked the papers and flung the briefcase not too far from where they stood. He folded some dozen single lined sheets and a glossy brochure and stuffed them in his pocket.

'Tchah!', he muttered, pulled them out and walked back to the car, gave them to the driver and came back to where Reddy stood as if made of stone while the small man hummed a song from *Maqbool*

'Uncle, you have seen this fillum, *Maqbool*? I seen it three times and I am going again tomorrow. I can recite all of Pankaj Kapoor's lines, even in my sleep.'

He did not hear that last sentence too well because a rock had slammed into his cheek. He saw stars circling furiously in his head; he felt the rush of blood and then the pain on his inflamed cheek. His heart was beating so wildly now he thought it would break free. He staggered, tears blurred his vision, but he knew that some heavy and blunt instrument had hit with extreme force. Then through the fog of pain and shock he heard the soft voice, faint but distinct.

'So uncle you want to put him in the newspapers? He owns them all; those writers, what they are called—editors? He says thank you all the same. Righto—anything to say? We can go?'

He did not hear their footsteps because of the roar in his ears. He fell to the ground, keeling away from the track into the thicket, his universe spinning as his heart screamed in agony as if caught in a tight grip, a stabbing pain somewhere behind his left shoulder convinced him that he had been knifed. Then he blacked out.

22

Sleep would not come; he felt listless, almost light-headed, like a leaf on a gentle wind. He would never go back he did not wish to meet them again. They knew too much. As the sole survivor he must move on, but where to? He watched the ceiling above his bed turn grey-blue at the first hint of dawn. He felt drowsy, his eyes drooped.

Morning came suddenly, sunlight streaming across his young-old face. He rose, stretched his limbs and sat near the window. He heard the busy chirrup of sparrows. A wind started up and he saw it; a clutch of red breasted robins trying to build a nest, unhurried yet intense, uncaring of the wind that kept tearing through their efforts. He wondered what he should do, Sunday stretched before him.

He sat there through the day, as the sun dipped into the Arabian Sea, the mellowing light washing over him. Stripped of all memory and longing, he watched a smog-filled dusk spread like a turbid river over the noisy traffic on Veer Nariman Road. Then he rode a taxi to Shuklaji Street. He walked aimlessly then turned into a dark alley and found himself in a cul-de-sac.

At the entrance to a single story building abutting the dead end wall he saw her, squatting on the shallow steps to an ill-lit passageway. A dim light cast a soft shadow over her face. She rose with a grunt he followed her into one of the rooms leading off the dank corridor. It was no more than a cubicle with a single bed and a sheet thrown over a mattress.

He sat next to her and without a word she held his hand and squeezed it gently but firmly as tears fell over his hollowed cheeks. She undressed him with feather-touch fingers, her eyes probing but not questioning his sorrow. Then she lay down, pulled up her sari and him down on her, calloused hands on his lean buttocks gently coaxing him on a journey deep into the unknown, unhurried and without pause down to the end of the earth where its fiery breath mingled with the rancid smell of passion. He exploded inside her, a cry of primeval release reverberating in his ears, and he knew eternity was a moment that died as it was born, again and again.

He put in his papers despite the entreaties of his managing director and Juliet Bissell, his tearful secretary. He walked out of his office building for the last time with his laptop. He packed a duffel bag with his clothes, some books, pulled the old battered tin suitcase of his father's memorabilia from a loft, watched the man from Personnel lock the apartment, signed a paper, smiled and rode a taxi to his childhood home in Colaba. The tenants had been kind enough to leave at short notice. He tiptoed into a desolate apartment, scraps of paper, old bills, mail order leaflets scattered over the empty floor of the drawing room, a dead cockroach, belly up near the window in the bedroom he had slept in as a child and set both the bags near the far wall. Off in the trees behind the building crows were noisily settling in for the night. A maid called out to someone. Nothing reminded him of anything; the walls simply enclosed space. He looked out the window facing the harbour, and the blinking lights of ships on the horizon waiting to berth, and Butcher's Island and the shadowy outlines of the Radio Club off to the left and he breathed deep and smiled to himself and fell asleep on the barren floor.

Next morning he washed in cold water, changed into a fresh shirt and trousers and sat against the wall facing the harbour with his father's notebooks, pencil in hand. Suddenly a picture took shape; a woman sitting on the steps of a tenement block on a dead-end street in the heart of the city, a dim light casting shadows on her plump and scantily clad body, mother earth, mottled and generous. He smiled at the recollection.

He put the notebooks away, gently shut the tin suitcase and hauled it down the narrow corridor to the other bedroom and slid it under a bare four poster bed and shut the door. Back in his room, cross-legged, facing the sun-washed harbour, the gentle tides lapping against the wall below, Mahesh booted the machine, opened a new file and typed the following across the top of the screen: "*A Chronicle of Ceaseless Love. By Mahesh Vats.*"

Postscript

Rajani

    With a handful of suspicions, some guesswork and a cupboard stacked with files, his widow would fill her heart with remorseful anger at Reddy's obsessions and his perverse mindlessness. Her feelings for her dead husband would congeal into an icy rage at the selfishness of desire, the desire for recognition from 'humanity', that cursed chaos he thought loved him. She had known of her husband's yearning and she tortured herself for having taken it lightly as a harmless symptom of regressive behaviour. As she settled into widowhood and old age, the rage died and she came to terms with her regrets and mankind's foolishness with an equanimity that amazed her younger son and his partner.

    She would spend the rest of her days with them as their elder companion, the one who laughed quietly, sank into the night and her corner of the world as if on cue so that they hardly felt her presence. Even when they moved to the suburb of Andheri and into a bigger, three-bedroom flat, she would know when to leave them alone. She was like some spirit, a friendly genie that put itself back into the bottle and they felt grateful for that. Never once, not even by a hint did she reveal to them the tortured road of self-discovery she had traveled after her husband's death. She saw the questions in her sons' eyes but she gave no answer. Hemu believed his father had been set upon by some "kulak thugs" for his writings in The Last Frontier; Sripad sensed a mad caper that led to his being waylaid by thieves. She just smiled; soon they forgot as their own lives became more tangled. She never judged them, not her sons, nor the young couple she stayed with. She simply offered her frail shoulder to cry on, a woman of steel each would miss when she died in her sleep, peacefully, without any fuss.

Deepika

For Deepika the death of her 'amma', that is how she looked upon Rajani Reddy even though she never married Sripad, created an emptiness she was never able to fill. Not with Sripad, her first love and only friend-in-need, the creator of her film persona, author of her most successful films and occasional bed mate two years into their live-in arrangement.

After a brief and intense relationship, Deepika had begun to get frightened at the prospect of marriage, a union that Sripad desperately sought to confirm his place in her heart. But Deepika's heart was like a cavernous, wind-swept hall in which nothing could stay anchored.

As her career escalated, taking her to the breathless atmosphere of stardom, she sought to fill her empty heart with lovers, only to throw them away like her last film's reviews. Her tremors ceased when her father died, peacefully in his sleep; she grieved briefly in an interlude between lovers. She was restless. She needed a new scriptwriter. Sripad, by now an indifferent lover had become an indifferent writer too.

Her success had turned him a failure. But they couldn't stay apart. He was terrified of another voyage and she had got used to him like a habit.

One day, at the height of her stardom, Deepika chanced upon a clothes designer working out of a bookstore in the Kala Ghoda area of south Mumbai. The lady in question— Deepika was struck by her energy levels—had designed dresses out of ethnic prints in a style that was neither Rajasthani nor Gypsy; something in between that struck a chord in the famous actress.

Poorni Collections was launched and Poornima Purohit became the city's darling fashion designer. She was to be featured frequently in the society pages of the city's dailies and magazines, her slender fingers round a glass of orange juice, accompanied by a man who looked an age between forty and sixty years with his shiny dome and weak eyes that peered out of rimless glasses.

Poornima

Deepika soon forgot her, moving her wardrobe closer to the designs washing ashore from London and New York. But Poornima had been launched and soon her husband began to revel in his wife's glory and fame. They moved back from their flat in Bhandup to south Mumbai atop Cumballa Hill, or more specifically, at the foot of it, in a high rise that also housed a professor of philosophy, an eighty year old gentleman who played Bach for Arvind in return for the latter lending his ears to an hour's lecture on Plato's Ethics.

Arvind could afford to keep two young managers to supervise the shop that had been bought off his old father by Poornima's earnings. Soon he lost interest in Konarak. He loved to chart Poornima successes by toting up her wealth that he invested in the stock market on the recommendations of his older brother, Amol. Afternoons, he hurried back to the old gent's dexterity on the piano. And in the nights he made love strenuously, even though Poornima was often too tired to respond. He did not care. He was back in south Mumbai; he had hated the suburbs. He was back to the life he had loved, one of lazy afternoons chatting of this and that. He did not know and perhaps would not have been devastated to know, that Poornima had taken his eldest brother for a lover.

Devendra's ardour for his youngest sister-in-law had not diminished with time. In his eyes she remained immeasurably ravishing despite the ravages of binge dieting that drained her of energy and colour. His palms would sweat profusely every time she came visiting the old patriarch, invariably midmorning when the women were shopping and the children, now grown, at college. One day, unable to control himself, he caught her by surprise; she let him run his furious hands over her, his lust almost singed her. Awed by the icy clarity of his longing, hungry herself for such violent and frightful devotion, she led this simpering child-man to her old bedroom, now used to store discarded furniture, bed-sheets and linen and the laundry, to a bed and a musty cover. She made love to him with such manic invention that he was sobbing into the night long after the event, even as his wife, his spouse of thirty five years lay by his side, weeping her dry tears.

Madhuri

Her decision to move to Pune with her mentally challenged husband took a minute. She had always wanted to shift there but Ranjan had resisted, pleading his career and Deepika's studies, or as it turned out, her attempts at finding herself. Then both the reasons vanished. Ranjan was given a premature retirement, his pension commuted; with the gratuities and the shares that Gandhi had assigned him and Deepika as co-signatory, the Kapoors were well off. Madhavi couldn't wait to pack her bags fast enough.

For a year she had nursed Ranjan, helped by a male attendant during the day. Her anxieties disappeared slowly; the male nurse troubled her but she bore his overtures with confidence and coquettish charm. She stopped her medication the day they were leaving for Pune, throwing the pills into the garbage can. Deepika was moving in with that Reddy's son. Her bags too were packed.

She never met Rajani Reddy. She had no desire to chat up someone who had clearly taken her place in Deepika's affections. With remarkable foresight, she knew that this frail child, her daughter, all set to leave the family home forever, would never find what she was looking for. She blamed her husband for Deepika's fate. She wished her daughter a long goodbye and turned cheerfully to wheel her husband back to his room. She heard Deepika shut the door behind her.

Then she changed into an orange and red-bordered electric blue sari, a red and gold blouse, applied some eyeliner, a fresh coat of ruby-red lipstick, struck a pose and pouted at the mirror.

'Okay Madhurani . . . Ready for the show?

THE END